RED CHRONICLES BOOK 4

# KENDRAI MEEKS

# PROLOGUE

## Brünhild

"But it's all in German!"

With that, I knew my daughter and nephew were up to no good. I could practically picture her behind the closed study door, my seven-year-old's ebony curls flopping around as her head tilted to the side the way it did whenever she was puzzled. *Like a confused pup.* I shuddered and banished the thought with haste. The last thing I wanted was to credit any lupine tendencies to my own child. Pietro didn't have any such quirks, nor had his mother, who was also an asenaic. What made my daughter so different?

I knew the answer to that question, however. *I did.*

Inside my study, the children continued their banter.

"Of course, it is!" Markus said. "We're in Germany. Did you think it would be in Farsi?"

"What's Farsi?"

"It's another language," my nephew said.

Only two years older than my Gerwalta, my cousin's first born thought he knew everything. For certain, he knew far more than he should. Markus had started reading at four and had yet to stop. The child was insatiable and his parents had quickly discovered that great care must be taken when leaving digestible materials around the house.

Gerwalta huffed. "Well, I've never heard of it."

"Doesn't mean it doesn't exist."

"Where do they speak Parsley?"

"*Farsi,* not *parsley.* And I don't know. In Farsistan?"

A pause, followed by a clunk as the pair took another book down from shelves I myself hadn't perused since being elected. The study had been my mother's when she, too, was Grand Matron, but books and administration had never been my wheelhouse. Execution was. I leaned in, just as curious as the children about what they may find.

"Look!" Markus said. "This one has illustrations."

"What are *iller stations?*" Gerwalta asked.

"No, not iller stations, *illustrations.* Pictures that go along with the writing. Smells weird though. Old. And… whoa! Geri, look! Your name is in this book!"

The door flew open without another moment's hesitation.

Filling the door, I invoked all the outrage I knew a mother should feel at catching children in the act of doing something forbidden. Planting balled fists on my hips, I glared them into guilt, and in its shadow, saw the two children diverge. Markus bristled, as if the only misdeed was being caught in the act. Gerwalta withered, her eyes cast to the floor as she shrunk back into herself.

*Like a shamed dog.*

The boy started to construct his rationalization, sitting in plain view with the ancient leather-bound book open on his lap. "We were just looking, Aunt Brunnie. You said yourself that we should read more about hood stuff."

"That is true, but that does not mean you should be in my study without permission." I turned to where my daughter cowered in the corner. "Come out, sweetheart. It's okay; I should have told you to ask first. This isn't like at home. Now that I'm Grand Matron, you'll just have to get used to me having things you cannot see. It's not because I'm trying to keep anything from you." *Liar.* "It's just because I owe it to the hoods and wolves under my command to respect their privacy. Now," I turned back to Markus, "what is it you've found?"

His pokey little finger landed on a bit of highly-embellished script. "Isn't that Geri's name?"

I bent over and took up the tome, surprised by its lightness, and began to page through the text. "Indeed, it is."

"Why does one of Grandma Sabine's old books have Geri's name?"

My eyes fell instinctively on my daughter, whose eyes shone bright with intrigue, even if she refused to ask the question herself.

The next page's illustration was of a lupine, his dual nature shown by having the head of a wolf and the body of a man, and a red hood beside him with a baby in her arms. "It's a testimonial of our ancestor, Helga the Restorer, about *Die Verräterin*. You both know this story."

All hood children were told a simplified version of the infamous Little Red Riding Hood. The real story, *not* the fairy tale. A werewolf and a hood had fallen in love and wed, despite her mother, the Grand Matron, forbidding their union. They had a child, which angered the Matron so much, she ordered all three executed. The wolf ate his bride's mother in defense. Helga the Restorer carried out the subscribed punishment in lieu of her mother, running them through with a silver spit and roasting them over a fire just outside the outer bailey walls.

*"Die Verräterin?"* Gerwalta stepped forward at last. "The one I'm named after?"

"You're not named after her," I insisted, stroking my daughter's cheek as I balanced the book on the other arm. "You just have the same name."

"But everyone says I am," the girl pouted.

"You're not. When they tell you that, just say what I told Grandmother Sabine: that your name in Old German means 'woman with spear.' It's a proud warrior's name, one which was common in our bloodline for centuries. It is time that it is so again."

It was a partial truth, but the child was too young to know the rest.

I pulled my hand back, flipping pages, finding ones less yellowed by age. They'd been added later, obviously, but why? After the details of the Betrayer's misdeeds and punishment, what more was there to chronicle? A great deal, it seemed, and it should have been no surprise. After all, my own mother had known the truth, that the babe born to Gerwalta Faust and her alpha mate Andreas Baron had not, in fact, been executed. That truth, concealed at the time with the aid of the powerful Dracule paterfamilias Igor Kharmarov, had been reintroduced to my mother shortly after she became Grand Matron. These pages bearing her penmanship documented the recovery of the lost bloodline, tracing the heritage back through the centuries.

The final entry tore at my insides.

> *On my orders, Brünhild visited Igor K.'s blooded-born, Inga R. She sampled young Gerwalta, confirming my worst fear. The vampire advises the child be ter-minated before discovery, a heinous act neither Brünhild nor myself are willing to entertain. It cannot be known for certain*

*what powers my granddaughter's blood will hold after she takes her fire, or even if she will survive such an ordeal. Her choice of mate is also highly likely to influence her nature, for such is the way of wolves. Brünhild has been advised that Gerwalta should be arranged to wed one within her own house, preferably someone unable to give her children, if one can be identified, so as to contain further iterations of her condition. To deny the child an opportunity for a full life weighs on me heavily, but the alternative is far too dangerous for us all. In the end, I blame myself for not acting sooner, and for my own contributions to the whole matter. The missteps of the House of Red, past and present, have resulted in a child that could empower our enemies and weaken our alliances. I will counsel Brünhild to do what's required so that our truths are never discovered. I pray this tainted blood dies away. There can be no defeat of the Ravens if ever they become aware of the child who never should have been.*

The plan fell into place without thought. "Children, go find the castellan and tell her I wish to have an inventory of everyone who had access to this room during Grandmother Sabine's tenure."

The young hoods looked at each other, quixotic.

"What's tenor?" the girl asked.

For once, her know-it-all cousin had no answer.

I placed the offending text on my desk and pushed the children toward the door. "It means during the time she occupied the office of the Grand Matron."

"Oh." Markus turned back over his shoulder. "But she was Grand Matron FOREVER. Like, before you were even born."

I nodded. "I know, and it will take Rebecca a while to put that list together, but I must have it. You're not to come back until it's ready, okay? In the meantime, practice your swordplay."

Markus let out a rambunctious laugh. "Swordplay."

Gerwalta paused, turning sharply. "Did we do something wrong, mommy?"

"*Mutter,* not mom." The ache in my heart brought a tear to my eye. "No, my dear, of course not. I just have work, is all. Now, go. I'll see you later for supper."

They scampered down the stairs then, the echo of their descent and laughter from their play growing softer with each step. I waited until even my sensitive ears could hear no more. Turning back to the study, I closed the door, locked it, checked the lock again. The book felt heavier when I picked it up the second time, weighed down by secrets. A few unspent logs still rested in the fireplace rack, perhaps where my mother had placed them before her death two months ago. Good, that meant they'd light fast and burn hot. As soon as I had the stack arranged, I placed the leather-bound text atop, held out my right hand, and brought forth a silver orb.

I burned our past under the light of a harvest moon, hoping that the embers did not carry forward in time to set us all ablaze.

# ONE

MARKUS

Triberg had never been a prominent town in history, but that didn't stop the tourists. I know, because one of the summers of our training spent in residence focused on local history, both ours and the hueys'. The kitsch-seekers started descending in droves in the '50s, right around the time the haze of second great huey war was settling down. Some came here because, frankly, it's freaking gorgeous. The mountains peaking up on the edge of town, the fall colors, the hot Berliners and Viennese college students flooding into the region to do some "male bonding..."

The Black Forest may have once been known for its isolation and, well, *blackness,* given it used to be so damned dense you couldn't see five feet into it, but nowadays, it was all about cuckoo clocks, alcohol-soaked cherries on chocolate cakes, and thermal pools. Is it any wonder that I loved trips to Triberg when I was a young man looking for other young men? Tourists are so easy to pick up, especially in a roman bath after a long hike through the countryside.

But what brings people to Triberg *specifically* are those waterfalls. I mean, I get waterfalls. Niagara is, like, one of the most impressive things God did with the earth. Even the Tahquamenon Falls by Aunt Brunnie's compound are crazy awesome. Triberg's are the biggest in Germany, and just a short hike from the parking lots at the base. You can hear them from every part of town, just like you can see the top of the cliff that rises above the valley from there, too. Believe me, if the House of Red had known when they built their homestead centuries ago that their beloved castle would be one of the most Instagrammed buildings in the whole of Badem-Württemberg, they would have avoided those falls like the plague.

Interestingly enough, avoiding the plague *was* one the selling points for building here, so far from any sizable population center. See, history lessons *do* come in handy.

Luckily, Schloss Wolfsretter (note: a fancy German frankenword meaning "wolf watcher," like we're some kind of damned lupine peeping tom) developed a bit of a reputation. The tourist guides even tell unsuspecting saps to be smart. "Former residence of a family made wealthy through ownership of the local silver mines, it is now a corporate retreat for a private religious order, and protects its borders aggressively. Take pictures from afar, but do not attempt to visit. You can find licensed postcards at the village gift shops."

But, you know, tourists... Some of them are dumb. A few still crawl up that mountain each year, either boldly driving up the paved road in their airport-issued Beemers, or attempting to hike it in through the woods. Every year, they're escorted back down at the end of a sword or axe. Not that they remember that particular fact afterward. My grandmother, Grand Matron Sabine Kline, wised up and hired a resident vampire. He does the hoopy-loopy thing and clears up huey memories. As a race, we may be old-fashioned, but we're not completely stupid.

I was six the first time my parents forced me to attend "Camp Wannawhackawolf." Geri was only four, but as the direct descendant of the leadership, her school breaks were sacrificed on the altar of hood bureaucracy since she was a baby. I can't really remember much about that summer except that it was the first time I'd seen a vampire, and they were cool as hell. Back then, the undead-in-residence was an old Welsh rabbit named Regina Flanders. She showed me how she could turn to smoke and made the one huey who lived in Schloss Wolfsretter think her underwear was a dinner napkin. Aunt Brunnie was *not* impressed, but I was. Though she wasn't officially supposed to encourage my curiosity about her kind, Regina sent me emails a few times a year with links to a few places to pick up insight. Which was, like, uber cool of her. Then, when I was thirteen, I showed up for summer training to be informed that Regina had "moved on to another opportunity."

Lucky her, I thought, because by that time, the "summer camp from hell," as we'd described it to our huey friends back home, had ceased to be anything Geri and I looked forward to. I mean, how many summer camps required its attendees to drill martial arts forms from four continents, to learn how to land an arrow in the heart of a squirrel from two hundred meters out, or to study semi-magical chants in half a dozen antique languages?

And did we ever weave a lanyard?

Not. One. FREAKING. Time.

Anyways, Triberg…

One big advantage of Hood HQ being a short drive from a big tourist trap was that you could drive around in cars worthy of a mafia flick and locals would just think you were an uptight banker from Frankfurt. The reason security freaks loved big, black SUVs so much wasn't hard to understand. They were sleek, powerful, roomy, but mostly, their shaded windows and boxy confines leant a certain amount of secrecy to the riders. Or so the theory went. As I pulled the Mercedes SUV to a halt outside the only vehicular entry gate to the compound, the last thing I was, was covert. Hard to stay secret when the only road traversable by a car wound two thousand feet up a mountain in plain view of the village in the valley below, the headlights a moving marker of my position in the night.

I rolled down the window. "Two fries, six cheeseburgers, and a kiddie meal please — extra ketchup."

A click preceded the tinny voice speaking perfect German that came from the box. "Name, clan, and sanjak, please."

Whoever was on duty either had no sense of humor or didn't speak English. Or both. I sighed, piecemealing together the broken language I'd been taught in my youth. "Markus Kline, House of Red, American Midwest under Brünhild Kline."

"Thank you, please hold." The speaker clicked as the castellan's office searched their schedules. Schedules I wouldn't be on, because screw them, I shouldn't need an official invite to enter my clan's ancestral home.

Another click. "Mr. Kline, we don't see authorization for your visit."

"Jesus fricking Christ."

"He's not on the schedule, either."

Inga rolled her eyes and crawled over my lap to get closer to the speaker. Her extended finger wagged at the box like it was a disobedient puppy. "I don't know who you are, but *this* is Inga Rosethorn, and if you don't open this gate and let us in right now, I will personally drain you with my own two teeth."

In German, she sounded even more threatening. And hot.

What? I'm gay, not dead.

The nerves in the voice of the on-duty guard were unmistakable. "Hold please." *Click.*

I fixed Inga with my best side-eye.

The vampire turned a blank expression to me, five inches from my face. "What?"

"Well, first..." I gently pushed her back to her seat. She

gave in. Of course, she did. There was no way a hood, even one with my brawn, could force a vampire to do anything. Not without a sharp sword or wooden stake, anyway.

"And, second," I continued once she was back in the passenger side. "Remember on the drive up when I said, 'don't say anything. Just let me handle it because you're going to go vamp psycho and piss them off?' That's the kind of vamp psycho I was talking about."

Inga crossed her arms. "What do I care about pissing off hoods?"

"Seeing as we're coming here begging for their help, I think the answer to that should be, 'a hella lot.' Unless, of course, you're thinking of killing them all."

"A hostile takeover of the compound?" She balanced her chin on a beautifully manicured finger. "How many do you think are inside?"

I wasn't sure if I should tell her because, one, duh, who gave up that kind of information to an outsider? And two, I was scared the number wouldn't dissuade her, and if that was true, yikes.

The speaker clicked again. "Matron Chin has authorized your visit. The gates will open momentarily."

I closed my eyes and grumbled a curse under my breath. I hadn't known Inga long, but it only took a few minutes in the company of the infamous 'Daughter of Dracula' to discover her arrogance. The simple victory would only fuel that fire of conceit.

"Psycho vampire, you were saying?"

"Shut it, Fangs."

The moon above was no more than a sliver in the sky. Tomorrow, it would be nothing. The castle had undergone some modernization efforts through the years, but unfortunately, that didn't include any sort of exterior lighting past the entry gate. The last thing the Matron Council wanted was any way for the hueys in the valley below to get a better view of what happened on the mountaintop.

Inga's eyesight, however, beat mine to Hell. "So, this is the infamous Schloss Wolfsretter?" She twisted in the passenger seat as the car pivoted up the switchback road. "Funny, I thought it'd be bigger."

"You've never been here before?"

Inga looked at me like I'd just said the most ridiculous thing in the world. "Is there a reason I should have?"

"Just, you know… You're one of the oldest vampires kicking it, and this is the center of the hood universe, so I just figured, you know, you big wigs getting together and such…"

"Vampires don't have big wigs," she said indifferently. "Except for Vlad, and then, only because he is a power-and-fame-hungry asshole who made himself renowned through infamy. I think Igor was here once, many centuries ago."

"Really?" I pulled the car into a spot alongside a half-dozen other well-intentioned stealth mobiles. "Why?"

Inga shrugged. "The list of things my father has done of which I know little is long and varied. He's always told me the knowledge of his acts would only be a burden, one he did not want to pass along to me. As time passed and I cultivated secrets of my own, I came to share that sentiment."

"I'm a little jealous of that. My mom tells me everything. And I mean, EVERYTHING. What she ate, who she played poker with, when her bowels are giving her trouble."

Inga's face curdled.

"Just saying, if your dad could give my mom a little

lecture on holding back, that would be just peaches and cream with me."

For the first time in our acquaintance, Inga's resolve broke. Her eyes went to her lap and her voice softened. "If he survives, I'll be sure to pass along the request."

A vampire playing the guilt card? That was new. "Look, Inga, I didn't mean to…"

Her hand shot up, halting my words. "No need for platitudes, Mr. Kline. Every child expects their parent to proceed them in death. Just because mine is immortal does not change that."

I leaned across the seat, placing a hand on Inga's arm. "I'm so sorry for your loss."

"My loss?" The vampire turned indignant. "Igor is still alive."

*Awkward.* I pulled my hand back. "But he was buried underneath half a mansion with a blood-thirsty, egotistical maniac who thinks he's the sultan of the vampire world."

"Tobias was also buried, yet Gerwalta knows he survived."

I didn't hold out much hope of that, either. "I'm not sure Geri even knows what day it is. She's barely come out of her room in the month we've been here. I'm all up for bitch-slapping her with reality if she doesn't get out of the denial phase soon."

"Gerwalta is not mourning Tobias."

"What do you call barely talking or eating while sitting alone in your room, staring at the ceiling?"

"I call it, 'coming to terms with a massive shift in your understanding of the world and your place in it,'" Inga said so plainly, I suddenly felt foolish. "She's spent her whole life being trained to hate the very thing she's found out she is. Even if she was rebellious and claimed to eschew many of those beliefs for herself, it does not mean others have. Not all hoods are as accepting as you are about her newly-revealed nature."

I looked to the castle, wondering if Yan was inside. "I do know something about having your nature judged by society."

"Then accept that Gerwalta knows what she's talking about." Inga opened the car door. "Tobias survives, as does Igor."

Rebecca Krantz was part security guard, part old maid, and three parts den mother. One thing she was not, however, was spry. Not that I held that against her. It wasn't like the olden days when the castellan had to actually be daytime caretaker and watchman for the castle, defending it with both sword and honor. Now, each sanjak was responsible for providing two hoods for a year of duty, young folk who staffed all the compound's needs, from security detail to custodial service. Even the cooks were hoods. Rebecca just sort of... kept everyone in line.

She was also the only permanent huey resident of Schloss Wolfsretter, and had been since she'd arrived as a teenager in 1945. By tradition, the Castellan had always been a human woman. A woman, because the hoods were a matriarchal society that held the so-called "fairer sex" as the dominant one. And a human, because no bloodline affiliation meant no bias towards or against any of the twelve houses.

She did have a soft spot for me, though.

"Bibi!" I threw my arms out wide on sight of the old woman looming in the doorway.

She feigned indifference, looking down her nose at me.

"Come to tease me again? Butter me up with flattery and try to woo me into bed?"

I let my face screw up. "But, Bibi… *You're* the one who hits on *me*."

"Damn right, and I'm tired of getting the cold shoulder. Now get over here and lay one on me!"

Rebecca's hands took a little tour south as she hugged me, letting my backside have a wee squeeze. Whatever. The old gal had survived a world war, the age of disco, and the holier-than-thou attitude of three Grand Matrons during her tenure. I wouldn't berate her for a little harmless pinch.

As soon as I was free, Bibi turned her attention to the slender brunette behind me. "And what about this one? Someone Yan's going to have to fight off?"

Inga examined her fingernails. "Not if he wants to retain his eyes."

Rebecca ignored the comment. "He's been asking about you, you know. Almost like he was expecting you, which I said was silly, since you were not officially recalled from Istanbul."

"Not my fault. I've been writing to Aunt Brunnie for almost a month, asking her to give me clearance so I could haul tail up here. Or at the very least, give him permission to hike down to RotHaus so I could just plain get tail. I finally got tired of waiting. By the way, Bibi, this is Inga Rosethorn of the House of…"

"Inga will be fine," Inga said, cutting in and holding out a hand in the modern custom. "You're just a human."

Rebecca's face soured, sensing a backhanded compliment.

"Never mind her," I said, putting my phone away again after shooting off a text to my boyfriend. "She's not great with her people skills. Listen, Bibi," I pulled the old woman aside, "why's Chin on duty? I thought Reyhan was in charge?"

"The Matron of the House of Black left a few weeks ago," Rebecca said matter-of-factly. "Apparently, there's been some unrest in the Bosporus."

I rubbed the back of my neck. "Yeah, we might have had something to do with that. Whatever. If Chin is the one here, then I need to see her and ASAP."

"Who's Asap?" Rebecca asked.

Inga cast her rolling eyes to the sky. "And I'm the one who's out of touch?"

Rebecca's spine stiffened. "Now, listen here, youngin'. I've been the castellan of this schloss since before you were in diapers."

Two gleaming fang daggers jutted out of Inga's mouth. "No, you listen here, youngin'," she spit back. "When I was in diapers, your great, great, great, great, great, great..."

My spidey senses told me to move the hungry vampire away from the blood-filled human. "And... we're walking. Bibi, page Chin, won't you? Inga's getting a little cranky. I'll need to get her home soon and put her down for a nap."

"But, Markus dear, the council is in session. Matron Chin won't come out, not unless it's an emergency."

"Oh, it's an emergency. Please, sweetie?"

The sugar sealed the deal. Rebecca grinned. "Okay, dearie. If you think it merits it, but they will want to know exactly what kind of emergency." She leaned forward, into the gossip, as it were.

I sucked on my lip for a moment as I paced out an explanation. "The slayers aren't extinct, but they will be without help. Currently, the twenty or so left are holed-up in Aunt Brunnie's house down in the village."

"Slayers? Well, I haven't seen one of them… Must be about fifty years, since that one stayed here that one time for a while." Rebecca nodded. "I'll announce you at once."

"Thanks, babe. Please also let them know that Ms. Rosethorn will be accompanying me in."

Rebecca clicked her heels like the soldiers of yore before shuffling off.

Inga swiveled. "I have no intention of appearing before the Matron Council."

She was kidding, right? "Then why in the hell did you insist… and I mean *insist,* that you come along?"

"To protect you in case the Ravens were lying in wait. They were not, and you made it into the compound safely. I am a vampire, it is not my place to assert myself in the midst of hood governance, as long as you'll get the council to issue them aid and defense."

"Hood governance?" I echoed. "Inga, this isn't the UN. You're not Belgium and I'm not Barbados, appealing for aid. This is a cross-section of the supernatural world coming together to prevent the exploitation of an oppressed and endangered… Oh, actually, it is kinda like the UN, huh?"

Inga ignored my screed. "As I said, not my place. I've lost too much time already. Now that I know the slayers will be protected, I must go."

"Go?"

She looked at me like I had two heads, neither of them particularly attractive. "To rescue Igor, of course."

"To rescue Igor?"

Inga spat what I assumed was an ancient Wallachian curse. "I swear, you are worse than a parrot."

"How in the hell are you going to rescue Igor? You can't kill a Raven without killing yourself. Plus, it's not like they're going to just be hanging out in Istanbul. They've moved on, and you have no idea where. It took you weeks just to find out which house they were in when you were in the same city, and that was only because I tracked them when they tried to kidnap Geri."

"Actually, I have some idea."

"Great then. Share with the class, Rosethorn."

"I am not your teacher, Mr. Kline, and I'm certainly not your friend."

"Which leads me to wonder, what *are* you exactly?" I crossed my arms, fixing her with a withering glare. "Don't think I haven't noticed the way your hungry eyes keep sizing up Geri. She might be too down in the pits of despair to notice, but I'm not. You could drink any huey in town. Hell, you keep drinking Caleb. I know, I saw the fang marks, even though he's trying to hide them."

The vampire raised an eyebrow. "Spend much time staring at men's necks, don't you?"

"Caleb is a hottie. I stare at his everything!" I retorted. "Stay on topic. What's your stake in this, Inga?"

The crack was fleeting. So fleeting I'd bet that she didn't think I saw it. But I did; that tiny flash in her eyes, a look of pain, a look that begged for mercy.

But a moment later, the stonehearted vamp swept away the cameo of humanity. She turned on her heel. "I will call if I discover anything about the wolf's whereabouts. Tell Geri that I promise that much."

Before I could get another word in edgewise, the daughter of Dracula became a pillar of smoke and dissipated before my eyes.

At which juncture, Rebecca returned. "They're ready for you, Markus. Have to say, the news about the slayers caused quite a stir." She scanned the bailey. "Where's that woman?"

Shaking my head, I made for the inner gates. "Stepped out for a smoke."

# TWO

## GERI

The sky cried openly, even if I could not.

More fall leaves rusted away by the day. I sat and stared out my third-floor window, as the eroding canvas of trees laid a carpet over the span of the village to the west, to a point where the earth swelled up from the valley floor. Beyond that, a mountain, one which seemed out of place with its stark cliff towering over the land below. Schloss Wolfsretter looked like building blocks arranged by a child at this distance: a rectangle, a cone, a few squares. In my mind's eye, however, I could see its marble entry way, the stone-floored council chambers with its antique throne and tapestries reveling of the glories of the House of Red past. I could envision myself running across the chess board of its inner bailey. Tasting hazelnut soup on my tongue and hearing the wind twist its lithe fingers up the cliff when I fell asleep at night, cloistered in the Grand Matron's residence at the top of the tower.

A few years ago, teenaged me had despised that place, saw it as a center for indoctrination that bred hate for the man I loved. Now, my heart ached for it, knowing that I might never walk its halls again. A werewolf hadn't set foot inside in half a century, as far as I knew. What sane wolf would? The ghosts of their ancestors may still haunt the corridors and passageways. If they were unlucky, they may join them.

The street beyond the walls of my mother's private villa away from the compound, RotHaus, glistened under the street lamp, a spotlight that stood achingly empty. Wishing to see Tobias's form fill in the shadow and stride toward my door was foolish on so many levels, not the least of which was that he had no idea this house existed. Even if he'd managed to escape the Ravens, how would he find me?

But he hadn't escaped. How did I know? I didn't. But in the quiet moments between waking and dreams, I felt his presence in a way that couldn't be explained by logic, sensed his desperation and loneliness. He was alive, but I didn't know why or for how much longer.

Amy walked up from behind, putting a hand on my shoulder. "They're going to say yes. They have to."

She'd confused my wistful street-staring for worry over the fate of the slayers. I couldn't blame her for it; it was where my thought *should* be. A month ago, we'd rescued the last members of a supernatural species thought to be extinct, from imprisonment by the very creatures they were meant to balance. If not for the Istanbul wolf pack, we'd never have made it out with our lives. Here, we were hardly safer than if we stood in the middle of the street, protected only so much as the Ravens feared venturing so closely to the center of the hood world. Our only hope was to get the Council of Matrons to accept the slayers as refugees.

Which should have been as easy as asking, but anything involving a single matron never was, let alone a dozen of them. Markus was the only righteous hood among us, the only one who could appeal to the council. But to do that, he needed an official invite. One we expected to come soon after he relayed a message to my mother that he'd returned from Turkey. One that never came.

"No, they don't." I wasn't being pessimistic; I was making a projection based on years of keen observation. "Hoods are very insular. Outside of dealing with wolves as much as they need to, they keep to themselves. It's like a cult."

Amy cocked a hip. "Then why send Markus to ask? Why don't we just keep running? All we're doing by sitting here is giving those vampire creeps a chance to catch up to us at as leisurely a pace as they want."

When I'd told my cousin I thought we were wasting time approaching the council, it wasn't simply because I felt defeated (which I did) or tired (which I was) or indifferent about what the hell they would decide to do (which I was earnestly trying to convince myself was true.) In the absence of slayers, there had been occasional appeals for help when a vampire got too big in his fangs for comfort, but only when another of his kind didn't solve the problem first. Now that the slayers were back, not extinct, and in need of consolation and protection? Great, but they wouldn't consider it their problem.

"We're here because this is our best hope of finding the slayers shelter," I said. "They need sanctuary, aid, resources. The women know how to use their power, but the men don't. Half of them can't even walk up the stairs without getting winded. They need rehabilitation, rest, and the money we were able to pool together is running out."

Amy, however, thrived on positivity. How could she not? She found a new boyfriend with the changing of the month, each time hopeful *he* was "the one" until the *homme du jour* proved a disappointment. That never ended the cycle though, one powered and buoyed by the fact that Amy always had faith in one time being *the* time.

The blonde crossed her arms over her chest. "Well, even if they do say no, so what?  If the hoods won't help, we'll just find someone who will."

"Like who?" I pulled my ebony hair, a rambled mess without definition, out of my face as I looked up. "The vampires certainly aren't going to do anything. Even if most of them are decent, none of them are going to take on the Ravens."

"The wolves then."

I scoffed. "Yeah, right, the wolves. Like that's going to

happen, them going against the Matron Council and their Machiavellian edicts."

Amy sat down beside me. "We help ourselves, then."

"*We*?" I fixed my friend with a withering stare. "Amy, you're not a part of this. You're not a hood, not a wolf, and you certainly aren't a slayer. Your best bet would be getting the hell away from us and setting yourself up off the grid for a while. Unless you want to discuss the process for becoming a vampire, I'd watch how we use the term 'we.' This is a supe crisis, and you're just a tourist."

The blonde's blood boiled, reddening her cheeks and sending her shooting from the room. A stray impulse told me to jump up and chase her, apologize for being rude. The wiser part of me knew what I said had been the truth.

Caleb slipped into the door, because apparently no one trusted me to be on my own for too long.  Great, yet another person with whom I had a complicated relationship coming to comfort/lecture me. I turned back to the window, but this time, not because I was looking desperately for any sign of Markus, but because I couldn't bring myself to look at the slayer who had confessed his love for me, asked me to marry him, then got cozy in the harem before my 'no' grew cold.

"You shouldn't be so rough on her, you know." He slipped his hands in his pockets, looking back over his shoulder in Amy's wake. "She's loyal, brave, compassionate, all things I'd take over mystical silver-wielding or sunlight-throwing powers any day of the week. Even if she does have the worldly concerns of a 1990s Teen Flick Drama Queen."

"She shouldn't be wasting time..." I cut myself off before I said something I couldn't take back.. "If Amy stays with me, I'm going to get her killed."

"What makes you think that?"

"The Ravens already tried to kill her once, and that was

before I knocked one of them off and stole all their gourmet meals."

I didn't have to be a bitch though. I'd apologize later. Again.

"Right. Okay. So, anyways, I've been sent in here to kick your ass."

I raised an eyebrow. "Meaning?"

"Meaning… It's time to stop moping. It's been a month since Istanbul, and sitting around being sad isn't helping."

I spun in my seat, making no secret of my anger. "We're not sitting around being sad. Our best shot at defeating the Ravens is with the backing of the Matron Council. Even if I think it's a waste of time to ask, Markus is right that we have to try. Your people are undertrained, underfed, and under some delusion that I can give them what they need. I'm just a twenty-two-year-old woman from a tiny village in Michigan, Caleb. I'm not capable of being a healer, a therapist, a trainer, or a general."

"And… what? You think as soon as the Matron Council bestows its magnanimity on the slayers, you're just going to pass us along and wipe your hands clean?"

My fists clenched so hard, I'd not be surprised to find I'd drawn blood. "I don't owe the slayers anything. In fact, it's just the opposite. I should have spent the last month hunting down the Ravens and rescuing Tobias. Instead, I'm stuck in the Black Forest, playing house frau."

"Bullshit. You might spend your nights here, away from everyone, but you're barely sleeping during the day. Amy says you spend hours when everyone else is asleep training yourself ragged in the basement."

"Of course, I am. I'm going up against a six-hundred-year-old vampire with a god complex and his four closest buddies. You don't overcome someone like that by knitting socks. Or should I just rush into where my mate is being held prisoner and wing it?"

"What makes you think Tobias is still alive?"

"What makes you think he's dead?" Anger crackled in my bones, an impulse to find something silver and push it into a weapon threatening to consume me. "You and Amy are just the same. You don't get that this is what *I* have to do, but I can't get to it until the Matron Council gets its *head out of its collective ass* and agrees to take care of you all."

The door leading from the underground garage opened, taking me to my feet and all the blood from my face.

"He's back."

Caleb, on edge of boiling over, threw the door open. "Good, let's go hear whether or not your terrible burden is over."

I was just about to dredge up another retort when Markus's booming voice called out across the house. "Oh, my god, seriously! Geri! Geri, your slayers are threatening to kill someone."

Caleb and I, drawn from the mire of our own conflict, exchanged a look of concern before rushing down the stairs. Markus, donning his red cloak like something had spooked him and using his body as a human shield, stood before a tall, slender man with dusty rose skin and hazelnut eyes. The scene did not explain itself, which forced me to demand to know what the hell was going on.

Markus kept his arms akimbo. "Hell if I know. All we did was walk in the door."

Alexandra, in all her gravidity, still held herself out as unofficial overseer of the group, and appeared willing to kick anyone's ass to prove it, pregnant belly or no. She stood a few feet away from Markus, balancing a solarium in the palm of her hand.

"That man is a vampire!" the slayer said. "We did not come all this way just to be taken again."

"Yan is NOT one of the Ravens," Markus insisted. "After everything I did in Istanbul to bust your asses out of Count Creepy's mansion, do you think I'd use you to open up an all-night buffet?"

Something needed to be done before things got out of hand. Only thing was, I couldn't figure out which side of the conflict I least wanted pissed at me.

Amy didn't have a side, or as had always proven to be the case, a filter. The blonde huey pounded down the stairs. "Oh my god, are you seriously telling me that despite all your radical superpowers, you all are still just as bigoted and ignorant as the rest of us?" The shockwave snatched the attention from the standoff, and centered it on her. "Markus, who is this and why is he here?"

But it was the vampire who answered the question, speaking in so gentle a voice, I'd have not heard him without superhuman abilities. "My name is Yan, the resident vampire at Schloss Wolfsretter. I'm Markus's boyfriend."

Amy's face screwed up as she eyeballed my cousin for the briefest second. Was she more surprised that he was gay, or that he was with a vampire? "Okay, *Yan*, my name is Amy, and I have to say, as the only non-supe in this house, I get where the slayers are coming from. See, they were being held hostage by Dracula and all, so we'd just kind of like to know... Are you going to hurt them at all? Because there's, like, twenty slayers here, and I'm sure if a few hit you with their weird sunlight things, you're going to go boom, along with all the rest of us."

Alexandra tutted. "Solaira do not harm slayers."

"Might blast all our clothes off, though," Caleb piped up from the top of the stairs. "Not that that would be a bad thing."

The vampire, perhaps sensing the de-escalation, and picking up on how the odds would be stacked against him, demurred. "I have no reason to hurt anyone. I am an honorable vampire; I do not drink from someone without their permission."

"Or without my permission," Markus added. When Yan gave him a *Really, that's what you want to say right now?* look, he clarified. "What, we're a couple now. I'm just saying, if you're going to suck on anyone's anything," Markus's hand shot up in to the air, "the line starts here."

Amy, blushing like a peach, turned to Alexandra. "If he were to try anything, can you end him immediately?"

The pregnant slayer bounced her solarium like a child's plaything. "In seconds."

"Good enough." The blonde dropped her arms to her sides. "Now, kids, we're all going to play nice until someone gives anyone a GOOD REASON not to. Okay? I'm talking injury, not insult, so everybody, chill."

The slayers grumbled, even as they began to break up and move toward parts of the house other than the large living room that had become a de facto gathering spot. Yan drifted behind Markus like a shadow as the latter made his way toward me.

"A word in private?"

I tried to keep the bitterness from my tone, but I'd never been very good at faking. "Why? We all know the Council said no."

As Markus reached the top of the stairs, he seized me by the arm and turned me toward my room, despite my still-body routine. "I said, 'a word in PRIVATE, Geri?'"

"Okay, fine. Don't be so dramatic."

Once the door was closed, Markus set about his briefing. "Okay, so the part you know: the request to offer the slayers sanctum was denied."

"You don't say?" I deadpanned. "I told you they weren't going to accept them."

Markus grinned. "But they *are* willing to accept them."

I shook my head. "What are you talking about? You just said the request was denied."

"The Council of Matrons has offered the slayers housing, provisions, and assistance with reacclimating to the outside world, in exchange for something."

I wracked my brain for the logic behind that lunacy. "For?"

Markus fixed a furrowed brow and glared. "For killing the Ravens."

I didn't have time to stop the cackle that erupted. "Ha! Is that all? What is this, the *Wizard of Oz*? They want to send a helpless, displaced people to take on the wicked witch?"

"We're not helpless." Caleb reappeared in the doorway, leaning against the frame with his arms crossed. "Overpowering vampires is what we were made to do. Each and every slayer in this house has the potential, they just need time and training."

"If you'll excuse an outsider's observation," Yan interjected as he came in as well, because apparently there was a party in my bedroom and everyone was invited, "at least one of them seemed more than capable—and willing— to kill me just a few minutes ago. Actually, at least one of the women was."

Caleb closed the door behind them. "That was Alexandra, who, by the way, says none of the males went through awakening ceremonies. They're wet noodles, like a nascent hood. Something I'll need to remedy soon."

Markus snickered, but Caleb just rolled his eyes.

"Get your mind out of the gutter, Kline."

I tried to subdue the crawling sensation that swept over my skin, remembering that I'd suffered the same at my own insistence until recently. How that had changed, I was still uncertain. But I'd made that choice for myself, and I raged at the idea of keeping another from their birthright by force. But this wasn't about me.

"The fact remains, they are… well, *nascent*. Even the women, who know how to use their power, haven't been trained in combat.  How could we take that kind of offer to them?"

"Okay, first of all," Markus said, "*we* are not offering them anything; the Matron Council is. And second, Caleb is right. This isn't an oppressed people, they were hostages. They're like us, Geri. They're supes. And supes don't get mad, they get even."

I balanced my forehead on the tips of my fingers. "What does Inga think?"

"Inga? Oh, she…" Markus's cheeks reddened as his eyes sought butterflies. "She, um… took off. To do recon, I think. She said she'll call if she finds out anything."

Damn her. What gave her the right to go look for her father, and leave me here to deal with the mess her brothers had wrought?

But since things were left to me, as everyone had

somehow decided I was the leader of this little party, I was prepared to lay things out as they were, without any heroic upsell. "I don't feel right about this. Markus and I have been trained as warriors all our life, and we barely managed to escape. And that was only with two Ravens on the scene. You can bet your ass that next time, they're bringing all their forces. Without the hoods standing beside them, the Ravens will shred them."

Caleb shrugged. "So we train them." He turned to Markus. "You said the council was willing to forward us some provisions?"

"Yeah. As far as shelter, they deigned to allow us to remain here at the RotHaus, though what any of them could do to make us leave, I'd like to know. It doesn't belong to the Matron Council; it's Aunt Brunnie's personal property. But the food and weapons they talked about would help. We do make some gnarly silverware, you know."

"Then we'll accept the offer," Caleb said. "And between the three of us, we can train them pretty quickly."

Yan leaned forward. "I can assist with pointers on the best attack methods that work on vampires. *If...* the slayers are comfortable with my presence, of course. And if they promise not to actually kill me."

Caleb clapped his hands. "Great, so it's all settled then. We'll draw up plans, break them out into groups, and get going right away."

Had they all gone insane? "Look, it's not that I don't care about the slayers, but I have to stay focused. The Ravens have Tobias, and I have to save him."

Markus dared my ire. "I don't see how those two goals are mutually exclusive."

Yan raised a finger. "I'm sorry, but who is Tobias?"

"It's complicated," Markus said at the same time I said, "He's my mate."

Markus tried to reconcile the two statements. "Tobias is the werewolf Geri found in Chicago two years ago when his mate was kidnapped and then killed by the Ravens. Indirectly, anyway. He was with us in Istanbul, but Vlad Tepeş took him prisoner."

Yan turned back to me. "Then how is he *your* mate, if *his* mate was killed? Werewolves mate for life."

Markus and I exchanged a look, one in which he asked permission to share my secret. I shook my head. The fact that he was asking, however, let me know I could trust my cousin. As much of a gossip as he was, if he hadn't told his boyfriend, he wouldn't unless I said it was okay.

"They do," I said while chastising myself internally to be more careful with my words in the future.

Yan's voice ticked up a note. "Did you mean 'mate' the way Australians use it, like friends? I can never keep all the variant forms of English in check."

"No, I mean I love him. And he loves me, I think, only..."

Of all the people I had no right to expect to come to my rescue, Caleb did. "The treatment the vamps were using on the wolves plays around with their hardwiring," he said. "We're not really sure what the consequences are yet, but when I was their prisoner, I overheard talk about undoing lupine societies from the inside out. Seems Vlad still has a bit of a chip on his shoulder about the way things went down in the Balkans back in his day. He blames the wolves and he wants revenge."

That seemed to put an end to the vampire's confusion, as he nodded once. I made a mental note to thank Caleb later. Hell, it wasn't really a lie, what he'd said. Vlad had told me as much, and I didn't have any reason to think Drac was lying. Still, something niggled at me. My attraction to Tobias was easy enough to understand, even before I knew I was part-wolf. Not only was he buff and hot in a rough-sexy type of way, he'd saved my ass too many times to count. But his attraction to me? Had I been imagining it in the early days? Purely physical, of course; I didn't dismiss for a moment his feelings for Kara. But still, could a bonded wolf be drawn to someone not their mate? Was there something in the archives that could explain the aberrant behavior?

The curiosity had my mind wheeling, and was about to take control of my feet.

"Markus, which matron is on duty at the Schloss?"

"Chin Zhu, why?"

Good. I didn't know Chin personally, but that made it more likely that she wasn't one of my mother's allies.

"Let the slayers know what the council has offered," I said. "I think it's a fool's deal, but ultimately, it's their decision to make. I need to run an errand."

"Run an errand?" Markus asked. "You mean you're actually leaving your room? Where are you going?"

"I want to see if I can appeal to Chin's better nature."

# THREE

Inga had told me that if Tobias and I were truly mates, one of us would know if the other died.

"But we never actually... you know," I'd said to the vampire.

Inga had merely smiled ruefully, the way only those grown wise with age could. "But you're some sort of wolf-hood chimera. I wouldn't expect the way mating works with you to be the same. In any case, you love him. I think there's a power to that that goes beyond whatever magic or supernatural talents we have. It's anchored in our humanity, and if that anchor slackens, you'd feel it. Just like I would, if something happens to Igor."

I'd stumbled for words. "You're not... You and Igor, I mean, you..."

Vampires couldn't blush, but she'd given it her best attempt. "No, Igor and I do not now nor have we ever had a sexual relationship. The love of family we feel has bonded us for centuries, even in the times when I was too pigheaded to accept it gracefully. That's why I feel safe telling you that if you feel Tobias is still alive, then he is."

He was. I could feel him somehow, like the warm feeling you had long after finishing a good meal. His existence fed me. But at the same time, I couldn't ignore the implications. If Vlad hadn't killed him immediately when we'd left, he had bigger plans for him. But what?

In the meantime, since leaving Triberg was on hold, I had another wolf to rescue. This one, from the pages of time and the shadow of infamy. Somewhere in my family tree was a branch upon which a noble lupine sat, maligned and overwritten by the so-called shame of *seducing* Gerwalta Faust. I intended to trim back those overgrown twigs and reclaim his dignity.

"Name, clan, and sanjak, please."

The voice piping through the speaker when I pulled up to the security gate of Schloss Wolfsretter wasn't one I recognized, but that meant little. Hoods from around the world and from every clan rotated through the House of Red's ancestral home.

"Gerwalta Kline, House of Red, American Midwest under Brünhild Kline."

"Gerwalta... Kline?" The tremor in the woman's voice was impossible to ignore.

"Oh, you've heard of me." I turned down the music playing on the car stereo. "I'd like to request a word with Matron Chin. I understand she's in charge at the moment."

Which begged the question, why wasn't my mother here?

"Matron Chin is in session, and..."

The gate attendee either neglected or didn't bother to turn off her microphone as her tongue turned to German, the Schloss's official language even if most everyone actually conversed in English these days. Despite the attempt at secrecy, I still picked up on a mention of "Die Verräterin." The notoriety of my 'betrayal' preceded me.

Good, knowing who they were dealing with would save so much time.

Finally, the voice came back full and steady. "Miss Kline, according to our records, you have been relinquished by your matron. Therefore, you have no official sponsorship or standing."

"Mom remembered to fill out all the paperwork, huh?"

She either ignored what I'd said, or chalked it up to rhetoric. "Relinquished hoods may not enter the compound."

"Right. Remind me, what's your name?"

The uncertain voice drew the answer out like taffy. "Beatrice Jones, House of Green."

That explained the vaguely British tone of her voice. "Beatrice, what does *relinquished* mean to you? Other than the fact that my own mother has disowned me, I mean."

"A relinquished hood is one who has had her powers revoked by her matron, and is rendered, as close as is possible, a huey," she said as though reading the answer from a book.

I beckoned a silver bangle on my wrist into action, holding my hand in the direct view of the camera just over the speaker. My influence liquified the metal, boiling it into a pool of cool liquid that swirled on my palm before it obeyed my command and took the form I envisioned in my mind's eye. The tiny, shiny Buddha didn't vary too much from the kind you'd find an any Eastern goods gift shop, with the exception of its prominent middle finger erect on its right hand.

"As you can see," I said, "I'm not relinquished in the way that really matters."

"That does not mean you're a righteous hood."

This chick really wanted to piss me off, didn't she? I plastered on my best fake smile and dipped my voice in honey. "Call Matron Chin, please, or I'm going to crash my car through the gate."

A new voice spoke. "Do that, and you'll be dead before

you can hit reverse."

*Bingo.*

Chin Zhu, a white hood from the lush valleys of China, had a history of disagreeing with my mother on matters of policy and practice. That she was talking to me took me by surprise, but I tried not to jump to the conclusion that it meant she disagreed with my banishment. It might, though, and if it did, she might be willing to agree to what I was about to ask. One could wedge open opportunities if only they knew where the cracks were.

Her German was pushed through a Mandarin sieve. "We are just about to retire for the day, Miss Kline, so if you would be so kind as to state your business succinctly, I would appreciate it."

"Thank you, Matron Chin, for your consideration. First off, I wanted to ask why the council refused to offer the slayers sanctuary."

"Perhaps Markus miscommunicated our answer on that. We *are* offering them sanctuary, if they agree to..."

"If they agree to anything to receive aid, it is not sanctuary," I interrupted. "If you have conditions, then what you're offering is payment. How is that fair? We thought the slayers were extinct for fifty years. Now we're dictating the terms of their rebirth?"

"*We* are doing nothing, Miss Kline. You are no longer a member of this community." A long sigh crackled through the speaker, and when Chin spoke again, her tone was more annoyed than authoritarian. "I'm not Grand Matron; I can't unilaterally decide to harbor the enemies of such a powerful vampire as Vlad Tepeş without your mother's approval."

"His enemies?" My voice shot up an octave. "They were his prisoners."

"I'm afraid that in this case, it's a matter of semantics."

"Slavery is never a case of semantics."

"Geri, please!" Chin huffed. "I want to help. Trust me, I do. But this isn't a dictatorship, and there are members of the council who aren't eager to set us up on a collision course with the Ravens, especially given the involvement of someone like you in the situation."

Had my mother spilled the beans about my true nature to the council? Had the Grand Matron of the legendary House of Red admitted her own daughter was part wolf and that our story of *Die Verräterin* wasn't entirely true? As much as I tried, I couldn't picture the proper Brünhild Kline giving up that kind of info without a fight. No, whatever Chin was talking about, it had nothing to do with Gerwalta Faust or my connection to her. What did she mean, then, someone like me?

Chin continued before I could figure out how to ask without giving anything away.

"Now, if the whole of your business was to come seeking resolution to a situation already resolved, then—"

Panic pushed my pulse into the red. "Wait, Matron Chin, I... I want to examine something in the archives."

"You know you can't..."

"Just for a few minutes," I interjected, even as I tried to keep the desperation in my voice contained. "Then, I promise, I'll go away and stop bothering you. Markus can be the liaison between the council and the slayers, but I really need to examine the logs of the condemned. You can be there with me if you want."

"Logs of the condemned? Why would you want to study the darkest parts of our history?" For someone not related to me, Chin managed to perfect the tone of a scalding mother.

"Miss Kline, this must end. You have no right to ask us for anything. I can't make you leave Triberg, but I can have a tremendous amount of influence in the council's discussion about the slayers. If you want us to help them, keep your head down and stay away from Schloss Wolfsretter."

"Five minutes in the archives. Please, Chin, I..."

The floodlights mounted above the gate flickered on, rendering me blind. My arm went up to block the assault, but as my eyes recovered from shock and the figures standing just beyond the gate began to take shape, I knew the discussion was done.

Hoods dealt with other hoods in the weaponry that made sense to us: swords, daggers, slings and arrows.

With humans, we used guns.

Which, oddly, would work on a hood too, especially if you managed to shoot her in the heart or the brain. But one didn't serve water in wine bottles just because it also quenched thirst.

I ground my teeth and the tires as I navigated the SUV through a three-point turn and headed back down the road.

# FOUR

I managed to get back to the safehouse without hitting anything more than the proverbial wall. And the steering wheel, several times. By the time I parked the car, keyed in past the security door, and made it inside the yard, rationality had abandoned me. I paced in the backyard, the grass still crisp with frozen dew, as the sky began to yawn in the east. I couldn't let the slayers see me like this; they were already on edge.

What I wouldn't give to run. In my youth, the mountain had been a playground for me, the only condition was never be seen doing inhuman things by all-too-human eyes. Now I felt like an animal caught in a trap, held in place by the slayers, and able to see an escape I could not obtain without chewing off my own foot.

In the corner of the yard sat a stack of hay bales, propped atop each other to create a target for archery practice. If I had my grandmother's dagger still, I'd hurl it over and over just to work out my frustration. Without it, I used a bit of silver I repurposed as a bangle to create a tiny penknife. The meek impact of so small a weapon didn't satisfy, but it still felt good to chuck it at something I could pretend was Vlad's face. When that failed to vent my ire, I turned to my fists, imagining the vampire was standing before me.

"So."

*Shoulder punch.*

"Many."

*Chest jab.*

"Damn."

*Groin kick.*

"Obstacles!"

One final blow to the side of the stack sent hay flying directly into Yan's arms.

I startled as the vampire dropped his catch and ran a hand over his brow to clear the debris. "Did you know I was here, or was it just coincidence?"

Met with the fact that I was no longer alone, my posture eased. Incrementally. "How would I know you were here?"

His bleached hair bounced when he jerked his shoulders. "From what Markus says, you are not like the other hoods. Perhaps you have some special ability to sense us, like the slayers."

"None that I've noticed." I didn't want to be rude, but I also wasn't in the mood to be hospitable. "Did you need something, Yan?"

The vampire restacked the bales with the ease of a waiter picking up a dropped spoon and setting it back on the counter. "Not me, *them.*" He pointed back over his shoulder to the house. "Markus says the slayers have come to see you as some sort of Jesus figure."

Even though I wasn't particularly religious, I still curled in disgust at the comparison. "I wouldn't say that."

Yan twirled his right hand in the air. "You know Markus. He's given to hyperbole. But at the very least, they hold you in great respect and have put their fate, at least for the moment, into your hands. You have great sway with them, and with their opinions of things."

"And this is leading…. Where?"

"I mean them no harm, Miss Kline," he continued from behind a twisty smile. "Like most vampires, I was under the impression their kind was extinct. I admit, their resurrection has me… curious. Perhaps in my questioning of their circumstances, I came off as aggressive. They have misinterpreted my interest for something sinister, when really, I am in awe of their survival. I was wondering if you'd be willing to say a word on my behalf, to set them at ease?"

I stepped forward to draw the silver penknife from the recesses of the hay, curling it back into a bangle on my wrist with a thought. "No."

"No?" He repeated the word as though unclear of its meaning. "Perhaps I have also offended you in some way? Or is it because I am a vampire, and one of my kind currently holds your lover hostage?"

"It has something to do with the vampire part, but it's not about me."

And then, for reasons I couldn't quite fathom, I began to lecture in the backyard of my mother's estate to a vampire who was basically a stranger and sleeping with my cousin.

"Hoods are raised to believe werewolves tiptoe along the edge of humanity, that lupines are only a hair's breadth from being consumed by their animal natures and going apeshit on hueys. Since the time I was little, I felt in my bones that wasn't right. I opened myself up to that possibility, so much so that I fell in love with one of them. My world hinged on his kiss, on our ability to overcome our natures and be together, despite traditions, biology, rules, my mother… And then—"

A silent laugh fell into my shoulder as I buried my head.

"And then, reality bitch-slapped me. All it took was one night for that illusion to break under its own weight. And that left me afraid. So very afraid, probably more than I even admitted to myself at the time. Not of lupines really, but of the idea that I might trust one of them—any one—with my heart, and suffer that loss all over again. Loving Tobias is the bravest thing I've ever done, and now... Now, I may have lost him, too. So, I'm learning that the fear is a good thing, Yan. It protects you. It keeps you from putting yourself in the path of danger. These slayers... Some of them spent their whole life under the Ravens' control, and for them, *every* vampire right now is a Raven. So, no, I won't 'say a word' on your behalf, because I know the danger of that. They *shouldn't* trust you."

I sighed, turning away from his sagging shoulders and pitiful frown. Great, I had to be an asshole, didn't I? Guilt condemned me to say something nice. Close to nice? Not so mean, anyway.

"Look, Yan, for what it's worth, they probably shouldn't trust me, either. I have no idea what I can do to help them."

"No, I... understand." As much as a vampire could, Yan folded in on himself. "Thank you for your honesty. It makes me wonder, however, if I should keep my distance, stay away from the house. At least until such time as I can offer more than my passing curiosity."

"What if that never happens?"

I didn't know if I was asking for his benefit, or for mine.

Yan only shrugged. "In my many years, I've learned that 'never', never happens." The vampire straightened out, before fixing me with narrow eyes and an amused smile. "If only more hoods were more like you, Miss Kline."

"Like me?" I guffawed. "Falling in love with their historic adversaries and given to violent outbursts?"

"Perhaps. Your crowd is far too straight-laced for my taste." He grinned. "Markus is an exception, of course. But no, what I mean is, I wish they all were so passionate about doing right, that they're willing to be ostracized to do so. You are an inspiration."

"Now that's a high compliment. And… one… I'm not completely at ease with."

"Well, then, Geri Kline, I hope you grow into the impression you've made on me through the years, because it is mighty, as are you."

My mouth dropped open. "What do you mean, through the years?"

But just at that moment, Markus emerged from the door on the backside of the garage. "Yan? Are you back here… Are you… Oh, Geri?" He held up when he caught sight of me. "I didn't know you were back. And with my boyfriend. Talking."

Yan, beaming at my cousin, crossed the yard, pulled the solidly-built hood into his chest and brushed a kiss against his lips. "Amor, I think I will run into town for a bite. Can I bring you back anything?"

"Greek sailor, if you find one."

The vampire grinned. "I would keep him for myself if I did. I think I will sleep up at the castle today. Your house is quite full with guests and I would not wish to cause you to accommodate another."

"I told you that it doesn't matter," Markus said. "We can sleep in that attic for all I care. Just don't…"

But the vampire didn't hang around to argue. One more quick peck on Markus's cheek, and Yan dissolved into a smoky patch that rushed over the grounds and out of the yard.

My cousin passed me the stink-eye. "Okay, what the hell? Why are you cockblocking me? Did you tell him he couldn't stay here?"

"No." I mean, I didn't say 'thou shall not commit adultery with my kin in the house of my mother' or anything. "What does he mean he's going to stay up at the compound?"

My cousin looked at me like I was stupid. "He's the resident vampire. You know, the one the Matron Council employs to wipe the minds of any hueys that see something they shouldn't? How did you think I met him?"

"Maybe using one of my methods? Work in his university research lab. Or be really old-fashioned: storm his house to free his prisoners," I deadpanned before realizing my attempt at sarcasm was probably the most honest thing I'd said all day. Which, of course, reminded me that the slayers—and Tobias—were in greater peril with every passing hour. And me? I could do nothing about it.

The weight of incompetence pressed down on my shoulders, pushing my back against the hay bales and my butt to the ground. "Why am I here, Markus? Why am I just... *hovering* here?"

Markus softened, leaning down next to me and putting a hand on my shoulders. "I'm taking it Chin wouldn't give you the time of day."

"I never even left the car. Shame for them, really. It would have made shooting me easier."

Markus's mouth dropped open.

"They *didn't* shoot me, obviously," I amended. "But they did draw against me, so... You know, three-quarters intent, or something like that."

My cousin mused a moment before saying, "Actually, it's a good thing they refused to let you in."

"Good? How in the hell is that good?"

Markus slid down on the ground next to me. "Because I'm willing to bet they don't know you're an asinine."

"*Asenaic.*"

His hand cut the air. "Whatever. The point is, your mother did everything she could to keep that secret, and no matter what you think of her right now, I don't think she did it for any other reason than to protect you. Outside of this house, hardly anyone is hip to that nugget, and maybe we shouldn't just go throwing it around willy-nilly."

"Duh, do you really think I was born yesterday?"

Markus buried his chin in his shoulder, his voice growing soft. "Well, I mean, you wouldn't have to *tell* them."

"Hoods have many great powers." I, for one, was totally digging silver wielding, now that I could do it. "But I'm pretty sure being psychic isn't one. How else would they know? Can matrons read minds and no one remembered to tell me?"

Actually, thinking back on a few times when my mother had caught me trying to sneak off and see Cody back in high school...

Markus gawked at me like I had just said the most idiotic thing ever. And he was a fan of Monty Python. "They'd know the way any hood knows when a wolf is near. They'd sense you."

Ice shot down my spine. "Markus Kline, are you telling me you can *sense* the wolf in me?"

He nodded. "I mean, not *all* the time." He ran a hand through his brown, wavy hair before cleaning it on his sweater. "It's weird, though, the energy... I mean, it's definitely wolf, but not consistent or very strong. I only get whiff of it when I'm as close to you as I am now. It cycles with the moon. Except when you're near Tobias, and then it gets crazy strong. Or at least it did that last week in Istanbul."

I looked into the distance, into nothing and everything in particular, seeing the light that lit the room, though the room had seemed empty before. "Because we're pack."

He laughed. "That's ridiculous. I mean, even if you *are* descended from D.V.'s kid, that was, like, more than three centuries ago. There's no way the tiny bit of lupine DNA you got is going to line you up for beta duties."

He had a point. Possible to have a few traits? Yes, very. Likely that it was strong enough to bond as pack? Unlikely. But the moment I said the words, I felt the weight of truth fall into my hands.

Markus continued, "I mean, what's next? You going moonmad if you two are separated for too long?"

I glared at my cousin. "You think I'm holding it together *now*?"

"I'm serious. If you're wolf enough to be in pack, that probably means you're wolf enough to be struck with lunacity." Suddenly, Markus's eyes brightened. "Have you tried taking your fur yet?"

I rolled my eyes. "Pretty sure if that were possible, it would have happened by now."

"Yeah, but you're different somehow, right?" He pulled closer, putting an arm around me. "I mean, even on a hood level. You can wield silver now, but you never took your fire. Maybe whatever happened to you that made that possible, also ramped up your wolfishness."

He could have a point. "It's possible. We'd never know for sure without proper studies. Test and control cases. Lots of lab work."

Suddenly, Igor's absence became tangible. What a field day he'd have with me in his lab now.

My cousin's face screwed up. "You're thinking too much like a scientist, not like a hood."

"What in the hell does that mean?"

"We're at least a dozen generations down the line from when Gerwalta Faust got Black Forest fever. You really think you're the *only* descendant?" Markus paused as his eyes filled with thought. "The line is actually on your dad's side, you said, right? From the yellow hoods? Don't you have any cousins from his clan? I'm sure if we got in touch with Pietro's family in Argentina we'd discover other aesthetics."

"*Asenaics.*" I shook my head. "Remember how we agreed I should keep this on the DL? I don't think reaching out to my extended family is down or low. Besides, my dad doesn't have any family left except my mom and me. My *abuela* was the only closely-related person on his side of the family, and she died ten years ago."

The hood beside me balanced his chin on a balled fist. "If we could look at the archives, we'd be able to trace back, then see if there were any special mentions of anyone in the annals who howled at the moon and hunted tasty villagers."

Humor finds no anchor on a soul worn down by sorrow. "That's what I went to the Schloss to request, but Chin wouldn't listen. Now that she knows what I was after, they're not going to let you anywhere near them either. I'm surprised they haven't ordered you to disown me too yet."

"Chin can't touch me. I'm still under the Grand Matron's orders to watch and protect you. Even if those orders came down because she's your mother and she's using the rights of the throne to benefit her own family, none of the Matron Council would dare to override Aunt Brunnie without good reason."

I wouldn't be so sure. The disgust in Chin's voice when she spoke about not acting on behalf of my mother still echoed in my memories.

"I wish there were some other source we could go to, but all the archives have been centralized at Schloss Wolfsretter since it was turned over to the community."

"You don't think ancestry.com would be able to trace back our family that far, do you?" Markus asked. I mean, we still paid taxes and bought plow horses and stuff."

"Doubtful." My shoulders slumped. "Right now, I'd settle for just knowing his name. Why, Markus? Why is Gerwalta Faust's name a firebrand of traitor to us, but her mate is considered so shameful we know nothing about him?"

"Probably because back in those days, no one cared about the wolves but the wolves." A tiny, sarcastic laugh escaped him. "Not that we've come very far since then."

We sat, letting our ambitions war with our adversity in the battlefield of our minds, until a cannon exploded behind my brain, taking me to my feet. "Oh my god, Markus, you're a genius."

"That's what I keep telling everyone."

I ignored his cheekiness. "Somewhere in my family tree, there was a baby born to Gerwalta Faust and a wolf whose name we don't know. We can't get to our records to see if it's there, but we can get to the wolf's."

"Great idea," Markus mocked, "except lupines aren't known for their archival skills. Before the Matron Council had the database, all that kind of tracking stuff just happened... ad hoc."

I grimaced, knowing Markus was right. The hoods had had to keep records. They had wealth, land, contracts, correspondences with kings and sultans. The wolves in most of Europe had been farmers or laborers, often making a living at the pleasure of their overseeing matron. The hoods, or *wolfsretters* as they'd been known back then, didn't treat the packs under their protection as anything much more than cattle.

Old fairy tales weren't told to inspire hope or recall legendary love. They were tools to sow seeds of fear and hate.

*Little Red Riding Hood* was used to tuck my kind's children into bed and implant in our minds how lupine leanings would corrupt us and lead to our ruin. If Gerwalta Faust's "crime" had led to an alpha's execution, the wolves would not have soon forgotten, either. Their histories might not record numbers and contracts like ours; likely they weren't written down at all. They were howled at the moon, barked in the trees, spun around warm hearths on cold winter nights...

They were oral.

"The wolves may have passed down the story, like we did," I said. "Only, the other side of it. A warning to their pups of the danger of letting your guard down around a hood. That's our next move, Markus. If we can't turn a light on the wolf, we're going to look for his shadow."

# FIVE

Pastels were an odd color choice for maps. The gentle yellows, tranquil blues, and pastoral greens used to color the different countries of Europe belied a history wrought with conflict, death, and hatred. True, the continent had been more or less peaceful during my lifetime, but then again, huey political boundaries didn't correlate much with ours. The supe map would be colored in radical reds, angry purples, and confusing grays, a swirling confusion of push, pull, and parry. Borders were fluid, set down in the cardinal directions based on the dominance of whatever pack claimed—and kept—territory.

Cities belonged solely to the vampires, as they had been since ancient times, their conflicts played out on urban turfs. Although in recent years, they'd spilled out from beyond those traditional hunting grounds. Thus, the whole reason Tobias came to Chicago from sleepy little Morpeth, Northumberland. If the slayers had still been around, would I ever have met the man I'd come to love? Did I owe my happiness to the imprisonment of a dying race? That I could only have him because his mate had been experimented on to the point of death by Vlad's supporters?

All things I needed *not* to think about right now. *Focus, Geri. This isn't just about you and Tobias. Other hoods could be in danger, and they may not even know it.*

Markus, Amy, and Caleb waited until sunrise before converging in the kitchen. On the floors above, the nineteen other slayers had divided the available rooms in ways that suited them, though the pregnant Alexandra had been granted a solo suite.

Markus briefed the other two on what both he and I

had already discussed.

"After '48, when Schloss Wolfsretter was converted from the residence of the House of Red to the administrative headquarters of the whole hood world, the pack that had been rooted in the Triberg area," he pushed his index finger over the very town on the map we currently occupied, "fractured into two packs and relocated. Most of them went here." His finger skirted to a region some 200km to the southeast. "The Oberstdorf Forest. But a few went in the opposite direction." His hand traversed down a minty green border region to a Pepto-Bismal shaded country. "To the highlands just below the Austrian border."

Caleb crossed his arms and leaned back in his chair. "Start with the bigger pack. More mouths, more opportunities for oral traditions to be handed down."

Amy nodded. "As a life-long gossip, I agree. If we drive crazy fast, we can be down there by nightfall."

"You know, Geri, this actually is one time when being relinquished is going to help you." Markus turned his eyes up to meet mine. "You're not a recognized member of the community, so you don't have to go through the formality of telling the alpha you're coming to the packland or letting the local matron know you're there. You can just wander in at your own risk."

I grimaced. "Yeah, but it also means you can't come with me. Most wolves are kind, but having a rogue hood show up on their land uninvited might leave me wishing I had backup."

Amy quirked her head to the side. "*Local* matron? You mean there's more than just Geri's mother?"

"More than one?" Caleb coughed a laugh. "The hoods are like a paramilitary organization. Very organized, very tidy, dividing the world into controllable zones of dominance."

"Actually, our current set up is something based off the

Ottomans," Markus countered. "One grand poohbah at its head, from the royal family, if you will, though all bloodlines *technically* have a claim. Then there's a council of advisors, and locally, each region has its own governor. The Ottomans are the reason we call them sanjaks, which unlike almost everything else, is so not a German word."

Amy's hand circled vaguely over the map. "So, you mean, like, the whole world is parceled out, and you guys… The House of Red?… are the hood royal family?"

"There's no one in Antarctica," I said flatly, vaguely motioning at the map. "Or most of Oceania. Australia has a few packs and a matron, but that's because of immigration. Lupines aren't native there."

"I like how you ignored the part about being royal," Amy said. "Does that mean your mom is…"

"The Sultan, the emperor, the master of the universe… Whatever way you want to think about it," Markus confirmed. "As long as she has the backing of the Council of Matrons, Aunt Brunnie's word is law to all the hood clans."

"Which, as you pointed out," I interrupted, "no longer includes me." I watched the light go out from Amy's eyes, knowing my friend had already been constructing some sort of Disney-inspired saga in her head. "Right, so that's my plan. I need a few hours of sleep, but then I'm going to set out for Austria."

The three people across the table blinked in rapid succession.

Caleb shook his head. "You can't honestly think we're letting you go alone."

"Of course, you're going to," I said. "The bigger need for security is here. If the Ravens show up while I'm gone, Caleb can lead the assault and Markus knows all the hideouts and escape routes from Triberg. And Amy can't come because, well…"

"Because Amy is a weak huey who will snap like a twig," she said.

A sheepish smile crossed my face. "I wouldn't have put it like that, exactly."

The blonde folded her arms over her chest. "Doesn't make it untrue, though, does it? No worries. After being attacked by a vampire, I'm not eager to be mauled by a werewolf, bested by pixies, or in anyway assaulted by whatever other creatures are out there."

Caleb turned back to his original point. "I'm pretty sure we don't have to worry about pixies, but there's still five Ravens left alive and they're going to be gunning for you. They might be thinking hard about heading into Triberg with the Hood HQ sitting right up the hill, but once you leave the Black Forest, who knows? Unless you're planning on not sleeping for two days straight or stopping to use the bathroom at some roadside gas station, you need someone to cover your six. You're *not* going alone."

I leaned back from the table. "I agree, that's why I want to take Yan."

"Oh! I'd love to go!"

All four spun the moment his voice called out, Caleb even balancing a conjured solarium on his open palm. Markus meanwhile pulled his hidden silver into a blade. Not to be outdone, Amy brandished a banana swiped from a bowl on the nearby counter.

Though, in her defense, it was a very *large* banana.

Yan wore a crooked grin. "You can put down the produce, Miss Popowitz. Potassium's effect on the undead is overhyped."

Markus, realizing his lover had entered without a sound, reclaimed his silver and circled the others, arms open.

"Sweetheart, what have I told you about sneaking up on me like that?"

"Don't, or you may inadvertently chop my head off?"

The male hood pushed the vampire's cheeks between his massive hands. "I mean, not *off*, probably, but still..." He graced a kiss over the vampire's lips. "I thought you went home. Have you been hanging out here the whole time?"

Yan's eyes landed on me, like a child constructing a cover story after breaking his mother's favorite vase. "I... um, changed my mind. I smoked in through the garage just before the sun came up. I've been hanging around in the heating vents."

"Heating vents?" Caleb's query wasn't directed at anyone in particular. "I never thought about it, but makes sense. Inga used to use the heating system at WWL to get all over the building. How are we going to defend against that, if the Ravens try to break in?"

"We can't," I said. There was no point in false optimism. It would get people killed. "This house wasn't designed for that kind of defense. Keep working with the slayers on sharpening their skills. For the ones who are in good health or haven't been through their awakening, start them working on some defensive forms." I jerked my head in my best friend's direction. "Amy, too. Just because she's not as strong as the others doesn't mean she should be left defenseless, in the event of pixies or whatever."

But Caleb wasn't distracted by my request in the least.

"You knew Yan was still here." The slayer's narrowed eyes focused in on me. "How?"

I huffed. "How else? Because he's a second pair of eyes

ordered to watch me."

The vampire dared feign confusion. "Miss Kline, I'm afraid I don't know what you're—"

"My only question," I interrupted, "is *who* gave the order? My mother or Chin?"

At that, the game came to an end. Yan grimaced. "Matron Chin."

"Wait, what?" Markus took a step back from his boyfriend. "Why? I thought that was my job."

Yan's hand rose to stroke down my cousin's cheek. "Because I volunteered. If it wasn't me, it'd be someone less amenable to presenting you all in a good light. I was strategizing." The formalities of lovers' reunion aside, the vampire turned to me. "As long as you can provide me a safe place to shelter during sunlit hours, I would be happy to accompany you to visit the Austrian packlands."

"She's not going to Austria, and she's definitely not going in the company of a vampire." Caleb planted his finger on the Oberstdorf Forest. "Geri, your chances are better with the bigger pack. If they turn out not to know anything, it's not that long of a drive to the other settlement."

"I don't care how short the drive is," I snapped. "I know it's irrational, but I'm going with my gut on this. Besides, the pack that's stayed further away from civilization is the one less likely to have given into modern distractions. The oral traditions would hold up better through the years."

"Actually, there's something to that," Amy said. "You know, I read this one article I came across about this remote valley in the east part of Turkey where the people speak a whistle language. Like, complete with verbs and nouns and stuff, only in whistles. I guess the sound carries, like, a mile over the valley. But now they're afraid the younger generation isn't going to learn it, since it's not the most efficient way to communicate anymore, given that everybody has a cell phone."

By the time the blonde huey finished, the rest of us sat with jaws unhinged.

Amy looked at her fingernails. "Why are you guys always so surprised when I know stuff? I'm not the Daphne of this Scooby gang, you know. Supes don't have exclusive rights on useful information."

I shook off my surprise before continuing. "Yan, I still would like to have you with me. A vampire can move with speeds I can't, maybe get us out of a critical situation. But this isn't hood business; any information I get isn't for her consumption."

"I'm already *not* going to tell her you're an asenaic," the vampire said with a wink. When my face morphed into a mask of shock, he pointed back over his shoulder. "I was back there, listening, remember? No, I'm just supposed to report if you try to make any contact with other *hoods*. I was very careful about what I was agreeing to."

Amy threw her arms out at that one, though. "Come on, Geri, you barely know this parasite—" Her eyes dashed to said *parasite*. "No offense." Then landed back on me. "—and you're just going to get in a car with him and drive off? What if he's just waiting for the perfect chance to kill you?"

Yan's hand splayed over his chest. "I would sooner destroy a Picasso."

I didn't think I was worthy of that level of reverence, but Amy was only being a concerned friend. "If his goal was to kill me, he would have done it when we were alone in the yard. Anyway, if Markus trusts him, I trust him. Only, I'm not sure how I'm supposed to keep a vampire out of the sunlight in a car?"

"I thought the answer would be obvious," Yan said. "You

are a hood. Encase me in silver."

I felt like I'd been asked to join a BDSM gang, when I had already said I didn't whip that way. "Can't we just use a Tupperware bowl or something?"

As if we had anything that Donna Reed in this house.

Yan shook his head. "I don't mind being trapped in something, but I must be sure it's sunlight-proof. There may be alternatives, but I'd prefer it this way. I know most vamps can withstand a few hours, but my skin is a little more… sensitive."

"And you're trusting me to do that? To entomb you in silver?"

"Of course." Yan looked surprised that I'd even ask. "Markus trusts you, therefore, I trust you."

"Thank you, Yan." I turned to my cousin. "While we're gone, put in some appearances at the compound. I don't want the council to forget that they still owe the slayers if the slayers agree to take that damned contract."

Markus nodded. "I'll do what I can. In return, make sure my boyfriend doesn't die."

"You mean die again?"

"Seriously, Geri." Markus's face drained of any jest as his hand wrapped around my forearm and squeezed. "He's my Tobias. Don't damage him."

I looked back over my shoulder, at the vampire who was now quietly watching with a cocky grin on his face. "I'll get him back to you unblemished. I promise."

# SIX

For centuries, supe intellectuals and philosophers had debated whether or not those once known as "dark ones" were still, or ever indeed had been, human. Opinions varied, bolstered by evidence and counter-evidence, varying degrees of facts, and even a few so-called divine revelations. Even the supernatural races were not immune from crackpots and self-appointed prophets. At the end of the day, since hoods, slayers, and werewolves could still *breed* with hueys, the collective summation was that, technically, we were only a different type of human.

Vampires, however, who could only infect hueys with their condition to create progeny, were classified as humans, but diseased. To me, the answer was simpler. A vampire could love and be loved, and was at liberty to make decisions based on will, not instinct, if they so chose.

Unconditionally, they were human.

*Maybe that's what drove Igor to study supernatural genetics*, I thought as I maneuvered the car through another gentle mountain curve. He was of an age when all maladies came with some level of social damage. What would it be like to live as a supernatural leper? Did he see himself as having some communicable disease, and see the slayers as a cure?

Retracting from completion of grand theories and biological classifications, even I admitted this was perhaps the oddest road trip I had ever taken. Under the light of the blazing sun, the others and I had agreed I'd be safe to drive on the main highway that led south out of the Black Forest region and over the Austrian border without my watchdog awake. As the sun dipped toward the horizon, however, and the purple shadows of the mountains stretched long over the highway, I turned to the urn-like container belted into the passenger seat beside me. To the untrained eye, it would look like nothing more than a full-sized coffee thermos, though without any seams. How would anyone suspect it held a vampire inside?

I reached across the divide, tapped a finger on the vessel and pulled the silver back up my arm, past my shoulders, and commanded it to plate the planes of my abdomen. I didn't want any of it in sight when I met the pack. The smoke held the container's shape only a moment, so concentrated that it looked like I'd only changed the color of the thermos rather than the materials it was made from. A blink, however, and the cloud swirled, taking on mass where moments ago there had been only miasma.

Yan stretched out long in the seat the moment he was reconstituted. "Thank you. It was getting rather itchy in there."

He put on his seatbelt, though I doubted a car accident would do anything to him. Unless it managed to take his head off, that was.

I turned down the retro German pop station I'd been listening to for the last two hours, more to annoy me and keep me conscious than to entertain. My annual Herbert Grönemeyer quota was full in one sitting. "We've got two more hours until we reach Zeihern. It's not completely dark yet, but the direct sunlight is gone. I have to stop for gas, and I'd feel better if I wasn't alone when I did so. You're not going to burst into flames or anything, are you?"

"A vampire doesn't burst into flames, we dry out, then scorch, then dissolve into dust," Yan said flatly. "The light is defusing quickly. I will be fine with this limited exposure."

"Groovy. So… Want to take turns changing the radio station or have awkward conversations about our lives?"

Yan shut off the radio. "Have you consummated your

relationship with your wolf lover yet?"

"Awkward conversation, then." I flicked on the right blinker as I merged toward the exit. "No offense, Yan, but that's none of your business."

He continued as if I hadn't spoken. "In the old days, these things were so much simpler to deduce. If we observed two creatures going into a room together for the day then coming out in certain unkempt ways, we could assume intercourse had occurred. Nowadays, though, your generation has no set rules for social engagement. You and Mr. Somfield, in fact, have been cohabitating for sometime without any intercourse occurring as best we can figure, but…"

The brakes cried to the high heavens as I slammed them down. As soon as I was assured there was no one coming up behind us and I wasn't blocking the exit, I spun in my seat.

"Who in the hell do you think you are, asking me that kind of stuff?"

Yan shrank back in his seat, finally rediscovering his shame. "Apologies. Time and isolation have made me unpracticed in the art of social convention."

"Ya think? My sex life is none of your business. How would you like it if I asked what you and Markus do behind closed doors?"

"Markus prefers keeping the doors open…"

My hand shot up. "Oh, my god, that mental picture is going to haunt me forever…" I tried to clear my mind. "How does that happen, anyway? And before you get into details I don't want to know or will ever want to know, I only mean how did the two of you end up together?"

"You *know* how curious he is about vampires, and since I came in to the employ of the hoods a decade ago, he's always been at me for details. I suppose in the last year or so we just sort of... clicked. It has not been without some negotiation. My position necessitates certain... *acts* which come into conflict with our relationship."

"No offense—I love my cousin—but he isn't the 'lie to my face and I'm okay with that' type."

"Oh, I don't *lie* to him," Yan rushed to clarify. "I've grown too old to put stock in the benefits of artifice, but both of us understand that our harmony depends on a bit of unscripted discord in the distance. I have no doubt he has his secrets as well."

Remembering that Markus hadn't told Yan I was an asenaic, I knew that to be true.

"Not that I'm going to answer, but why would you ask me about sleeping with Tobias?"

Yan's eyes brightened. "Ah, so you have—"

"STILL none of your business."

He drew inward. "One of the things that brought Markus and I together is our interest in the other's peoples. Just as Markus is curious about vampires, I have always been curious about wolfsretters. *Hoods,* as you say currently. I've endeavored to learn as much about your history as I can."

The full implication of what Yan said took shape in my brain. "What do you know about what really happened to Gerwalta Faust?"

"The only record I've ever encountered about those events was one penned by her sister, Matron Helga Faust. But there are... rumors."

My ears perked up. "Yeah?"

Yan nodded. "That the Betrayer wasn't Gerwalta Faust at all, but her mother."

That didn't make any sense, even if I didn't buy the commonly-held version of the story as true. "How so?"

"As the saying goes, 'history is penned by the victors, the truth buried with the victims.' Have you not ever wondered why Helga is called 'the Restorer'?"

I chewed on my lips as I moved the car back into drive. "No, but I guess I should have. Anything you can add to that?"

His hands flattened on his legs, rubbing his knees. "One story I heard was that Gerwalta Faust's mother, Gunda, had a last-minute change of heart about her daughter and saved the baby from harm, staging its death and secreting it out of Schloss Wolfsretter."

Hope fluttered in the pit of my stomach, making me dizzy. "Do you think that's true?"

"Oh, yes, Miss Kline, I do. It came from a very reliable source not given to spreading gossip."

"Yeah, who?"

"Igor Kharmarov."

Holy shit. Igor? Had he known the whole time that my ancestor survived? How? The answer to that question would have to wait until the next time I saw the professor again. If I *ever* saw Igor again.

Yan leaned forward, examining me across the divide. "Are you okay, Miss Kline? You've gone pale."

"I'm fine." I wasn't. "Call me Geri, though. And do you mind if I give you one word of advice before we get to the packlands?"

"Of course not."

"Don't ask any of the lupines about their sex lives."

# SEVEN

We left the car parked on the side of a dirt road and moved with lithe steps across grass crisped with frozen dew. Ahead lay six cottages clustered in the midst of a clearing, braced by several utilitarian structures. A little further up the hill stood the remnants of an ancient barn, moist and moss-covered, looking like one of the postcards the summer tourists gobbled up. The style was similar to ones still seen at intervals in the Black Forest, though fewer of the structures remained with each passing decade.

A half moon peered over the mountains, lighting the settlement.

"Which house do we try?" Yan asked. "Or do you suppose the pack is out running?"

I closed my eyes and inhaled, testing the air for hints, sending my senses coursing over the landscape. Then, I felt it. That little tug, a quiver which grew into a wobble in my gut. They were there, up the hill and concealed by the forest, roughly a kilometer away. They'd been moving in the opposite direction, but the moment I reached out to them, I may have inadvertently changed that. Suddenly the pack was on the move, closing in fast. But not all of them. Several of them were closer. Much closer. I didn't need any supernatural powers to know that part. The frosted, lit windowpanes of one of the residences gave it away to the naked eye.

"Markus ran this pack through the database. Four males, six females, four cubs ranging in age from two to thirteen. Two females are with the two younger cubs inside the biggest house." I lifted a finger, pointed to the two-storied structure that lay furthest from where the road ended.

Yan's jaw dropped. "Remarkable. Your senses are so well-tuned as all that?"

"Actually, I'm just using deduction." My finger flicked up. "That's the only house with its lights on and smoke coming out the chimney. You should know, though, that the rest of the pack is charging toward us from that ridge up there."

"I can hear them," Yan concurred. "I am surprised you can, though. I know hood hearing beats a human's, but it is nothing compared to a vampire."

No sooner were the words out of his mouth than the first lupine broke through the tree line, only eight hundred meters to our right. She was tailed by the rest in quick succession, the pack moving in a way I'd rarely observed myself except in nature documentaries. Their circular formation complimented with yips could only be interpreted in one way: they intended to kill.

"We have a plan, right?"

The nerves in the vampire's voice were undeniable. Wolves and vamps didn't often cross paths due to their different habitats, but the archives of our peoples included a few times a pack took on a lone vampire and ripped it to shreds. A single vamp may be stronger, but a lupine was just as fast and, in a group, could pull down anything.

"Kinda." I pushed Yan behind me. "Not sure this is going to work, so be ready to smoke unless you want your throat ripped out."

"I can't smoke when I'm scared."

Brave of him to admit as much.

"Besides," Yan continued, "Markus loves kissing my throat."

I readied myself to move. "So didn't need to know that."

A wall of barks and growls fell over us, an onslaught that pushed every button my hood instincts had. *Strike them. Slay them. Damage them.* I lectured my wolfsretter brain, in German even. *No! This will work.*

Or so I hoped.

It was funny. All my life I had listened to the drive of my nature pushing me to act in ways prescribed by breeding and genetics, and never considered that wolves did the same thing. And since new revelations had me seeing everything from a new perspective, I figured the right thing to do might be the *opposite* of what instinct demanded.

"Yan, do exactly as I do when I do it."

My eyes would be glowing silver now, but there was nothing I could do about it. The wolves ripped up ground. Twenty meters. Fifteen meters.

Behind me, Yan's voice shook. "Geri?"

Ten meters.

Five.

"Geri!"

"Now!"

In the blink of an eye, I folded in on myself, dropping to the ground, burying my head down between my arms, assuming a fetal position on the ground. One of a vampire's greatest strengths was the ability to move with superhuman acuity. Gravity didn't pull on Yan any harder than it did me, but I still heard the thud he made even before I'd assumed my position.

The pack surrounded us, and for a moment, when a few pushed their snouts into my hair and clothing, one even nipping my ears, worry gripped me. Would they attack, would they bite? Would they *kill?* One raked a paw across my head, hopefully just to get a better view of my face. No further comment from Yan, so either he had a remarkably high pain threshold, or the wolves hadn't touched him.

"Explain yourself."

The man's scorched voice, drenched with the thick accent of the Austrian mountains, told me that at least one of the wolves had shifted back into his human form. I fought down the impulse to look up and continued to kiss dirt.

"My name is Geri Kline, relinquished hood of the House of Red, disavowed daughter of Matron Brünhild Kline," I said. Or at least, I hoped I'd said. I'd been raised to speak basic German, but fear was getting the better of me and I wasn't sure I'd said it right.

A lupine's hot breath huffed against my ear as I awaited response. Without my eyes, my ears became my only view of the scene. Quiet whispers wove together in a tangle, the unfamiliar threads of voices difficult to discern. The gruff man—he must be the alpha—spoke with a female. It was the woman, not the man, who addressed me next.

"Why do you travel in the company of a vampire?"

To my relief, Yan answered for himself in German perfected as though god damned Goethe himself were drafting a new work on the vampire's tongue.

"It is my honor and privilege to accompany Miss Gerwalta Kline into your beautiful packlands. I yield to the grace of your Konigswolf, offering my respect and vow that I am here without issue, seeking no claim but a hope for friendship."

I cried out as a firm hand twisted my hair in its grip and pulled me to my feet. I couldn't help but whimper, even as I told myself to do so was to broadcast weakness.

*But you* are *weak, Geri,* a little voice inside me mocked. *A strong hood would not have thrown herself like pearls before swine.*

The naked, middle-aged woman who held me at arm's length didn't seem interested in roughing me up though, or of actually causing pain. In fact, she looked at me… confusedly, with deep earthen-colored eyes and skin nearly as fair as the snow that topped the nearby mountains. Her appearance struck the eye, gave me pause for a reason I couldn't quite put words to. It wasn't beauty, per se. No, it was some sort of power I sensed from her. She was gentle, but formidable. Dominant. Powerful.

"Your name is Gerwalta?"

"Yes, ma'am." *Ma'am?* "Like the Betrayer."

The woman's face curled. "Who?"

Not all wolves knew of the hood legacy, it seemed. In fact, not all hoods knew more than the name, like a title of a book they'd been read as children rather than a real person, an archetype of evil without the need for context.

"Gerwalta Faust," I clarified, "the Betrayer."

As we spoke, other wolves shifted back into their huey forms, one of whom, a young woman who couldn't be but a year or two younger than me, leaned into the wolf who held me captive.

"It could not be coincidence," the first said.

The other woman clicked her tongue. "Coincidence is never coincidence." She turned back to me. "What business does a relinquished hood and a vampire have in these packlands?"

They were never going to believe me. "I came to learn your stories."

She laughed, turning to the gravel-voiced man and finally releasing her hold me. "Did you hear that, Lukas? She says she wants to hear our stories. Lies! A hood wants to hear nothing from a wolf but 'Yes, ma'am' and 'no, sir.'"

I tried to wet a mouth that had suddenly gone dry. "Please, I've driven all the way from Triberg just for this. All I want is to talk to you, ask you a few questions."

The young woman smiled and stroked my cheek. "And we will do our best to answer."

Lukas took half a step forward. "Ann-Marie, you cannot possibly—"

Ann-Marie snapped her fingers and gave Lukas a vicious scowl, silencing him, making him sink back. How curious a behavior for an alpha.

"The road from Schloss Wolfsretter is long," Ann-Marie continued. "Come. I think dinner is just about ready. Go to the alpha's home. We will dress and join you shortly."

By this time, all the wolves but two had scratched back into human flesh. As though Ann-Marie were a grand marshal leading a parade, they all fell into line behind her, six naked bodies walking through the crisp Alpine landscape as though strolling across a Brazilian beach in the height of summer. The two in fur pulled up the rear.

Or *rears,* as the case may be.

Yan drew himself beside me, his eyes fixed on a rather svelte male who looked to be in his early thirties. "Are they always like this? So liberated? So nude?"

I nodded.

"But you don't seem fazed by it at all."

"It gets old after a while."

It didn't.

"Really?" The vampire grinned. "So when you see Mr. Somfield…"

In an instant, my face flushed. I had, of course, seen Tobias shift from fur to flesh before, but that had been in a time when we'd either been battling for our lives, or before we'd admitted our feelings. Thinking on it now, I didn't picture myself being so blasé the next time.

Yan clapped me on the shoulder. "Save your breath, Geri. Your pulse says it all."

Lukas opened the door to the largest home as the others filtered to the other residences. The scene we found was enough to melt the heart: playtime for a chubby-faced toddler and an older girl, perhaps a sister, who must have only recently gained an ability to take fur. She darted between her wolf and her huey forms, drawing the little boy's squeals with each iteration. Inviting flames leapt about the fireplace, bits of bundled pine branches hung on the walls, and I'd bet twenty euros that all the wood furniture and embroidered cushions were handmade.

"At ease," Lukas said to the two attending shewolves as they leapt to their feet, instinctively seizing the children and shepherding them behind them. "They are guests. The hood is Gerwalta Kline, the vampire is her chaperone."

Both women's faces blossomed into silent smiles, and one with luxuriously long and thick black hair said, "Look at her eyes! How curious."

I blinked my surprise, suddenly self-conscious and uncertain how to respond.

Luckily the other, her hair bobbed short and blond, spoke instead. "Like the hoods." She fixed me with a diagnosing study. "But I don't sense—"

"No, wait." Something shifted in the air around us, and the shewolves grinned. "How odd."

Yan needled around my side. "I don't suppose you ladies would be willing to speak on what you're experiencing?"

The blonde wolf's smile soured. "I'm sorry… You are?"

The vampire stuck his hand out. "Janus Sousa, born of the Varanasi Creche and of the Rajani bloodline, currently resident vampire employed at Schloss Wolfsretter."

None of these facts seemed to meet with lupine approval, as they both eyeballed the proffered hand for a few moments before turning their attention back on me.

"Is your name really Gerwalta?" the blonde asked. "Like, honestly? It's not just a pet name you picked up?"

"A pet name?" My face curdled. "Not unless someone really hated me. *Which* my mother does, so…"

The blanket of awkward I'd just thrown out settled, dampening the conversation. Luckily, it was at this point that Ann-Marie returned, wearing a black knit poncho and blue jeans. "Ladies, I wonder if we might borrow the room for a few minutes?"

Both the women ceased staring at me and turned to the children, still engrossed in the pleasures of the young girl's quick-change routine.

Ann-Marie settled on the couch, inviting me, and I'd presume, Yan, to take up the nearby chairs. "Before anything else, I have to ask what brought you to *us*?"

How to answer it in a way that wouldn't put the wolves on the defensive? "Are you familiar with the hood stories about the Betrayer?"

Ann-Marie grinned. "You mean Little Red Riding Hood?"

I grimaced. "Kinda, but not exactly the Grimm Brothers version."

The shewolf exhaled and fell back into the couch. "Why don't you tell us the hood version of the story, then?"

"Well, it's not a version. It's the actual story. Back in the 1600s, a hood of the House of Red became the mate of a werewolf from the Triberg pack. *This* pack's ancestors. It's the biggest crime a hood can commit."

"No huntsman and his axe, then?" Ann-Marie's eyebrow arched.

I curled in on myself. "The story *we're* told as children is that they were hunted down by the Red Matron, chopped into pieces, and roasted on silver spits over a fire on *Feuernacht* as punishment, but I don't think that's true." I knew it wasn't, but I wasn't about to cast out all my secrets. "I'm hoping your version of the story gives an alternative picture."

*And his name. Please, I just want to know his name.*

"Let me see if I understand." Ann-Marie smoothed out the bottom of her black poncho over the tops of her legs. "She both chopped her own daughter into pieces *and* roasted her over a fire, you say? If you'll pardon the pun, it seems a bit of overkill, doesn't it? But the hoods are given to violence. I should have guessed their version would end with blood and torment."

Yan perked up. "Blood?"

Ann-Marie ignored him. "My ancestors would be appalled to know how the hoods have corrupted their story."

My head sped again, though I tried to pull back the anticipation. "Are you saying that this story *has* been passed down in your pack?"

"Do tell." Yan inched forward in his seat. "And please, emphasize any parts that include blood."

Ann-Marie took to her feet, and I was suddenly aware of how the gaze of the only wolf who remained behind, Lukas, rose with her.

"Geri," the young woman held out her hand, as though she and I were schoolgirl friends. "Might I interest you in a walk, just the two of us? I don't believe you've ever visited these packlands before. They really are quite beautiful, and I'd be honored to show you."

My instincts screamed at me to say no. *An unfamiliar, young wolf with an unusual sway over the pack wants to get you alone. It cannot be for any good reason.* My head jerked in Yan's direction, though if I expected to find any counsel in his eyes, he left me wanting. He watched with an invisible tub of popcorn. Hoping that being alone with Ann-Marie would let me be more open about the reasons I'd come, I swallowed my fears, reached up, and accepted the shewolf's hand.

# EIGHT

Winter came earlier at higher elevations. Despite the fact that it was only mid-October, we'd not had to climb far up the mountain to find snow beneath our feet. Wolves preferred forested regions (insofar as the packs that lived where it ever snowed at all) in part because the tree tops offered refuge against the accumulation of the white stuff. What did float between branches and firs to the ground was protected from the sunlight, reducing the chance the surface would melt in the day, only to refreeze after sunset. A space up ahead where the timberline met the cleared land came into view, but it seemed so odd that the wolves would build their residences so in the open, a fact I remarked upon as we walked.

Ann-Marie smiled. "A bold move on our part, perhaps? Who would ever think a pack living so in the open would have so much to hide? But that's not the story you came to hear, is it?"

"Does it have anything to do with why you all fractured off from the wolves who settled in the Oberstdorf Forest?"

"Indeed. The schism resulted from a difference of opinion. Curiously, Geri, do you know why your clan fractured and went to America?"

Honestly, I'd never given the thought a moment's consideration. "Probably the same reason a lot of Europeans were moving around that time: the hope of a better life. There were already wolves and hoods in America, of course. The Orange Clan, the first lupines...They're still around, but not as many. Mostly in the plains states and southwest."

"I've read about this, native peoples pushed out of

their lands. Why should supes be immune from such cultural shifts?"

She mused in silence for a moment, though I didn't know if it was because she needed to digest the thought or she was hoping I'd say something. But the question was rhetorical, wasn't it?

Finally, Ann-Marie continued. "I know why you're here, Gerwalta Kline, daughter of the Red Matron. There's a reason you came to us for stories and not the Oberstdorf Forest."

I drew to a stop to fix her in my gaze, but without pausing, Ann-Marie pulled me onward.

"Let's keep pace. I should try to get back home sooner rather than later. I know it makes Lukas nervous when I'm out here alone."

Because she was young? A woman? Alone with a hood?

As if she'd heard my internal question, her face broke out into a drunken smile. "He wants me to be his mate, made a formal offer a week ago. I think he's afraid if he isn't with me every second, he'll miss me giving my answer."

"And do you know your answer?" I asked.

Her head bobbed. "But if I told him right away, what fun would that be? Ah, yes, we're almost there."

I trudged on. Up the mountain slope, tall pines dusted with snow created a verdant crystalline view that disguised a measure of both breadth and width. As far as I could see, there was nothing ahead to arrive to, other than more trees. "I wasn't aware we had a destination."

Ann-Marie grinned, her eyes scanning the treetops. "Anytime one moves forward, it is always with a destination, whether or not they are aware of it."

"You're very philosophical for a wolf."

The statement crossed my lips before I'd had a chance to bite my tongue. Instead, I bit my lip, waiting for a rebuke that I was totally owed. Instead, Ann-Marie let out a single laugh.

"I'm sorry," I scrambled. "I didn't mean to—"

Her hand rose, cutting me off. "No need. You were raised a hood, I was raised a wolf. We both have been forced to believe that the other should fit a certain mold, and it confuses us when we meet with experiences that make us question who the other is, for it also makes us question who *we* are. Besides," she turned a warm grin my direction, "I could also say that I've never met so kind a hood."

Even the indirect insinuation left a mark, one I couldn't slight the shewolf for. Through stories I'd heard from Tobias, and after the Matron Council's rejection of the slayer refugees, I had begun to see my own people with an outsider's eye.

Feeling a shiver that had nothing to do with the cold, I pulled my jacket tighter about me. "You didn't think I was too kind when Yan and I arrived earlier. Your pack looked like it was out for blood."

"That was not about you being a hood." Ann-Marie drew to a stop, as did, it seemed, the falling snow, the wind through the trees, and the rotation of the earth. "That was about an unknown wolf venturing into our packlands."

When I'd used my ability to detect the wolves, I hadn't realized the feeling went both ways. But it wasn't like I was about to come out and admit that. Ann-Marie was going above and beyond to be hospitable, but who knew what she'd do if she knew I could summon her kind. "What unknown wolf?"

"You don't need to hide your secret from me. In fact, you can't. I perceived you the moment you drove up our access road. The others did not, of course, but that's to be expected."

"But I am not of your pack."

Asenaic or no, I was still certain the other laws of lupine nature applied. Wolves had a tremendous sense of smell. Their vision was pretty keen as well, though it paled in comparison to a vampire's. Where the "super" of "supernatural" really came into play, however, was in their ability to communicate while in their animal forms. *Not quite psychic,* Cody had once explained when I'd asked about it. *But we have a sense of each other, both in terms of what we're trying to say and where we are. If another member of the pack is inside my house, I know it before I walk in the front door.*

But the skill wasn't omnipresent. Like a closed-circuit system, that power only extended to members of a pack. Or so I thought...

"True, you are not," Ann-Marie admitted. "Nor are you of my pack, and how could you be? But I think a hood mother would not name her child Gerwalta casually. It would have made you a pariah among your people. The Grand Matron is exceptionally brave, I think, to do this. But it doesn't matter. Even if your name were Philomena or Tsa-Tsa, I would suspect you were of my bloodline. Let's keep walking. We're just about there."

Walk? How could she walk with that kind of bomb thrown at my feet?

"Your bloodline?" My head shook without consideration that it may seem insulting. "That can't be. I'm a hood."

"Who also has a wolf ancestor."

My mouth felt like someone had stuck an overly starched, dry washcloth in it. "Are you descended from Gerwalta Faust?"

The young woman blushed, took me by the hand and coaxed me onward in body, but away in mind. "Oh, dear, no. But my ancestor was the brother to the Guardian's mate. Just a few more steps, now, Geri. Come now, it's just over in that glade there. You'd never know it, but until a century ago, there was a hunting lodge here, one with a splendid summer garden. It's all gone now, of course. But the marker remains. My pack thinks the forest itself protected them, growing around it."

"Ann-Marie, please." I seized back my hand. "I don't want to be rude, and I sure don't want to come off sounding like a hood, but I demand you to tell me what you're talking about. Who is the Guardian? Where are we walking? How did you know we have a common ancestor? Have the wolves known this whole time that Gerwalta Faust's baby lived?"

In short, why was I lied to all my life, while others knew?

The shewolf looked as though she had a secret threatening to bust through at any moment. She pointed to a place behind me, over my right shoulder.

"Read it."

I spun.

At first, I'd thought I'd been put on. What lay before me was just another tree, even if deformed, like some superhuman force had bent it to his will, compelling the trunk to bulge and bubble about four feet off the ground. But as I let my eyes relax, *words* began to take shape. The plaque may have once gleamed, but now its silver was exposed, tarnished. My fingers danced over it as my powers reached out, calling to the silver that lay in the pine's embrace, asking it to shake off its age and weathering. Where a moment before the letters could barely be perceived, they now shone out, reflected in the ambient light of the forest.

The Old German script proved so embellished and elaborate, it was a barrier to understanding. Perhaps Ann-

Marie sensed the trouble I was having; a moment later the shewolf was at my side, her finger bouncing along with each elucidation while still keeping sufficient distance so as not to be burned by the element which was a poison to her kind.

*"Here lieth the body of A. Baron, born 16 April 1662, aged twenty-five years, died 12 November 1687, and wife, born 3 December 1666, died 12 November 1687, aged twenty-two years. May they be together in death as they were so briefly in life."*

Impossible. *"This* is Gerwalta Faust's grave?"

"Pah! Gerwalta *Faust!"* Ann-Marie chuffed. "This is the grave of Gerwalta *Baron.* She and your ancestor didn't have some casual *fling.* They were desperately in love, enough to rebel against both their traditions to be together. And when the hoods attempted to punish the entire pack for that perceived sin, it was Gerwalta who negotiated the peace, and kept them from being destroyed. This is why we call her the Guardian."

"But my people, we call her the Betrayer. We..."

The words caught in my throat. That word, *Betrayer.* I'd heard it, spoken it, thought about it all my life, and never really understood. Every hood knew Gerwalta Faust's story, that she'd committed the biggest crime for one of our kind by becoming the mate of a wolf, but that hadn't been her betrayal, had it? *That* was not the act for which she was forever branded in our histories as Die Verräterin.

"She started a civil war."

"She started a *revolution,"* Ann-Marie clarified. "She encouraged wolves to stop accepting their suppression and demanded hoods cease their tyranny. The Matron did not seek her death because she'd mated a wolf. Gerwalta died because in her heart, she became one of them. Even now, my indirect connection with the Guardian earns me prestige in our pack. No doubt you picked up on how they defer to me, or how in awe they were when they learned who you are."

The tears didn't make sense, but what did anymore? The woman who I'd been raised to revile, with whose namesake I'd been cursed and branded… was someone completely different than I thought. And knowing that, I didn't know who I was, either.

Embarrassment flushed my cheeks, heated my temple. I leaned into the warped pine, one arm rising to give my forehead a place to settle as my free hand traced the letters of the plaque.

"A. Baron," I read in time with my ghosting hand. "Ann-Marie, is there any chance you know what his n—"

"Andreas." Ann-Marie anticipated the question. "Andreas Baron, brother to Stephen, from whose line I am descended. That, by the way, is a secret I am trusting you to keep."

"A secret?" Confusion warped my features as I turned to the shewolf. "Why would you need to keep *that* a secret?"

For the first time in our discussion, the kindness in Ann-Marie's face fled, as did the color. "Because, according to *hood* history, neither Stephen nor Andreas had surviving descendants. Andreas and Gerwalta's child roasted on a silver spit over a full moon fire, and Stephen was killed when Gerwalta slayed him on the steps of King Ferdinand's castle. But you and I are proof that never happened. I am protected here, away from the other packs, with the grandsons and granddaughters of a few wolves who believed my grandmother's life and lineage was worth protecting. Someone did the same for you. Do not work to undo that too quickly. The day may come for wolf and wolfsretter alike to know the truth, but that time is not now."

"But I—"

I didn't know, and as words became escape artists, my

thoughts hid away, making my mouth agape without purpose.

But Ann-Marie was not done. She took my hands in hers. "Wait for it. Don't try to talk. Just let your mind quiet, and the thing you must know will in turn, make itself known. Deep breaths, Geri. That's it. Now—" She gave my arms a little shake. "Ask it: the same question that has burned within me since I was a little girl and my father told me the truth."

I searched my heart, searched my mind, both reeling and racing and driving my thoughts in a million directions. Across the web of confusion, one thread pulled taut, and I grasped it.

I looked to the shewolf, the tremble in my voice flattening. "Why did the matrons lie?"

"I've told you my truth." Ann-Marie leaned forward, squeezing my arm. "Now go find yours."

# NINE

"So anyway, I guess Ann-Marie's grandmother came from Ireland when she heard the pack would be moving away from Triberg. She said by then, the wolves had lost Andreas Baron's side of the story, and her grandmother thought it was a good time to be reminded, since they were going to be out of the shadow of Schloss Wolfsretter and all. That's what caused the pack to divide. The ones who believed her came down here, the rest ended up in the Oberstdorf Forest. By the way, did you know there used to be more wolves in Ireland than people?"

"Actually, I did." Yan put on the blinker before changing lanes. "I have to wonder how Ann-Marie knew about the graves, though. Or how they ended up here when the Betrayer was executed in Triberg."

My head quirked to the side. "I didn't think about that. She thinks—like you heard—that Gerwalta's mother must have taken the baby and fled. If Andreas and Gerwalta's bodies *were* burned, there would be nothing left but charred bones after. Moving bones is much easier than moving corpses."

"They are."

He spoke with an air of confidence that sent a shiver down my spine. I shouldn't ever forget that while Yan seemed to be a pretty passive and go-along-to-get-along type of guy, he had lethal capabilities that could cut me down at the drop of a hat if I wasn't vigilant.

He must have sensed the mood shift, as he took one glance at me, plastered on a huge smile, and moved the conversation to lighter fare. "Sounds like the two of you bonded right away, then."

"We did." I looked out to the horizon, where a thin line of pink sliced the blanket of night. "Sun will be coming up soon. I should... um, put you in silver, I guess."

"Probably best if I pull over first." Yan laughed silently at his own joke. "I saw a sign a few kilometers back that said there's a service station coming up. I'm okay with a little bit of sun until then. Besides, Markus likes a man with a nice, golden tan."

Good. Not about the tan; I couldn't care less what my cousin's proclivities for his paramours were. But even though I didn't want to admit it out loud, I liked having someone to talk to. Someone who didn't have a dog in the whole hood-versus-lupine show was especially welcomed. No pun intended.

"What did you do, by the way, while Ann-Marie and I were out?"

"Mostly, I entertained the pups."

"Meaning?"

"The kids returned when you left, and I don't know...." He shrugged. "They'd never seen a vampire before. They wanted to see my fangs, know if I really drank blood, if I hated garlic... The usual. But I was happy to answer. And bless the parents, they encouraged the curiosity rather than shame or dissuade it. For such an isolated pack, they are amazingly progressive."

"That's not surprising, seeing as they also call Gerwalta Faust the Guardian instead of the Betrayer."

"One man's terrorist is another one's freedom fighter, as the saying goes." He was silent for moment, before slipping in, "Still..."

"Still?"

The corners of the vampire's mouth notched downward. "Please don't misunderstand. I'm glad to hear you've gotten a fresh perspective on your ancestor. I believe that will help you deal with the trials you have coming. But something about what you've learned... It creates more questions in my mind."

"Such as?"

"Ann-Marie said Faust led a revolution against the hoods."

"Yeah, so? Every culture in the world has had uprisings. Why should supernatural ones be any different?"

The vampire turned, even as he guided the car off the exit ramp. Just in time, too. The first crimson ray of sunrise peaked over the mountains, stinging both our eyes. Only in Yan's case, his actually turned red.

"Why doesn't your history record anything more than this one betrayer, and not a movement? Who was doing the revolting and why?" he asked. "What would victory have looked like, and did they achieve it? And most importantly, who was her enemy, and who, her ally? That is probably the question that gnaws at me the most. One rebelling hood does not an insurgency make, after all. There must be a greater context to the events of that era. One, it seems, that may still be having ramifications now."

"Maybe." Any sense of satisfaction I'd gathered during my visit dissipated. "Were you a journalist in your human life? You got a thing for framing questions."

"No, I was a steward under the Portuguese flag."

"Like, on an airplane?" He didn't seem that young. That was, he didn't *look* much older than his mid-20s, but way of dress and manner of speaking didn't suggest he'd been too long a vampire. Based on his formality, I was actually guessing later Victorian era.

"No, not an airplane." He pulled into the station and up to an empty pump. "You said Vlad was surprised when he bit you to discover you were an asaenic."

"Yeah, he said he didn't think any of us truly existed."

"And the most famous asaenic, you've recently learned, was born right around the time the Ravens were entombed," he said. "You don't honestly think that's a coincidence, do you? I mean, Gerwalta Faust's story is infamous enough in supernatural circles that the Ravens would have undoubtably been aware of at least the possibility. Even if they hadn't known contemporarily, they must have heard since resurfacing in 1945."

I bit my bottom lip, remembering what one of the female packlings had said. *Coincidence is never coincidence.*

"I suppose so. But maybe he just meant he knew it was possible, just not likely. Hyperbole isn't the sole art of the hueys."

Yan clicked his tongue. "Or he wasn't talking about what you thought he was talking about. Think about it, did he actually say he thought *asenaics* were impossible?"

My brain tried to pull out the details from a detritus of emotional trauma. "I... can't remember. But if he wasn't talking about asenaics, what was he talking about?"

"A wonderful question."

I rolled myself through a stretch before getting out of the car. "Maybe it's time to pay the matrons another visit, shake them for the truth. Or at least, as much of the truth as they know."

He grinned. "Shall we storm the castle? I've been

employed at Schloss Wolfsretter for over a decade now. It's been a good run, and I would enjoy the distraction."

"I was thinking more like sending Markus to appeal to their better natures. You know, with threats of violence and the such."

Yan rolled his eyes. "What makes you think my Markus would rise up against his own? Other than having an unnaturally strong interest in vampires and their history, there isn't a rebellious bone in him."

I kept talking as we got out of the car, doing the pass-and-gas routine. "What do you call him taking on the Ravens with me in Istanbul?" I settled in behind the wheel. "A peaceful protest?"

"I call it following orders." Yan closed the door behind him, trapping in the interior of the vehicle a subtle odor of singed hair. "Your *mother's* orders, as you'll recall, to aid you in whatever mad quest you were undertaking insofar as to keep you from harm."

"Maybe, but I don't think my mother ever anticipated I'd take on Dracula himself. If she had, she'd have probably told Markus just to call when I was killed."

"Of course, she anticipated you facing down Vlad. Or, at least, planned for the contingency."

"You almost make it sound like she was trying to help me. Trust me, she wasn't. I'm quite sure Markus also had orders to kill me if the escape from Vlad's took a turn for the worse. It's part of the unofficial hood handbook; the scorched earth policy. Now—" Making sure no one was watching, I pulled down the silver grafted to my arms under my sleeves. It pooled in my hand, then took on the form of a jar. "Ready to play Aladdin again?"

The vampire crossed his arms and frowned. "You give your mother too little credit."

"On the contrary, I credit her with a great deal, just very little of it to do with my welfare or happiness. Now," I tapped the container, "smokie-smokie."

He closed his eyes. "Okay, but only because I do not savor a hellish sunburn. We shouldn't let this go. I have a feeling what happened back then has a lot more to do with what's happening now than you might think."

"I do too. But all those answers are at the end of this drive."

# TEN

## AMY

"Oh, god, I— Ahh!"

Caleb was beside Alexandra in a flash, but for all the good it did, he might as well have taken his time. She was pregnant, not under attack. Unless slayers had some sort of "do not break water here in this totally badass training gym hidden behind a secret wall in the basement" power, I didn't see what his Flash impersonation achieved.

*Show off.*

Caleb braced her. "Alex, are you okay?"

The gravid (isn't that an awesome word? I picked it up reading Bronte. It only means pregnant but it sounds so much more... intellectual) woman squatted against the wall, holding her bulbous stomach like a bowling ball. Or at least, like the way *I* held a bowling ball.

"I'm fine." *She didn't look fine.* "The baby kicked. Very hard. And possibly, ruptured my spleen."

Caleb drew Alex to her feet with a great deal of tenderness as he spoke from the side of his mouth to the dozen or so slayers working in the space. "Okay, everybody, let's call it a night. Hit the showers and grab some dinner before you turn in for the day." Then, once they had filtered out, he said to Alexandra, "I told you, you shouldn't be down here. You should be upstairs, relaxing. I know you're a badass chick, but you're also carrying the future of our race in there, and she gets preferential treatment. Hey, Barbie?"

He was talking to me. Of course, he was talking to me.

I raised an eyebrow. "Yes, Buffy?"

Caleb grimaced. "Can you help Alex back upstairs? I'm going to practice a few more forms before bed."

I mockingly inspected his backside. "Your *forms* look fine to me."

Caleb pointed toward the door, even as he turned away. "Help. Alex."

Alex put a hand on my shoulder. "No, Amy. I'm fine. The pain has passed, and I don't want to become a burden for anyone. I'll be fine."

And with that, the toughest pregnant chick I'd ever met waddled out the door.

I tried to draw from my limited prenatal knowledge, which claimed extensive breadth on the first 15 to 30 minutes of the process and was a little vaguer on the latter parts. "Alex is huge. Shouldn't we, you know, start making plans for the delivery? Is there some kind of special slayer OB-GYN or something? It's like a regular birth, right? Or do you guys have tentacles or something that fall off when you get older?"

"Yeah, like fifty of them. I still have one." Caleb worked his body through a series of blocks and jabs. "Markus has asked the hoods if they have a midwife on retainer, one familiar with supe birth. Turns out, their staff physician serves that role. She'll make herself available when the time comes, if we're still here."

I wasn't a werewolf; I didn't have hackles. Still, I felt mine rise. "What do you mean, if we're still here? I thought the slayers accepted the contract, that we were staying."

"They did, but you see what they're like," Caleb said, turning to me, his bare chest so very *glisten-y*. "The men can't even conjure solaria, and the women don't know how to use them properly. *None* of them has any weapons or combat training. They're not ready to take on a clutch of vamps with centuries of strength and experience behind them."

"You guys literally make liquid sun. How hard can it be to hurl it at something?"

"Oh, ye of little…" His eyes went to my chest. "Well, not those."

"Ha ha, a tits joke. I never heard one of those before. Now answer my question."

Caleb picked up a towel and dotted it against his forehead. "Fine. It's like this: a solarium only has a ground life of three to five seconds, and vampires are quick enough to dodge out of the way if the assault isn't made close enough. They'll have to know how to strike hard and run fast before we encounter them. And if the Ravens come here first…" Caleb swallowed. "Then they'll be hardly more able to defend themselves than you are."

Heat flooded my face. "No thanks to you."

"No thanks to me?" Caleb threw the towel against the wall. "I'm sorry, Barbie, but did I miss the part of orientation where you were my responsibility?"

"You told Geri you'd help me learn how to fight." I crossed my arms over my chest. Not to push up my cleavage, but *que sera sera*.

"*Geri* isn't my boss. And since she broke up with me, she's not really my anything. I'm being nice because the welfare of my people needs me to be and because we're both after the destruction of the Ravens, but you can bet I'm skipping town the second that's no longer true. Besides, Geri already taught you basic self-defense, and that's about all you're going to master as a huey that will stand any chance."

I took two steps forward; Caleb eyeballed my advance with some sort of malicious glee. "So you're saying if I kick you in the balls, it will hurt just as bad as it would a human male?"

"Of course, the anatomy is the same. We just—"

*Thwack!*

"What the fa— Owwww…"

There are times in life when you wish you could just roll back your memories and frame a picture. Seeing smug, self-important, cocky Caleb double over would have gone up on my fireplace mantle, if I lived to have my own place again.

"Why did—" A terrible wheezing noise. "—did you—" A delicious cough. "—do that?"

I bent at the waist, bringing myself eye-to-eye with him. "I was trying to see if you were right. Guess you were. All I have to do is kick a vamp in the nutsack and I can run away screaming. Oh, unless he's smoke!" I shot to my feet. "Then what the hell do I do?"

Caleb shook his head, braced his knees for support. "I wasn't…" *Hack.* "Damn that was hard."

"That's what she said."

What? I couldn't help it. He left that window too wide open not to crawl through. Even though I very much wanted Caleb to choke on his own tongue for treating me like some defective teacup that couldn't hold a cuppa, part of me lightened when he grinned at the joke.

Gasping, he righted himself. His recovery time was miraculous. Next time, I might want to kick him twice. "I suggest you do the same thing you do with men: date them.

That sure seems to get rid of them fast enough."

"Oh, and here comes the sequel."

But before my hand could connect with his cheek, he'd fetched the assault from the air, holding my arm in place.

"Amy…" So he *did* know my name. "Can I tell you a little secret?"

"A supe with secrets? How novel."

A momentary flicker of his customary annoyance, but it faded in a blink. "I wish I could teach you, but some things vamps do a huey could never counter. Smoke, for example. A slayer can push it away with solarium blast, but since you can't summon those—"

My confidence dripped to the floor, taking my righteous posture and the tension in my arm along with it. I dropped the attack and turned to leave. "No, I guess not. Sorry I kicked you in the balls."

"Amy, wait—"

No sooner had I turned to leave than he was before me.

"Not that I enjoyed having my testicles against the back of my teeth, but I guess I deserved it a little. I haven't been very nice to you lately, or like, ever."

"No, you haven't, and I don't get why." I spun on my heel. "Even when I thought Geri was crazy for not hooking up with Tobias—before I understood why, I mean—and she was dating you, I was telling her to put her big girl panties on so you could take them off. It wasn't like I was trying to undermine you or anything."

He buried a laugh into his chest. "Geri's right. You don't have a filter."

"And... you're right back to insulting me in the blink of an eye. So, bye."

"Shit, no, I wasn't insulting you."

This time, instead of rounding me, the bastard tugged me back by the arm. I was two seconds from a second attempt at a ball-drop chaser when his words alone stopped me.

"You've already mastered your weapon."

My hand paused at my side. "What weapon?"

"This." He motioned vaguely to my body. My *whole* body, from top to toe. "This façade you've got where people believe this is all you are: a materialistic, man-eating, dumb blonde. But really, it's like your shield. It keeps back the danger until you gauge your enemy, find all his weaknesses, and exploit them. And that honesty you have? That's your sword. No, it isn't going to overpower a pair of fangs, but a warrior learns to choose his battlefield. Yours is interaction, relationships, and I'm willing to bet you're undefeated there, aren't you?"

Only when my lungs cried out for air did I realize I'd stopped breathing. What the fuck? What the actual fuck?

"If you mean, did anyone ever break up with me instead of the other way around, then the answer to that is a brilliantly red hell no."

He crossed his arms, examining me like I was a piece of art in which he'd just found a heretofore unnoticed brush stroke, framing the muscles of his chest. Caleb had, like, one percent body fat, but damn, it didn't make him look bad.

"It's because all you've done so far is sparring," he said. "Practice runs with opponents you knew you'd best. But be advised, Amy Popowitz, you're working up to something, I know it. You're going to find a worthy adversary someday, one who's going to hit you blow for blow, one who's going to pin you to the mat and get a few blows in before you even realize what happened. And you know what?"

His arms fell to his sides and my jaw went to the floor as Caleb stepped in closer. The no-man's land between us suddenly became a one-man land. One man who was crazy hot. And half-naked.

And touching me.

The slayer's heated breath parted my lips, the angle of his head tilt demanded me to reciprocate.

I managed to lick my bottom lip. "What?"

An inch, a half an inch, a quarter of an inch. My eyes closed…

And reopened to him, six feet away and laughing.

"Oh, come on, Barbie!" Caleb struggled not to double over. "Did you really think I was going to kiss you? I'm still nursing my broken heart here."

Oh, he so didn't want to try to out-burn me. "Actually, when I passed your room yesterday, I heard you nursing something else. Pretty sure it wasn't your heart."

I hadn't, but by the way that smile fled his face told me I'd stumbled on to the fact by dumb luck. Might as well play it for all it was worth. "Which is odd, because aren't you sharing a room with Mikael and Ezekiel? Or were they watching?"

"They were asleep, and I haven't… You shouldn't have…" Red as the dawn, his wide cheeks burned. "If you tell *anyone*…"

I put up my hand to end his suffering. "Chillax, Buffy. My lips are sealed."

His frame relaxed.

"If…"

And again, he was a wall of nerves and steaming eyes. Oh, it did my heart good.

Caleb asked, "If what?"

"If you stop putting a huey down and help me learn how to fight."

"Stand around and observe all you want, but I kinda got the weight of my race on my shoulders here. I don't have any extra time to…"

I cupped my hand, made a rude gesture, and winked.

"Okay, fine. Fine. But don't expect me to go easy on you just because you're—" He motioned finger quotes. "—fragile. And top heavy! Get a damned sports bra or some duct tape or something. But mark my words, Barbie, you'll regret this. I'm going to be on your ass more than any of your fly-by-night boytoys ever were." In a flash, he reclaimed the towel he'd thrown against the wall and tossed it my direction. "You've got a little bit of drool there on your chin, by the way."

"Hey, if I wanted you to kiss me, then you'd be—"

And then, he was.

And damn, he was good.

Or so I was beginning to suspect. By the time I'd actually become conscious of his lips on mine, it was over, and he was glaring at me.

Because that's what you do after you kiss a woman hard and fast, you *glare* at her.

And just as I was about to lay into him for daring to be so bold, and yell even more at him for making it so brief, the door to the training studio opened.

I pushed the asshat in his asschest to get him the assaway from me.

"Oh, good, you two are going at it." Geri walked in, Markus trailing right behind.

"What? No, we weren't. We're—"

Panic told me to get distance, but then I realized there was distance, a great deal of it. I was standing alone in the middle of the room, and Caleb was in the corner, mocking forms.

Geri's eyebrow rose. "So, you're not training? Because this looks like training, and I should know."

"Nope, this is training," Caleb said, punching the air. "Amy's great. Really progressing, keeping me on my toes."

"Really?" Markus asked. "Because to my eyes, all you two have done in the two days Geri was gone was bicker and bitch at each other."

"Like he said, I'm keeping him on his toes, and you don't do that with casual pleasantries," I said. And then I changed the subject, because I so did not want anyone spinning any sentence that would diagram Caleb and I in the same compound subject. "So, did they know anything?"

"You could say that."

Geri ran a hand through her hair, shaking out her ebony locks. God, why did she get supernatural powers *and* supermodel hair? It wasn't fair. She and Yan then launched into a summation of their discoveries, and with every sentence, Caleb and I took turns dropping our jaws.

"And so..." She folded her hands together. "After Yan and I talked about it in the car, we think it might be worth trying to find the other asenaics by looking for anomalies in *huey* history."

Caleb's face screwed up. "Why? I don't understand why that's what this all led to."

The vampire and the hood exchanged a look, but it was the first one who talked. "Because while we do not have access to the hood archives, we do have access to the internet. And knowing what we do now, that the lupine version of the Betrayer's story mentions at least one prominent huey, we might find threads that will at least point us in the right direction."

"But you live up at the Schloss, don't you have access to the archives? You know, somehow?"

Why were supes always so cloak-and-dagger? I pushed Caleb back, trying to ignore the jealousy of my other body parts toward my fingers. "I think what Nancy Drew here is trying to say is, can't you just go all smoke monster and look in these archive thingies, even if you're not supposed to? Assuming you're not supposed to. Are you supposed to?"

The man tried to diagnose me with a cocked head until a moment later, he shook off whatever thoughts had been going through his head. "No, I'm not supposed to, and yes, of course I have. But the archives are not what one might call complete, especially the further back you go. Until recently, the different bloodlines operated more or less independently, and without a universal method of cataloguing or the same priorities of what should be written down, there's big blank spots in the histories. For example, I can tell you that now, knowing the name of Geri's wolf ancestor, there is no mention of his execution in the list of the condemned. To clarify, huey history is no different, but much more of it has been digitized."

"We might find nothing," Gerwalta added. "But we're going to look just in case. Every day, those asenaics are more in danger. I'm not sure how long the Ravens can go without feeding, but it's been six weeks now. Unless there are other slayer harems they have in other places, they'll need to feed soon."

Caleb grabbed a towel from a stack on a shelf and went about dabbing off his glisten. It was a crime worthy of jail time. "Let me take a shower, and we'll get to it then."

# ELEVEN

## GERI

"I think I found something."

As though moving through well-rehearsed choreography, everyone stood and circled around Amy's computer.

I squinted, trying my best to comprehend what I was seeing. "Okay, explain."

The blonde huey expanded the view of the scanned document on the screen, pulling out the details of highly embellished text. Letters took on definition, but definition brought no clarity.

"Seriously?" Amy blinked rapidly. "None of you read French?"

Caleb, Markus, and I exchanged expectant looks that fell away when the truth became clear.

"I'm only good for English, German, and some basic Spanish," I said.

"Me, just the first two," Markus added.

Caleb took on a cocky grin. "English, Turkish, Hebrew, Spanish, and Romanian."

Amy held up a finger. "You forgot Pomposity, which as I understand is a common dialect of Bastard."

Any hope of Caleb explaining the sudden hostility that had grown between him and Amy in the last few days was met with the latter only shaking his head in a "don't ask" type of way.

Rather than dig any deeper to unearth that mine, I stayed focused. "Amy, can you read it for us?"

My huey friend beamed. "Of course, Geri, I'd be delighted." Then, turning to her screen, motioning to bits and pieces of the image as she spoke, Amy began. "So just a little north of here is a region that's gone back and forth between France and Germany through the centuries. I figured since all of you probably had the Germanic sources covered, I'd skim through French archives and see if there were any unusual events or mentions of things in the 1680s. And here—" Her right index finger zeroed in on the swoopy text "—I found a letter from the Bishop of Alsace to the Cardinal Montblanc written in the year 1685 which reports a rash of livestock deaths throughout Southern Germany by, quote, 'a pack of abnormally vicious wolves.'"

Markus and I exchanged knowing glances.

Caleb stood erect. "This isn't news to you two."

I shook my head. "We all know that one; we think it's where the Little Red Riding Hood fairy tale came from. There was an anathema alpha—"

"Like Ayşe in Istanbul?" Amy interjected.

"Exactly, like her," Markus confirmed. "Female alphas used to be considered some sort of defect that made the wolf dangerous. I don't think that's true, of course, but this one actually was. She was able to lure away betas from a dozen packs to make her own family. The House of Red tracked her down and killed her before she managed it. Unfortunately, not before they ate their way through the countryside."

Caleb turned to me. "And what about the betas she

lured away? What happened to them?"

I shrugged. "They went back to their packs, I guess. I don't remember hearing anything different. If they had been killed as well, our stories would have boasted about it. Through history, hoods have been pretty decent at sticking to our own laws about when we could use lethal means to curb wolf behavior, but our ancestors prided themselves on putting down the slightest infractions with brutality."

Amy spun around her chair while also spinning her eyes. "Oh my god, you guys really *can't* see the forest for the trees, can you?" She stood, passing to the sink and drawing herself a glass of water. "Geri, didn't you say this shewolf you met in Austria, that her ancestor was Andreas's brother, who supposedly died?"

"Yeah, so?"

"So?" The glass lingered at her lips. "If Andreas was an alpha, isn't it possible his brother may have been a beta? And if the House of Red was involved in tracking them down, then isn't it possible Gerwalta Faust could have been the one to let him get away?"

As she finally tipped back the glass to drink, her long neck stretched and her throat bobbing with each swallow, I tried to stitch together her logic.

And then, I did.

"But that would mean she let him go on purpose." Every revolution starts with a single act of rebellion. "But why would a hood do that? If she'd had been caught at that time, she would have been exiled. Or worse."

Caleb rubbed his chin. "But she *was* caught and killed. You guys tell the Betrayer story like it took place over a couple of days, but the chick had to have time to fall in love, get knocked up, and pop the kid before the ax fell. Why is it so ridiculous to think the love story started earlier than you think, too? Or is it told in your books that one day, Gerwalta Faust came down with the must-mate-a-wolf flu and went searching about for the cure?"

Amy pointed at the slayer. "Only you could take a beautiful fairy tale and reduce it to getting knocked up."

"Well, that's what happened, wasn't it?" Caleb said, defending himself. "Ergo, we are here."

It didn't seem possible that could be coincidence. But then, something triggered in my brain. I went back to my own computer and went about searching the web, even as the others looked on with concern. When I found what I was after, I flipped the screen around.

"The wolf of Ansbach?" Markus read the title of the article aloud. "Oh, come on. We've disavowed that one for centuries. That was just village idiots getting their superstition on."

Amy swooped in, eyeballing the text through squinted eyes. "In 1685, the same year of the letter I found? Except if that graphic's to be believed, that guy... um, werewolf?... actually ended up dead."

I turned the computer back, looking closer at the accompanying picture of a human-bodied wolf dangling from a scaffold. "Obviously it's not Andreas or his brother, but if there really is a connection between Gerwalta Faust and the wolf epidemic, this might have been part of it. We can never really *know*, but it feels right to me."

*Coincidence is never coincidence.*

"If only we could get into the archive, then..."

The computer dropped to the table as my chair flew out behind me. Startled, Amy coughed, choking on the water mid-swallow. Markus and Caleb were beside me in a moment as I turned my face to the front door, gaging the distance of the uninvited guests I sensed outside.

In my peripheral vision, Caleb turned to my cousin. "Markus?"

"No idea," Markus answered, even as he leeched the silver hidden beneath his clothing to form a two-pronged knife. "Geri, who is it? Do you know?"

Did I? One was coming closer but moving at too steady a pace to be covert, and too leisurely to mount an attack. Not that whoever it was would stand any chance if he were. There was only one of him, and three of us ready to kick ass.

Three and a half, if you included Amy.

"Amy." I spoke without turning. "Tell the slayers to shelter down. Quickly."

Without asking a question, the huey obeyed, scurrying to the stairs.

Caleb rounded my right side. "Shelter from what?"

Not vampires; that he'd be able to perceive.

Before I could answer, though, the approaching party finally came close enough for Markus to pick up.

"A wolf," he said.

I shook my head as proximity delivered clarity. "Two wolves."

Markus squinted. "No, I'm only getting one. He's not dodging around or anything. He's making a straight line for the front door. Could it be… Geri, you don't think—"

"It's *not* Tobias," I said, cutting him off. "But I know these two. I've felt their presences before." Definitely the one, and I thought the other, though I just couldn't place either. "I… God damn it, really?"

Light brightened the grand room as Caleb conjured a solarium. "Tell me who it is, or I'm going to blast them back across the Rhineland."

No time for a witty retort. No sooner had I turned to the slayer than the doorbell rang.

Which marked the first time in fifteen years of staying in the house that I had ever heard it.

Caleb did a double take. "Well that's unexpectedly civilized." Then, raising his voice, he called out, "Who's there?"

Silence for a moment, and then an unsure timbre reached through the wood. "Hello? I'm, um… I'm looking for Geri—Gerwalta, I mean. Shit, you think she's really here? I'm looking for Gerwalta Kline. Is she… Dude, are you sure this is the right house?"

Markus honed his weapon and made his way to the door. "What is *he* doing here?"

"He who?" Caleb asked. His solarium stayed at the ready, just in case.

I was on Markus's tail. "My ex-boyfriend. Who will be leaving as soon as I see what idiot wolf is with him and how they both knew this house even existed. Markus, wait. Let me answer."

"I can hear you, you know," Cody said from the stoop. "And you shouldn't call this guy an idiot. It's very disrespectful."

My movements arrested, drawn up in the fantasy. Could it be Tobias? The energy I felt was wolf, but weak, barely perceptible. But that didn't make sense. How would Cody have found Tobias? And why would he tease me with it if he did? Why would he be that cruel?

Oh, yeah, that's right. Because Cody was an asshole who kicked me out of his packlands for having the audacity to refuse to kowtow to his edicts like I was some god damned wolf.

Forget that I kinda was.

A head full of steam, I reached for the door, prepared to waylay into whatever bastard wingwolf my ex had in tow.

"Cody Ryland!" I bellowed. "How fucking… dare… y…"

But the insult died on my tongue when the beaming, warm, welcomed man standing outside stepped forward.

"Hola, cariño," my dad said. "We need to have a talk."

# TWELVE

Caleb stared at Cody like the werewolf was some piece of abstract art, the meaning of which he just couldn't grab.

"You're her ex?"

Cody nursed his beer. "Yup."

Caleb shook his head. "It's just that you're so muscular and rustic and brawny and… and nothing like me."

My father, sipping apple tea, turned pleading eyes on me. "Who is this man, and why does he smell like an Abercrombie & Fitch?"

"This *man* is Caleb Helsing," Caleb answered on his own behalf. "And FYI: it's Kenneth Cole."

"You're the slayer she was talking about last summer?" Cody took one look and hacked a laugh. "Wow, you are *so* not her type. But tough break. I was pulling for you."

"Me, too. Even asked her to marry me," Caleb boasted. "I understand you did that once too, right before you slept with one of your packlings."

"Caleb!" Shit, I so didn't want to deal with an arrogant slayer and a back-woods alpha butting heads right now. "Caleb, you should probably track down Alexandra. Make sure the red alert didn't stress her out too much. Markus, give Amy and everyone else the all-clear. I need to speak to these two alone."

Minor grumbles followed, mixed with Markus recounting the details of the dramatic history of my first hood-werewolf romance, the last sentence of which I perceived being, "so they found other ways of expressing their feelings…"

Cody eyeballed the pair until they were all the way up the stairs and out of sight. "You were really engaged to that guy?"

"No!" Even I was shocked by the insistent tone. "I mean, he proposed, but I was already planning on breaking up with him before then. But let's talk about you." I spun a chair around and sat cowgirl style. "First of all, Papa. Let's start with… I don't know, maybe with my whole life being a lie and work up from there."

"You've learned about our… unique heritage, I take it." My father folded his hands atop the table. "I think you are hyperbolizing, niña. Very little of your life was a lie. Your mother and I only kept one tiny truth from you, and it was only for your own good."

"Really, Dad? The Betrayer's baby survived, a secret that I could maybe overlook if I wasn't her namesake and, it turns out, her descendent. We have wolf blood in our veins. How is that a tiny truth?"

His gaze cast off into the distance. "I was supposed to be the last, so that the line would die with me. But then I met your mother, and…" He made a vague gesture with his hands, something that seemed to say 'one thing led to another…'

Which was fine. I so didn't need to know the details of my own conception.

I crossed my arms. "She wouldn't have married you if she knew. You know she wouldn't have."

"Oh, no, cariño, she *did* know," he said. "It was how we met. She was sent to Argentina to deliver the edict that I would be forbidden to have children. Your grandmother relented, saying she'd permit just one more asenaic, hoping her strong bloodline would wash away any lupine leanings.

We did not expect the wolf nature to manifest in you to such a degree. It has varied throughout the centuries, sometime reinforced when different asenaic branches partnered. We kept you in the dark, hoping to marry you off to a hood who…"

"Hood begets hood," I said. "Yeah, I remember that line coming up often when I was dating the bastard who broke my heart." My eyes flashed to Cody. "No offense."

The instigated werewolf threw up his hands. "Your mom's words, not mine."

My father, crestfallen, continued. "You have always wondered how I could stand by while your mother grew stricter by the years. It is because *she* is my mate, niña. I am bonded to her, and I love her no matter what she did to me, or what she did to you." His hand sought mine across the table. "I saw the pain it caused you, every time, and I suffered with you."

The little girl inside me who longed for her father's comfort melted, if only for a moment. Until, that was, the woman I'd become seized back control. I leaned back in my chair, crossing my arms over my chest and turning my attention to the alpha seated to my father's left.

"And you?" I said to Cody, jerking my chin. "Why are you here? Last time I saw you, you were kicking me out of your packlands."

My father turned on the alpha. "What?"

Cody guffawed. "I mean, she didn't give me a choice. She questioned my authority in front of the whole pack."

"She is a hood!" my father said, his Latino-hands-of-reinforcement bobbing through the air. "That is her nature."

"And I'm an alpha," Cody shot back. "Geri was causing some of my wolves' fealty to falter. The pack knows her, loves her like one of their own, and believe it or not, some of them actually think I'm a bastard for mating Lisa, just like Geri, even though I only did it because of alpha's prerogative. I was going to have wolves going rogue if I didn't do something." Then, the focus of his rationalization swung my way. "But I've never stopped caring about you. And then when Pietro came to ask me to come along, letting me in on your secret... I realized how much it all made sense. Your instincts on lupine nature, your ability to understand some of our wolfish, how we were so attracted to each other..."

"Well, guess what? You finally got your wish!" I said. "I don't love you anymore. I only love—"

Even the pain of saying his name cut deep across my tongue.

"Tobias." Cody grinned. "And that's great, Geri. I'm glad to hear that. Only, Little Red, you know that's a dead-end street. Tobias already had his mate; his heart is always going to belong to Kara. It's obvious to anyone you two are good friends. Great, even. But it will never be more than that. I'd hate to see you throw away any chance of a full life."

"Oh, my god." I turned to my dad, and away from the unspoken words I knew Cody wanted to say, *by falling in love with another werewolf you can never have*. "Mom banished you."

Pietro's eyes grew wide. "How did you know?"

"Because if you were still getting communiques from a matron—*any* matron—you'd know what Markus reported to the council a few days ago." I crawled to the edge of my chair. "Vlad Tepeş has some personal, historic beef with werewolves. He's exacting his revenge by unraveling their mating bonds using some sort of genetic therapy. He wants to destroy them from the inside out, and he doesn't care how long it takes. Tobias's mate was one of his victims. He undid her mating bond."

"Does it affect both mates, or only the one subjected

to this…" Pietro's hand turned circles in the air. "…therapy?"

"We're unsure. When Kara died, Tobias still went through the same pain I've felt in other wolves who've lost mates. But was he unaffected?"

I remembered both the kisses we shared: one under the full moon in Paradise, the other moments before I'd lost him in Istanbul. I remembered that he loved me, had loved me for who knew how long before either of us had said anything.

*It's not just because of the serum…*

"He must have been," I surmised.

Cody barked a laugh. "Be that as it may, genetically altering all the wolves in the world would take decades, centuries maybe. If old Drac really wanted revenge, he'd just kill them. He seems more than capable."

I held up a finger. "You're thinking like a mortal, but Vlad doesn't. In his opinion, the wolves undid his country, his family, and his legacy, so he's going to do the same to them. A vampire has the luxury of time, as long as he has the right kind of blood for fuel."

My father narrowed his eyes. "What do you mean, the right kind of blood?"

I didn't know how many hoods were in on the vampire secret that they were not, in fact, immortal, that after five centuries or so, death would still claim them as it did any creature. Unless, of course, they fed off other supes. Even in such circumstances, I wouldn't betray the whole species for the sins of the few.

"The Ravens have a… condition," I said. "And the only treatment is supe blood. Werewolf blood works, slayer blood is better. But the best blood is asenaic." I met my father's eyes, seeing the understanding form within. "Like the kind that comes from the descendants of Gerwalta Faust and

Andreas Baron."

My father's olive skin blanched. "This is why your mother was so worried about them finding you. All this time, she led me to believe it was because they wanted revenge."

"Revenge?" For the first time in this conversation, I was the one left in the dark. "For what?"

"For their capture," my dad said. "The Ravens were trapped for many centuries, encased in silver urns crafted by the House of Red, and kept in the vaults of Schloss Wolfsretter."

Though I knew the sky outside to be as clear as a bell, I had no doubt that lightning had just struck my brain and stopped my heart. The world came to a halt, then just as soon, sped up again, all too fast.

When I could find the words to speak at last, my hoarse voice surprised all of us. "What do you mean, we trapped them in silver and kept them at the Schloss?" A dry palate made talking difficult. "Igor told me Inga trapped them with the help of some Wallachian lupines and entombed them in some air-tight wall."

My father blinked his confusion. "The first time, yes. I understand that is what happened."

"The first time?" I balanced my temples on my fingers. "The *first* time?" I repeated, louder, even rudely.

"Yes, the first time. The slayers found out about it, and blamed the wolves for interfering in their affairs. They discovered where the crypt was and opened it, intending to obliterate the Ravens, but they were bested. After that, the House of Red took a contract to trap them in silver urns. The silver was even blood-claimed, so that none might open it."

Cody verbalized my unspoken thoughts. "What is blood-claimed silver?"

My father's eyes went to the table as he shook his head. "A barbaric practice, one long banned. A hood can become the sole master of a piece of silver by threading the metal through her veins and passing it through her heart. Once upon a time, it was a rite of passage when a hood took her fire and was presented her silver medallion. As a demonstration of becoming righteous, they blood-claimed it. I have read that the pain was excruciating. There are even stories that some died from it. But as all hoods can command silver and form a plethora of deadly weapons, it is a way for us to gain an advantage over other members of our race."

My thoughts turned back to the sword I'd been gifted by Vlad in Istanbul. It had felt different from any other silver I'd ever handled, almost like it had its own memories. Could that have been it?

"Looks like you got yourself mixed up in some deep shit, Little Red." Cody grinned. "Makes me glad you got Tobias here protecting you." He scanned the room. "Where is he, by the way?"

"Wherever Vlad Tepeş wants him to be," I retorted. "He was taken prisoner when we freed the slayers."

My father's eyes nearly bugged out of his head. "What?"

"I guess that hasn't gotten to you either, then." I folded my arms over my chest. "So, tell me, Papa, if you didn't come here because of my mate's disappearance and not because Mom told you to, then why did you come? More importantly," I turned on Cody, "Why are *you* here? I hope it's not for an apology for what I said at Kim's wedding, because you're not going to get it."

The werewolf clearly wasn't ready to mend fences, either. His acidic gaze fixed me long and hard as he drew another pull off his bottle of Schwarzbier before saying, "I'm here because of Amy."

"Amy?" Okay, that I hadn't been expecting. Why would

my ex-boyfriend care anything about my huey friend? "What does Amy have to do with anything?"

"She took off to Istanbul with you back in June, and she hasn't contacted her parents since," my father filled in. "By the time late July rolled around, her mother got worried enough to hire a private investigator, who found out your friend emptied all her bank accounts the day before you left, hasn't used any of her credit cards since the first day or two you were gone, and other than going through passport control when you landed in Turkey, hasn't triggered any official records in three months."

Cody took over from there. "When the PI showed up in Paradise and started sniffing around for clues last week, that raised the packs' hackles."

"Oh my god." My head turned to the stairs, as though I expected to see my bubbly, blond friend there. "I had no idea. I never even asked her... I mean, how would that come up, anyways?"

Cody grunted. "Maybe by you being a little less self-involved and remembering that the people around you have their own lives, that this isn't some sort of dramatic play where all the characters enter and exit the stage just to move your plot along."

My father growled. Actually growled.

But the alpha wolf wasn't impressed. "What? We agreed we were going to give it to her straight, didn't we?"

"Straight does not mean cruel," my dad snapped. "*Niña*, what Cody means to say is, especially where hueys are concerned, you have to be far more appreciative of the fact that they do not come from our world. They have attachments that will follow them if you bring them in."

But it sounded like Amy had been trying to break those attachments. Meeting her parents, I understood she and her father didn't have the greatest relationship, but she seemed to get along with her mom okay. Why would she cut them both off?

"I'll talk to her, ask her to reach out to the folks with just enough information to pacify them. I'm sorry that hueys infiltrated the packlands. But that still doesn't explain why you came all the way to Germany. I mean, you could have called. My phone number is different but Markus's is still the same, and I'm sure mom told you he was with me."

For the first time since they'd arrived, my father's face curdled. It was up to Cody, the fount of cruel truth, to explain.

"I'm here to make sure Amy does what needs to be done. And in the event that she doesn't, *assure* she's convinced otherwise. And if it turned out that she hadn't phoned home because of some terrible fate, I came to make sure any evidence went away."

I blew a raspberry. "What were you planning to do, eat her?"

His dead stare made a chill run the length of me. "If needs be."

My spine electrified. "Well, needs *don't* be. Amy's fine. Like I said, I'll talk to her. So, now that's out of the way, I'll trust you two to find your way out."

"When you're up against both the Matron Council and Vlad Tepeş?" my father asked. "Absolutely not."

"I'm sticking around, too. Tobias may not be my packling anymore, but that's only an official thing. He's my friend, and I'm going to make sure he's rescued." The alpha let out a gravelly laugh. "Oh, Geri, you just have to have some lupine in your life or you get into trouble, don't you?"

I was too tired to deal with sexist, wolfish crap. "You sure that Lisa's going to be okay with that?"

"She'll understand. She cares for Tobias, too." The empty bottle thudded on the table. "So, where do we start looking?"

I turned the chair around. "We don't. He's not my focus right now."

The alpha went wide-eyed. "Maybe you don't love him as much as you think you do, then. If it were my mate—"

"But it's not," I said, cutting Cody off. "Despite what you think about how self-absorbed I am, the truth is that I have others depending on me right now. For one," I jerked my chin, "the houseful of slayers upstairs. Maybe the last of their kind, and considered by Vlad to be stolen property. The Matron Council in their *magnanimity* refused sanctuary. Instead, they offered them a contract. Full social and financial support, but only if they agree to kill the Ravens."

My father's jaw dropped. *"Dios mio.* Surely this edict was not issued with your mother's knowledge."

"Who knows?" I said. "Markus says Mom hasn't been in residence since right after we left for Istanbul, and she hasn't been checking in, either. I don't suppose either of you know where she is?"

The men exchanged puzzled looks.

Cody stretched out in his chair. "She was in Paradise over the summer, but since the middle of August, your aunt has been overseeing the roost."

A fact I was sure his pack was thankful for. Markus's mom was slightly less regimented than her older cousin, *my* mother. Still, even a kind warden is still a warden.

I continued. "Matron Chin is sitting in the big chair right now, and she's not too interested in anything Markus has to say. I tried getting in, but no-go as I'm officially relinquished."

"And the slayers?" Cody asked. "Did they take the contract?"

"Of course, they took the contract. They have nowhere else to go. Or at least, their best bet for the moment is near the hoods. The council might be refusing to grant them humanitarian support out of the kindness of their hearts, but we all know that if the Ravens stride into Triberg and try to get away with anything, the hoods will have their heads."

My father nodded. "Yes, which is why you should not feel guilty about leaving here to go find Tobias. The slayers will still be shielded by the proximity to the Schloss."

"I *am* leaving, but you see, there's another group of people counting on me for protection. And they're in even more danger, because they don't even know it yet."

Cody and my dad exchanged a questioning glance, but neither knew what I was talking about.

"The other asenaics, the ones in Spain," I said. "Since Vlad discovered I exist, and since I'm currently out of his reach, he's going to have to find the next best thing if he wants to continue his... his therapy. You might have been the last asenaic in the Americas, Papa, but there's still others of our line in the Old Country, aren't there?"

At least he had the guts not to deny it. "But I do not know where. My line comes from the north part of the country, and this is all I know."

I pursed my lips. "We need to ask Inga Rosethorn."

My father narrowed his eyes. "What do asenaics have to do with her?"

"The same condition that Vlad has, she and Igor do, too." It wasn't the whole truth but it would suffice for now. "And the two of them have been treating it for years with trips to Spain. Igor was also taken prisoner by Vlad. I'm not sure if vampires are susceptible to torture, but if so, it won't take long for the Ravens to find out. That's why I'm going to Spain. It's not the most likely place for me to find Vlad."

And since I doubted he'd leave his prizes behind after I'd robbed him of his harem, I could assume Tobias and Igor would be going along for the ride.

My father stood. "I will go with you."

"Dad, no. I'm going to be traveling light. You'll only slow me down."

"Fi! *Me* slow *you* down? Don't be ridiculous. Besides, your Spanish is not so good."

"What are you talking about, my Spanish is fine."

"You think that because you only speak it with me. I know what all your mistakes mean. When do we leave?"

I grinned. "Just as soon as I can pack up the car and get supplies together, which should only take me until morning. Oh, and talk to Amy, of course. I'll just go..."

Without warning, a scream rent the air: a terrifying, shrill cry that took me flying through the house and up the stairs.

Footsteps pounded behind me, even as a voice in the back of my head warned about the slayers finding yet more strangers in the house. None of them would have noticed, however, because they were all too focused on the huffing woman in the midst of them when I got to the third-floor hallway, being braced on one side by Caleb and on the other by Amy.

Alexandra's face broke into a smile as she caught sight of me, even as her teeth clenched. "Geri, I think it's time."

# THIRTEEN

At some point, coffee would cease to substitute for sleep. I couldn't have drunk more of the stuff unless Starbucks introduced an IV Latte. Hour eighteen came and went, with no more babies in the house than there had been when Alex's labor had started. The screaming had started in the thirteenth hour (my father and Cody agreed as the self-declared senior experts in childbirth, that the first part of the labor didn't really hurt that much). The slayer women took shifts, two or three at the time in the impromptu birthing suite that heretofore had been Alex's bedroom, to fetch ice chips, refresh the water basin, or give Alex a new hand to squeeze the blood from as she suffered through the pain.

Dawn, however, arrived in eerie silence.

No one spoke. I suspected because none of us wanted to acknowledge the obvious. But as I finished my sixth mug and set it on the coffee table in the great room, truth took on a mass that refused to be contained.

"Something's wrong."

My father on the sofa beside me pulled me into the wing of his embrace. "We do not know that, *niña*. Have faith, all will be right."

A door opened on the floors above, bringing with it a fresh swirl of scented air. Antiseptic, I'd been told, as well as some aromatherapy oils because, apparently, hood medical care had caught up to the 1970s. Petunia Creed (whom Caleb had already nicknamed Patchouli Reed) pawed down the stairs on lithe feet. Doctor though the slender woman in her early sixties was, she was also a hood of the House of Green. Like all supes, her physical appearance belied her years, as did her endurance since she'd arrived at the house.

We shot to our feet as though a head of state had just entered the room. When she chose to address me as the point person for all that was going on, I had to wonder why. Still relinquished, I had no right under our customs to expect more than a curt nod. Even my father, merely exiled, had status over me.

"She sleeps between contractions," Petunia began without precursor. "But she's growing weak."

Caleb stepped forward. "And the baby?"

The green hood side-eyed the slayer. "Are you the father?"

"Me?" Caleb stuck his thumb into his chest as his face burned crimson. "No. No, definitely not."

"Shame, that," said Petunia. "The genes would be strong. The baby, as far as I can tell with the limited instruments at my disposal, endures, but that could change quickly. I rarely recommend sending one of my patients to a huey hospital, but at this point, I believe it's the prudent choice. I, of course, am not familiar with slayer delivery norms, and none of the females above have attended the birth of one of their own, but most hoods deliver in an eight- to ten-hour window and I can't imagine it's much different. I suggest she be taken to the hospital in Lahr as soon as possible."

Amy pivoted, making for the stairs. "I'll put together an away bag."

Markus headed to the garage. "I'll warm the car and pull it out in front. Should I put the back seats flat so she can lay down?"

Petunia nodded to his disappearing form. "Yes. A few blankets and pillows will also help keep the bumps of the road from causing her too much pain."

My father took the acquisition of sufficient linens and throw pillows as his duty, speeding off to a closet where we kept such things.

That left Caleb, Cody and I, looking to Petunia for marching orders.

"Does Alex know about this recommendation?" I asked.

The physician bobbed her head. "I advised her of the risks, both to go or not to go. She agreed with me that it was better safe than sorry. A slayer birth is a rare event. She said there had not been one in the fifteen years she was held as one of Vlad Tepeş's harem. We need do all we can. We should have made arrangements for this at a private clinic in advance."

"We weren't expecting her to give birth for a few more weeks," Caleb said. "According to Alex, she's only eight months along, and barely."

Petunia chortled. "Eight months, my eye. If anything, she's overdue. I'll want to move her between contractions in as easy a way as possible, and I'll need the help of that cousin of yours, Miss Kline, to carry her down just as soon as he's back."

Cody stepped forward. "I can do it."

The midwife looked at the alpha like she wanted to deliver a knock to the side of his head.

"What do you think I'm going to do, run away with her, eat her?" Cody huffed. "I just want to help."

Caleb stepped in closer. "Take him at his word, Nurse Ratchet. If Geri trusts him, then he deserves it."

Petunia's eyes rolled to the ceiling as she turned back toward the stairs. "A slayer and alpha, vouched for by a relinquished. What is this world coming to? Fine, come along. Miss Kline, I'll trust you to make sure this whole kit and caboodle goes off as planned. I will phone ahead to the hospital and let them know to expect us shortly."

We looked like a circus train driving into Lahr. Two cars, each full of fretful twentysomethings, supplemented by one senior physician smelling of the Grateful Dead and one middle-aged Latino looking like Antonio Banderas's slender brother.

The silky black SUV took the lead, deference given to the transport of the woman actually in labor. As instructed, the back seats had been laid flat, and my dad proved he had missed his calling as an interior designer by making use of sheets, pillows, and blankets in a short space of time to make it as comfortable of a bed as could be had. The shaded windows made my seeing Alex impossible during the twenty-minute trip, but I hoped that Petunia and Amy, both of whom were beside her, had found a way to comfort her. Yan had also rushed down to the house just before the sun had arisen, advised that his telepath services may be needed.

"Who's the vampire?" Cody asked from the backseat.

"His name is Janus Sousa, but he goes by Yan." In the passenger seat beside me, Caleb assumed responsibility for answering. "He's employed by the Matron Council at Schloss Wolfsretter. He swirls the memories of any hueys who manage to get into the property or who spread rumors they shouldn't."

Anya, a willowy reed of a slayer woman who'd been Alex's friend in the Istanbul harem, perked up at that. "So that's true? Vampires can change memories?"

The werewolf turned on the slayer. "How can *you* not know that?"

Affronted, Anya choked out her answer. "We were only

taught what the Ravens wanted us to know, and had little contact with the outside world. All of us were born in the harem, or arrived there as children before our parents could train us. In fact, until Caleb arrived, we believed that only female slayers could conjure solaria."

I caught Cody's eye in the rearview mirror. "They were prisoners."

The werewolf became very sheepish. "Oh, um... Damn, I didn't know. I'm sorry. I'm just surprised, you know? I mean, like, you never saw them using that power?"

"It doesn't work on us any more than it works on slayers or werewolves," I said to a crestfallen Anya. "Don't feel ashamed that you didn't know. I mean, Markus and I had an extensive library of information on the natures of all supes, and neither of us had any idea slayer pregnancies only last eight months."

The polarity of the atmosphere changed with Anya's giggle. "That I *do* know. There haven't been any successful pregnancies while I was in the harem, but there were several stillbirths. Nine months, more or less, just like hueys. I remember because that ninth month, the pregnant *haseki* would always be put into a private suite. Never did any good, though. The baby always died."

Reading the anxiety that hatched over Caleb's face, I leaned across the front seat to place a hand on his knee. "It will be fine. Alex is going to deliver a strong, healthy baby. She hasn't endured so long just to lose it."

His eyes tracked the car in front of us. "I hope so."

I'd spent more time in hospitals in the last few years than all the years previous collectively. What struck me was how similar the experience was, whether it was Marquette, Michigan or Lahr, Germany or even Chicago. Maybe the sterile atmosphere could only result ultimately in the same bland-but-functional environment?

A pond of taupe-colored fabric chairs was docked around a pine-paneled table holding an odd collection of fashion magazines, newspapers, and well-worn children's books, the chairs numbered just enough to seat us all. Markus and Yan, noodled together, thumbed through a copy of the German edition of *Cosmo*, I eyeballed a local newspaper published in Munich, and Cody tried to make sense of a picture book in which two kids bounced on a dragon's tummy.

A cell phone rang.

Caleb pressed the device to his ear. "Halo? ... Ah, Inga, how kind of you to remember that any of us exist. Thanks for saying bye, by the way. ... Hmmm? No, nothing too much, just sitting at the hospital, waiting for Alex to give birth, you know, just shooting the breeze and all. What?" His eyes surveyed the room. "No, it's just us here, no one else. ... You sure about that? Fine, just a second." He lowered the phone to his palm and pushed a button on the screen. "Go ahead, you're on speaker."

"Have you all lost your minds?" the eerily-sedate voice of the vampire demanded without pretense. "You've taken a slayer to a huey hospital? Are you insane?"

"It was her choice, and advised by the hood physician," Caleb said, holding the phone up. "She's been in labor for a whole day at this point."

"Let it be for thirty days!" Inga shouted. "But let it be in Triberg! Do you have any idea what you've done, exposing her to outsiders and having her registered in one of their computer systems?"

"Do you think we're a bunch of first-time supes?" I asked. "She's here under an alias, one created by the Matron Council. They've given new IDs to all the slayers."

A pause suggested Inga hadn't counted on that. But the vampire proved she had more than one arrow in her quiver. "What of the doctors, though? If they do any basic blood work on her, they're going to figure out she's not human. Hell, they'll suspect something's wrong when her pulse and blood pressure are so irregular, and that's going to results in tests, notes, data in medical systems..."

Yan leaned in toward the phone. "I am here to make sure the hueys take no notice of Miss Alexandra's abnormalities, nor that they have any memory of her when we leave."

"Who..." A pause more pregnant than the slayer we'd arrived with. "...is that?"

Yan shrank back, suddenly silent. But Markus wouldn't stand for any slight of his boyfriend.

"*That* is Yan, and he's going to make sure everything is kept secure. Don't worry, we got things covered."

Inga's voice became alarmingly pinched. "Yan, who?"

The black-haired vampire buried his chin into his balled-up fists. "I am blooded of the Varanasi Clutch."

"I see," said Inga, followed by a space during which I could practically visualize the woman examining her fingernails with disdain. "I will arrive back in Germany tonight, and come directly to the hospital. If there is a single doctor left in that facility who even remembers what Alex's hair color is, there will be trouble. Do you understand, Watcher?"

Yan licked his lips. "Yes, Dracule, I do."

"Good," the vampire cooed. "I thought you might. Now, get that baby born, and as soon as I arrive, we leave, whether the doctors think she's ready or not."

And without a further word, the connection dropped.

# FOURTEEN

My gaze shifted between cutting and curious when I turned eyes on Yan. Even surmising that the Varanasi and Dracule had some kind of tension didn't do me much good. After all, the Ravens were Dracule, and I had a whole Texan cattle industry worth of beef with them, despite Inga and Igor also being born of that clutch.

Any chance of follow-up would have to wait. Petunia arrived right in time to catch our shell shock but to keep additional bombs at bay.

"The doctors agree that we've waited on the natural thing to happen long enough," the green hood said. "Alex is being prepped for the operating room. She'll be going in in the next ten to fifteen minutes, just as soon as the epidural kicks in."

Caleb stepped closer. "And the baby?"

Petunia's face blossomed. "She's a strong little lass. But she is showing some signs of stress, so it's good we got here when we did." Then, the glow of her cheeks faded. "Only…"

"Only what?"

Who asked? Who didn't?

She frowned. "The OB-GYN asked Alex permission to perform an ultrasound. Poor child hadn't had one, she said. The image was…" As Petunia's voice drifted off, Yan rounded the lobby. "I'll start containing the abnormality."

My pulse pounded. My breath hitched. Something was wrong, and it was my fault. "Abnormality? What kind of…"

Instead of illuminating our understanding or alleviate our worry in the least, Petunia turned her staunch expression square on me. "Alex would like to talk with you before it's too late."

The weight of collective stares threatened to collapse me.

"Me?" I asked, just as surprised as any of them. Anya had gone in with her the moment she'd been wheeled off, after all, so it wasn't like she was alone. "Why me? Caleb should be there; he's a slayer. Or Amy; she's been helping Alex pick out baby furniture and names. I'm... I'm..."

What? A hood? A no one? Relinquished?

But I knew what I was. I was a broken woman who was beginning to fear her mate was dead. I was bad luck. I was a malcontent. I was the last person Alex should want at her side as she welcomed her first-born child into the world.

I felt my head shaking before I'd even realized I'd said no.

Petunia planted balled-up fists on her hips. "Miss Kline, perhaps you've never been present at a birth before, but here's a helpful tip. Whatever the mother wants that's not a danger to her baby or herself, she gets." The elder hood pulled the surgical mask back up over her mouth. "I'll come to retrieve you in a few minutes when we're going into the OR."

As the midwife made her exit, I suddenly felt like I was the one in need of medical attention. My heart was going to thud right out of my chest.

Markus put an arm around me. "No worries, cuz. It's easy. You just tell them to breathe and push."

Caleb slapped Markus upside the head. "Alex is having a c-section, Einstein. The doctors are going to remove the baby surgically."

"You mean, they have to cut into her whoo-haa?" Markus's face curdled. "Oh my god, I'm so glad Yan can never do that to me."

As the boys bickered and Amy rattled something off about the shortcomings of the female body, I gathered my courage. I'd taken on ruthless vampires and stood up to my alpha ex, but facing a mother giving birth was twisting me into knots. One thing Alex did not need was to be the one reassuring *me* everything was going to be okay. Time to step up and get my act together.

"Caleb?"

"...I mean the biology alone would be impossible, so..."

"Caleb!"

The slayer snapped to attention, wide-eyed. "Geri?"

"I don't suppose you're aware of any slayer birth traditions or anything?"

He guffawed. "We don't give birth to aliens or anything. Plus, how the hell would I know?"

"There's the naming ceremony," Markus offered.

Leave it to my cousin to have some forgotten piece of historic slayer lore in his head but be completely clueless on what a caesarian section was.

"How does that go?"

"Yeah, Markus." Caleb crossed his arms over his chest and cocked a hip expectantly. "How does that go?"

"During the first sunrise after the birth, you're supposed to hold up the baby to the first light of dawn to introduce it to its birthright, while proclaiming its name. Usually it's something done by the dad." He frowned. "Hey, do we even know who the dad is? Seems like that should have come up by now, but I haven't seen Alex being particularly Jane Brady with any of those slayer guys."

"When I asked her once, the only thing she said was that it didn't matter," Amy chimed in. "He's dead."

Another bitter inheritance this child would be born into.

Caleb got a sly look on his face. "I don't think it was a slayer, though. Probably some huey staff the Ravens had. Anya and the others say that Alex never got together with anyone in the dungeon as far as they knew, and there wouldn't have been much opportunity, you know."

I shouldn't be spending one brain cell on trying to puzzle out something that wasn't any of my business, but it did draw my curiosity. Given that the slayers were so important to Vlad, surely he would have been eager to, for lack of a better word, breed them. Would he have tolerated a hybrid? Was he so desperate for any of them to reproduce he'd accept any pairing that resulted in a child? Or was it possible that Alex had found a way to have a little happiness, confined as she was? Although, frankly, her restrictions hadn't seemed as bad as the other slayers'. Vlad exulted Alex over them all, doting on her, treating her with her own personal care and tenderness.

The same man who held my mate bound in silver and wanted to kill his own father. How very … odd.

"Well, at least we know that Vlad didn't knock her up."

Amy slapped Cody's chest quicker than I was able to. The blond huey didn't fear the big, bad wolf one single bit.

Returning to the room, holding a mass of pink scrubs, Petunia cleared her throat. "It's time, Miss Kline. Take these. You'll put them on over your clothes after you scrub up."

*If any of these people hurt Alex or her baby, I'll flay them with their own scalpels.*

I put my hand against the wall to steady myself, flooded with a sense of protection that perplexed me.

"Miss Kline?" Petunia's callused hands had a remarkably light touch. "Is something wrong?"

"No." *Yes.* "Just had a weird moment there, a little overcome." *Like I needed to protect something with my life.*

Petunia patted my shoulders. "Stress, perhaps. And I bet you haven't gotten anything past those lips but coffee since this whole episode started yesterday, have you?" She helped me regain my balance. "You're lucky you're relinquished. That wolf of yours from America... He's got a peculiar type of energy. Took me a while to get used to it, too. Makes me wonder if all American lupines are like that. The ones back home in Wales aren't."

What the hell was she talking about, *peculiar energy*? But then I remembered what Markus had said, how he could sense me now at times, the way any hood could sense any wolf when they got close enough. I hadn't thought about that when we called the hood's physician down from the castle. Cody's arrival, it seemed, had come at just the right time to serve as camouflage for my true nature.

Petunia gave me a gentle nudge toward a set of swinging doors at the end of the corridor. "Come along, now. This young one has waited long enough."

I yielded. "Petunia, thank you for this. For being here for Alex, even though she's not a hood."

"Pash! A baby is a baby," the old woman said. "I can't blame it for its parentage."

In the back of my mind, I wondered if she would have said the same thing back in 1687, if she'd been asked to assist in the birthing of my nameless ancestor.

In the OR, the medical staff moved with deliberate speed around Alex, stopping only a moment to acknowledge Petunia and me. The slayer's head stuck out from a surgical poncho, a tent that was tied down at the level of her shoulders and fanned out toward her feet, opening her most private areas to the inspection of the doctor and two nurses busily preparing a slew of instruments on several trays.

To be exposed in such a way to strangers. What more would this creature have to endure?

"Geri." She managed a smile, even as her voice cracked. "Thank you for coming." Then, moving her gaze and tilting her chin the slightest, Alex spoke to Anya and Petunia. "Can we have a moment?"

Anya let go of Alex's hand. "Of course." Petunia pushed a palm to Alex's cheek, telling her she was a brave woman, a mother of the future light. Despite this passing in English, I suspected at least one of the nurses wondered what the two were getting on about, as she stopped in the laying out of instruments for a fraction of a second.

As a hood and as a woman, I knew that's where the truth often revealed itself: in the slivers of time between understanding and obfuscation.

I assumed the tall stool at Alex's side, still warm from its previous occupant, and took her hand. "It's almost done now. Pretty soon, you're going to be holding your baby."

She grinned. "I have been holding her for eight long months."

"Yeah, but now you'll be able to put her down, too."

"Miss Denver." The doctor leaned in over the top of

the tenting, looking the slayer in the face. His English proved good, even if heavily accented. "We will make the first incision in just a moment. If you want your guest to stay, it is okay, but if you want either Miss Anya or Petunia back, we should ask them in now."

"I'd like Anya," Alex returned, "but if you would, just a moment?"

The doctor nodded, then went back to his position down the bed. "But quickly. We do not want to cause you or the baby anymore stress than is necessary."

And I'd add myself to that list. "I don't want to rush you," I said, "but it seems you have something to say to me. Best just to say it then."

The jerk of her chin was so minute, I'd have missed it if I didn't look for it. "I want you to know that I didn't hide the truth because I was ashamed. I hid it because I didn't know who I could trust. Now I know, I can trust you."

Where was she going with this? "Of course, you can."

"My baby, Geri..." Her eyes drifted down to the regions of her body now embargoed. "The life she would have known if you had not helped us—"

Thank god she was cognizant to mind her words with an audience. "When you liberated us from Dracula's harem" might have changed the temperature of the room.

"The opportunity she will have now, possibilities that would have been impossible before... What I'm trying to say is, will you do us both the honor of being Mina's godmother?"

The skin on my nose crinkled. "Who's Mina?"

"Why... The baby, of course."

"Oh? Oh! Oh, goodness." So much for that naming

ceremony then. Either Alex wasn't aware of the tradition, or the absence of a father had encouraged her to make do without.

I didn't really understand where this was coming from. I mean, yeah, the gratitude made sense, even if it landed on me with a wallop as a reminder that, in exchange for the slayers' freedom, Tobias had lost his. But did she mean would I be some sort of protector? A godmother? An executor of a vast slayer estate Alex had heretofore failed to mention should something happen to the mother and until little Mina turned twenty-one?

Part of me hesitated, and I recognized that part, at last, for it was: the selfish me who Cody had so accurately pointed a finger at (not that I'd ever admit that to him). Remembering what Petunia had said, that a pregnant mother gets whatever she wants as long as there's no harm in it, however...

My hands wrapped around Alex's. "Of course, Alex. I'd be honored."

The slayer didn't need to conjure a solarium to shine. "Thank you. You have no idea how much that means to me. Now, I hate to push you along, but I have to see to this one little thing."

I couldn't help but laugh. "If you insist. I'll send Anya back in on my way out."

Which should have been the joyous end of a long and arduous day, but my true nightmare was only just about to begin.

The hall was empty as I hit the linoleum floor, smelling vaguely of antiseptic and lemon. I'd managed to break my fall, but couldn't move. All four limbs worked to keep me right, even as my frame shook from tip to toe. As the first cries of a new soul who claimed the air as birthright and her life as her own filled my ears, the ground beneath my palms tilted. *She's mine*. The voice in my head chanted it, declared it, repeated it like a mantra as old as earth itself.

*She's mine.*

*I am yours.*

*She is ours.*

Three voices, all of them singing in perfect harmony.

The first voice, mine.

The second, and how I did not know but knew it was utterly true, was Mina's.

And the third...

The third was Tobias's.

My eyes shot up, as though he might be standing there, with his worn-out jeans, scratching the five o'clock shadow that showed up at 9 AM each morning, while offering me a bowl of dumplings. The hall remained empty, but my head remained full.

"Tobias?" I asked.

Aloud? Or was it just in my mind? I didn't know.

"She's ours, Geri," he answered. Or did he? Could he? "The pup is pack."

He had to be talking about Mina, but that was impossible. Mina was a slayer. How could she be—

Alex never talked about the father.

Vlad had treated her like a goddess.

The pregnancy had only lasted eight months.

A werewolf, free of his mating bond, could love again…

Finally, the realization took me to my feet. "Tobias?"

I blinked, and suddenly, what I was seeing wasn't the hospital my logical brain knew I was in, but a small, square room built of ancient rose-colored brick, smocked over at intervals by beige stucco. I was on the floor, my hands bound behind me, while Vlad and another male vampire sat on cushioned, baroque-styled chairs.

"Once I have its lover, then the plan will all be in place, Massimo. It will give us the tools we need to be both masters of life and death."

Massimo, the archetype of a Byronic beauty with his prominent jaw, ebony locks, and olive skin, clutched the top of a silver-crested cane anchored before him. "You assume, Vlad, that we all want such things."

Vlad blinked. "Are you saying you want to die?"

"I am saying that I have very little left for which to live." The man shook his head, then passed me—Tobias?—us?—a sympathetic gaze before turning back. "Why live forever without purpose, when you can die happy with pride and with love?"

The man rose, and Vlad followed.

"You and yours may take shelter in my clutch, as requested, but I suggest you depart for Spain as soon as you've made arrangements. In the meantime, you *will* observe to my edicts while in Venice. We adhere to modernity, Vlad. No drinking to excess, and erase the memories of those from whom you do imbibe. Tourists work well, especially those who themselves have had a little too much to drink."

The fingers on Vlad's hand flexed. "You presume to lecture me on remaining discreet?"

Massimo's eyes shifted to where we were huddled on the ground once more. "You travel with both your sire bound by oak and an asenaic in bondage, Dracule. Such acts in our world draw attention. I bid you good evening."

And with a tip of his fingers off his forehead, Massimo (and his walking stick) became smoke and flew away.

Vlad, chest heaving, anger in his eyes, turned on us. "You'll pay for your words, wolf. You were told to *remain silent.*"

When I spoke, it wasn't with my voice, but Tobias's. "Even if I were rendered mute, my heart will cry out for her so loudly, the deaf would hear."

"Is it torture or love that's made a poet of you?" Vlad stomped the four paces it took to cross the room. "And I do detest both the love and poetry of amateurs."

Without warning, the vampire's fangs latched onto our neck, the pain rippling through my body. Our screams rang out, walled in by brick and bitterness. The vampire pulled what he desired from us, then retracted, then... was just gone.

Our breath heaved. Our wounds bled. Our hopes withered. The brick sent a chill through our body.

"I will find you. I will save you."

Did I say that to Tobias? Did he say it to me? I didn't know. A moment later, bitter, toxic fumes filled my nose. I blinked, and suddenly, the brick wall was gone. The pain was gone. I was still here.

In the hospital, with a very concerned doctor muttering something in German to me that didn't register.

"I'm fine," I said in English before remedying with, "*Mir geht's gut.*"

She seemed doubtful as she explained that she'd just come up the hall to find me on the ground. "Not unconscious," she said. "Just staring blankly. Miss, do you need medical attention?"

I shook my head as she helped me to sit up. "I just need food. I haven't eaten anything in… two days?" I said.

We both turned as the doors of the OR behind us opened and a beaming Anya, draped in the requisite cleanroom attire, peaked out. "Tell everyone, Geri! It's a girl! A healthy, beautiful, baby girl!"

# FIFTEEN

The redhead's delicate eyelashes fluttered open.

Alex's movements were slow, but the doctors had warned they would be. She'd gone through nearly twenty-seven hours of labor from start to finish, then endured a c-section. The staff said she'd be healed enough for release in three to five days. The staff didn't know supes healed in half the time of a huey.

Ignoring the vampire hovering over her bed, Alex's gaze searched the room and found me sitting in a nearby chair, rocking a sleeping Mina.

"Is she okay?"

She was better than okay. Holding Mina felt like I was holding home in my arms, and she wasn't even mine. I gave the slayer a smile. "She's perfect. Absolutely perfect."

Inga pushed an index finger into Alex's chin, directing her attention back. "You have some explaining to do, sparky. Who else knew the father was lupine?"

Alex tried to sit up, but one painful shift of her frame told her why that wasn't a good idea, and she surrendered back to the bed. "Vlad knew. Timur, too. Other than that, I don't know."

"And what about the wolf?" Inga asked. "Do you know who he was? What pack he was from?"

"What pack he was from? The wolves that the Ravens held.... Ahhh... Ahh!"

Yan flew to the bed, putting a hand on Inga's when the latter's fingernail drew blood. "Perhaps you can remember, Miss Rosethorn, that Alex is not our enemy. She has committed us no wrong, and she is recovering from major surgery."

Violet eyes flashed anger. Then, with glacial coolness, Inga's features eased. Her hand dropped back to her side as she feigned clearing her throat, waiting for Alex's answer.

The slayer shook her head. "I speak English, Ukrainian, Turkish, and the Raven's form of Romanian. The wolf spoke none of those."

Something about that answer set Inga at ease, and I itched to know what. Regardless, now wasn't the time.

The recovery room door opened, and a short man with a pot belly and brown-rimmed glasses bustled in, carrying a clipboard. "Miss Inga, madame?"

"Yes, Doctor Altz?"

Earlier in the morning, Inga had marched into the hospital like Patton arriving to the front, despite the sun lingering overhead. A quick arrival was worth the sunburn she'd endured, it seemed. Within five minutes, all the doctors and nurses that Yan had already corralled and began to process were under *her* sway, taking each of their breaths from her sighs.

Yan had looked simultaneously impressed and ill.

Dr. Altz flipped open that charts. "As you predicted, the patient's blood pressure and pulse are slightly elevated, but steady. The baby, however, seems to have the opposite result. We're concerned that her temperature is low."

"I wouldn't worry about it," I said. "A wolf's temperature runs slightly cooler than a huey's."

Speaking up only brought Inga's attention back to me, the last place I wanted it to be. The vampire had been shooting me daggers since she'd shown up.

"What happened, Geri? Igor raved all about your amazing ability to sense wolves at a distance none of your kind ever had. How did you not sense the baby?"

I'd been pondering that myself. "The only thing I can think of is that Alex's body—a slayer's body—created some kind of barrier that interferes with whatever it is that lets me do that. As soon as Mina was out, I could sense her."

"Any of you had any other insights?" she drove on. "No inklings? No nudging suspicions? Any visions?"

At the word *vision* I almost spilled about what had happened to me in the minutes after Mina had been born, but instinct told me to hold back. Besides, it probably had been a hallucination. Wolves weren't telepaths in the traditional sense; neither were hoods. There were no precedents for any supe saying they'd actually inhabited the mind of another and seen with their eyes.

"None," I said instead. "I assumed – we *all* assumed – that the baby was wholly slayer."

Before the vampire could follow up her line of questioning, I launched into one of my own. "Alex, it sounds like you met the wolf, but if you couldn't speak, how did you two... you know, come to an understanding about what was to be done?"

The woman in the bed blushed. "The act of procreation does not require words, as you know."

Embarrassment became a flame in my cheeks, but luckily Alex wasn't in a position to see.

"Vlad had offered me the option of having—what is it called?" Alex's eyes drifted through the air, searing words.

"An injection?"

*Artificial insemination* seemed too course a term to say while holding an infant. "I understand. But you didn't choose that. Why?"

The slayer's fatigue pulled at the corner of her eyes. "I did not survive in the House of Tepeş by being ignorant. I learned when to listen, when to be deaf, and when to ask questions. I've spent years making Vlad feel he was my living god. He trusted me. Once, when he thought I was asleep in his bed, I overheard a phone call he took."

I tried to ignore the implication, even as my mind raced to judgement. But how was that fair? Alex had been worse than a prisoner, she'd been a slave. Whatever advantage she made of her limited choices wasn't for me to berate; I knew from experience that knowledge was power. She'd have done it not only for herself, but also to keep the other slayers as safe as she was able. Martyrdom didn't always mean the death of the body. Sometimes it meant the death of the soul.

I placed Mina in the clear plastic bassinet the hospital had provided and made sure she was tucked in tight. "Do you know who he was talking to?"

Alex shook her head as I took a chair at her bedside. "A vampire, for certain. Vlad said something about how he wished he could destroy his father, but he'd need a miracle to do it and survive. You know that about them, right? That vampires who kills a member of their own bloodline kill themselves in the process?"

I nodded. "Yes, Igor told me."

A faint smile ghosted her face, then flitted away. "Right. Then, whomever he was talking to told him something that made him happy, exceedingly happy. To delight Vlad when he is in such a mood is to sift diamonds from mud. I pretended that I just woke up and asked what the good news was. When he explained he'd learned a way to kill Igor and explained how, I asked for the honor of being the vessel. Vlad agreed, saying if any of the slayers could seduce a wolf to lie with them, it was me."

"That sounds like my brethren," Inga hissed. "I'm sorry that happened to you, Alex, but I don't understand what you're getting at."

"Of course, you don't," Alex said. "Like all vampires, you don't want context, you only want what you feel is critical. But you never understand that humanity is where the context lies."

Inga choked on the retort, taking none too kindly to being lambasted.

Perhaps because she was so tired or just tired of acquiescing to vampires, Alex continued unabated. "My people have clung to our stories. Maybe you would call them legends, and maybe that's all they are. They've been handed down for so many generations, it's impossible to know what's true and what's made up. One talks about a lupine who took two wives: one slayer and one hood. Both bore him children. One night, a vampire descended on them, eating first the lupine, and then his wives, and then he came to the children. First, he consumed the blood of the babe born to the hood, and it gave the vampire incredible strength, fueling him with power. Then, the vampire ate the child of the slayer, whose blood made him weak, and eventually, killed him."

Inga mused a space before saying, "If this is true, it would change things radically."

Alex's head angled as she took me into view. "At first, I carried the child, hoping that the story was true. I would sacrifice a child born to such circumstances to save my people. Then I was rescued, given a chance at a life, a real life, with my child. Now, the last thing I want is to lose her to them. Please, Geri, swear you will protect her."

I moved to the edge of the slayer's bed, pulling her

hands to mine. "Of course, Alex."

Behind us, Inga paced. "If that story *is* true, it means Mina would be... Would be a way to kill the Ravens. The child must be harvested at once."

I shot up from the bed and spun on the vampiress. "What?"

Inga blazed with hope. "Just think about it, Geri: the Ravens arranged for this baby's conception with the intent of drinking it. All we have to do is let them."

I was in front of the bassinet before I realized I'd even moved. "No one touches the baby."

The temperature of the room had shifted, and suddenly, we were no longer three women with fates bound by a common enemy. I was pack, a status extended by virtue of blood to Alex, and Inga... Inga was a jaguar, stalking the young I protected.

"Come on, Geri," she said, creeping forward half-step by half-step. "Don't you want your *mate* back at your side so you can finally be together? You and I both know killing Vlad is part of that process. The other Ravens are tough but not undefeatable; we've already proven that. With Vlad, the rest will fall in short order, but we must kill him. Let me take the baby. I can still leave tonight if I move quickly."

"We're not doing anything that is going to bring a lick of harm to this child." My arms went wide, but not in a mere display. As the vampire dripped toward me, I called out the silver hidden under my clothing, fashioning it into a chakram. I'd never fought with the Indian weapon before, but the circular throwing ring had an edge as sharp as a sword, and could be used up close as well – both advantages when fighting a vampire.

Inga blinked thrice. "My, my. Been doing some research, or did someone watch *Xena*?"

No idea what that meant, I answered instead by positioning my weapon. "We are not using this baby as a weapon."

"Why not? She's not that precious. Alex got knocked up by a wolf; it shouldn't be hard to get another slayer to do the same."

Revulsion roiled my insides. "Their race is dying and you want them to be some kind of anti-vampire breeding factory? Not to mention what that does to a wolf."

"We'll use unmated wolves, then. Since they automatically love whomever they first bed, what's the big deal? Besides—" Inga held up a hand. "We don't even know if it will work. Worst case scenario: I use Mina as a peace offering, Vlad takes me into his fold again, and then I can work from the inside to destroy them."

Across the room, Alex labored to sit up. She did better this time, propping herself on her elbows. The sedatives they'd given her during the c-section were wearing off, but that didn't mean she was in any state to anchor a battle. "Give me one shot and I'll end this discussion."

"Don't move, Alex, or you'll rip your stitches. Don't worry, I'm not letting her touch Mina."

The vampire flexed her fingers, cracking each knuckle like a string of fireworks. "I tried the nice way, hood. Now we do this my way."

And before I knew what had happened, I was flying through the air.

# SIXTEEN

## AMY

Someone had brought their pug to the hospital, and when I'd nodded off, it had crawled up into my lap and made itself at home.

No, wait. Check that. It was Caleb. *Caleb* had crawled up into my lap and made himself at home. Or at least, his head had.

"Get off me." I pushed him practically onto the floor.

He startled awake like all supernaturals... uh, *supes* did: leaping into full battle position. What was it with this crowd, did none of them have to rub the sleep from their eyes and spend five slow and confusing minutes trying to figure out which frat boy's bachelor pad they'd passed out in drunk the night before? Every time they were shocked awake, they expected Lord Voldemort to be attacking.

Luckily, he hadn't conjured a solarium, because that probably would have really freaked out the thin, middle-aged woman dressed like an LL Bean commercial in the chair across from us. I mean, I knew that since Inga had arrived, she had all the doctors and nurses involved with Alex's case sequestered and Criss Angel-ed, but down here in the main waiting room, it was still clueless hueys.

Which, for once, didn't include me.

I rolled up my copy of *Der Spiegel* and hit the slayer on the thigh. "Who gave your head permission to be on my lap?"

"What? I fell asleep." His stance eased. "And if you want to give me permission to put my head somewhere else, by all means."

Luckily, German middle-aged auntie didn't seem to speak English. I, however, did. What the hell was it with this guy? How could you so openly flirt after you'd just had your heart broken? Besides, totally inappropriate innuendo was *my* thing. Caleb Helsing was beating me at my own game, and he didn't even like me.

By the way, what was there about me *not* to like?

The slayer sauntered to the automatic coffee machine. "How long was I out?"

I turned my wrists out to him. "Do you see a stopwatch?" My eyes went to the clock over the world's most pristine goldfish tank. "It's five-thirty. Morning or evening, though? We've been at this hospital so long, I've lost track."

He shoved a coin in the slot, and automatically a disposable cup popped into existence underneath the dispenser as it spouted out liquid humanity. "Morning. The sun is about to rise. Probably why I fell asleep. That, or you bored me to death."

"Believe me, Buffy, if I could kill you by talking, I'd never shut up. Now, stop being a self-centered bastard and get me a cup of coffee, too."

"Your wish is my command, Barbie."

Despite the lip, he did as asked, shoving a scalding plastic cup into my grip a few moments later. Inspired by joe, I finally untwisted myself from the awkward position forced by trying to sleep in a waiting room chair, bending at the hip, elongating my frame, puffing my chest out to stretch my lower back. I did *not* miss how Caleb's eyes clung to me during the whole procedure.

"Didn't Inga get here, like, three hours ago?" I asked. "I thought she'd just go through and mind zap all the particulars and we'd be out of here." I took a survey of the waiting room. "Where are the others?"

"Cody and Pietro are sleeping out in the car," Caleb said between sips. "Markus and Yan are upstairs, helping to run doctor and nurse interference."

"Why? Is there something wrong? Is the baby okay?"

The slayer shook his head and then, annoyingly, crossed his arms and beamed at me. "You're very cute when you're concerned with someone beside yourself."

I stood and shoved a finger into his chest. His very solid, very defined chest. "I'd say the same of you, but I don't know what that looks like."

Those soft lips curled into a mischievous grin, one I wanted to smack off his face.

With my lips.

Hot coffee scalded my hand as Caleb threw me against the wall, knocking all the wind from my lungs. I'd had aggressive lovers in the past, but this was borderline Christian Grey-level shit and I was not having it.

Especially not in these clothes.

But no sooner had I drafted a witty way of saying "fuck you" that simultaneously said "fuck me" then I figured out Caleb wasn't attempting to ravage me. Not unless a slayer's idea of getting to first base was to paste you to the nearest flat surface with their backs pressed into your chest.

Which begged the question: were slayers' danglies on their frontside like ours, or to sleep with Caleb would I have to reinterpret the term "reverse cowgirl"?

"What the f—?"

*Boom. Crash.*

I'd never heard anything about earthquakes in Germany, but it would have been hard to miss the way the whole building shook.

The slayer peeled himself off me and shoved me toward the exit just in time to see LL Bean high-tailing it likewise. "Get out of the building, now!"

Caleb almost managed to get away before I grabbed him by the collar and dragged him back. "What's going on?"

"Fighting. Not sure who. Go to the car in the parking lot. Send Pietro and Cody in. Might need their help. Hurry!"

In a blur, my hand was empty and Caleb was gone, leaving me unprotected, and worse, unravaged.

Sigh… Maybe I should try to sneak out of the house and hit up the local bar scene when we got home. Apparently, I *needed* someone again. Always did, eventually, and it had been… what, six months since that graduation party at Delta Mu Xi?

Did Triberg have a bar scene?

Ignoring the throbbing of my scorched fingers, I instead focused on the destruction of my last pair of blue jeans as I headed toward the exit, all while things were crashing somewhere behind me. All around, frightened chatter turned into panic as patients and hospital staff alike fled the building.

I turned to look up to the three-story structure, knowing Geri and Alex were on the second floor. Right where a bright light flashed moments before the windows blew out from one side of the building.

"Holy—"

Women screamed. A child cried. I looked up, only then realizing I'd fallen to the ground, a moment later to be pulled to my feet.

Cody shoved keys into my hand as Pietro whisked by. "Get the car ready. We might need to make a quick getaway."

"They're still up there." My head jerked to the place where a patch of wall had simply ceased to be.

But Cody didn't wait for a reply. He flew as fast as two feet allowed, running the opposite direction of the crowd.

This was bad. This was super, mega bad. Some serious shit was going on upstairs, and they wanted me to go start the car? I looked over my shoulder and found it parked just twenty feet away, past cement barriers that would keep me from bringing it much closer. The key fob had a remote starter. As long as I didn't lose the keys, it was fine.

Slipping them inside my pocket, I circled back.

The good news was, Lahr was in the middle of nowhere. Nowhere being the Black Forest region. Well, technically, it was sort of on the upper northeast side, but there weren't many people there. Caleb said Inga had created a safe zone around the area where Alex was recovering. Other than Geri, Markus, and Yan, there shouldn't have been anyone there when whatever exploded went boom.

Oh, except a poor, helpless baby.

I wasn't exactly what one would call "interested in kids," but just because I didn't go gaga over mini-humans didn't mean I'd let one get hurt if I could do anything about it.

As I reentered the building, I came to the sudden realization that I really had no idea where to go, other than up. Luckily, the steady stream of people heading in the opposite direction gave me some clue. Near the stairwell, a man wearing a security uniform, his chest pumping and his face uber white, talked over a red phone. He held out a hand as I passed, saying something very German.

"Sorry, I no *sprechen*."

"Explosion!" he warned in an accent so heavy, I'd have to pay extra fees to take it on a plane. "You no can go in the—"

I hit the stairs and didn't hang around to hear the rest. At the top, I could turn right, down a sterile hallway, or left, down a sterile hallway with a window at the end. The glass in the window was still intact. I thought that was as good a reason as any to hang a right. A few doors down, I heard growling. A few more steps, a thundering voice wove into the mix.

"… can't let you do this."

Caleb? My feet picked up the pace, as did my heart.

I rounded the corner and passed a door. Like, one on a wall, only not hung by hinges. The smoldering rectangle bore a perfect shape to fit into a frame that now stood empty.

On the side of the room without windows, or really, much of a wall anymore, was Geri, holding a bundle of pink blankets clutched to her chest, winged by Markus and Pietro. Yan and Caleb stood in front of the trio, the slayer balancing a solarium on his hand. Also, there was a wolf. Like a massive, hulking, would-make-my-mother's-chihuahua-shit-itself wolf. Alex was still in the hospital bed, and from what I could see, unconscious.

Inga's back was to me, but I'd learned enough about supes in my limited time to know they all probably knew I was there. Hearing me or smelling me or their earlobes tingling or something… The supernatural really got the royal flush of hands when it came to the five senses.

And… that made me wonder what Caleb's mouth could taste like.

"Silly slayer!" Inga hissed. "Don't you see? This is the solution! That babe has the power to kill the Ravens. All I need to do is present it to Vlad, and finally, your kind will be saved."

"We are *not* sacrificing a baby!" Caleb snapped. "Back down or else."

Inga crossed her arms. "Are you going to kill me, Caleb? You couldn't do it when I found you, and you're even more compromised now. Now, hand over the baby. I don't want to hurt anyone."

"Hurt anyone?" I'd never heard Geri's voice so worn, so broken, not even when we left Istanbul. "You killed Alex!"

My racing pulse went still as I sucked up all the air in the room.

And surprisingly, *that's* what drew the vampire's attention.

Inga spun. "Why, hello, Amy."

Caleb looked past the vampire. "I told you to wait in the car."

"Alex is dead?" No, that couldn't be possible. She'd just given birth. She'd just gotten free, god damn it, all to die here, in the middle of the Black-Fucking-Forest? "How? When?"

I closed my eyes against the sting of tears, but in doing so, also closed them against the signs of danger. I flew forward. When I opened my eyes, I was five feet farther into the room then I'd been before, and Inga had me trapped, one of her blood-red fingernails at my throat.

And that's when it hit me, I was going to die.

"Caleb!"

*Caleb*? Why the hell, among all the people in this room, was I singling him out.

"It's okay, Amy." He inched forward, but Inga dug her nails deeper into my skin, and then under it. A hot line of blood trickled down my neck, soaking into my shirt after rolling over my collar bone.

"Careful, Caleb," Inga warned. "Little Amy is just a huey. I could kill her before you had a chance to blink."

The slayer cocked back his weapon. "You do, and I'll kill you here and now."

"Like I said, how? Share a secret, Amy?" The vampire's lips hovered next to my ear. "I've had a theory that this is part of the reason that Caleb is such a manwhore. His solarium has performance issues, so he bangs everything with a pulse to feel like a man."

Anger fringed my fear, burning away its fumes. "Probably why you're so jealous," I said. "Having no pulse, he never gave you the time of day."

The vampire's chest shook with laugher. "Oh, I do like you. I'd hate to kill you. Geri? Give me the baby, and that doesn't have to happen."

I locked gazes with my best friend, shaking my head. "Don't you dare, Kline."

Geri nodded. "I won't, Amy. I won't."

The wolf—Was *that* what Cody Ryland looked like with fur?—chuffed.

I turned my eyes back to Caleb. "Throw it."

His eyes went blank. "But it will kill you."

"If you don't give Inga the baby, she's going to kill me

anyway," I said. Even if what the vampire said was true and Caleb's supernatural power had performance issues, it had to hurt like a son of a bitch, right? "Besides, I got nothing to live for. No job, no home, no boyfriend. My father hates me, and my mother thinks I'm the reason he hates *her*. Saving a baby from a wacko vamp would at least give my death some purpose, even if my life has added up to zero net gain."

Said vamp tugged me a step backward. "The girl makes sense, Caleb. Now, *hand it over* or I'll take you too, Geri. Your blood could keep me going until Doomsday."

Geri got the fire of the gods in her as she put a hand forward and morphed silver into some kind of ball. Because the best kept secret in history is that you can kill a vampire by bowling at it.

My friend sneered. "To the death, then, Inga."

*Amy's* death. I mean, that's what they meant, right, being that I was the hostage du jour? I closed my eyes, trying to buy my sales pitch. I could see my mother weeping her crocodile tears in my mind's eye, but I could also see Geri, actually crying.

Fine, I'd die. At least I'd be the hottest corpse ever.

The grip around me loosened and the floor smacked my ass suddenly. A moment later, I found myself sitting in a puddle of something dark and crimson. A thud next to me drew my attention. Turning my head, I found a body without its own.

Pietro Kline stepped away from the non-human shields that had gathered around the baby. "*Gracias, Dio.*"

Was he smiling? Grimacing? Having gas? Any of those was possible based solely on the half-grinning, half-kidney-stone-passing expression he wore.

I followed Pietro's gaze, swiveling, my arm losing its grip

from the slick sheen of blood pooling out over the floor. What I saw didn't makes sense. A red hood, brown hair pulled into sober braids that twisted like a crown around her head, and a silver sword dripping red.

An actual, fucking sword. In the post-op recovery room.

At the end of the woman's arm, the head of Inga Rosethorn, frozen mid-bitch. She (the sword-wielding badass, not the decapitated vampire) looked down on me, both literally and, I felt in my huey, huey soul, figuratively, and asked, "And who in the hell are you?"

# SEVENTEEN

## GERI

I stepped past my father and fixed my mother with the most acidic glare I could manage. "Her name is Amy Popowitz, and she's my friend."

My mother ground her teeth. "Markus, explain."

Markus cleared his throat, even as he pulled his silver away from the twin daggers he'd fashioned in the heat of battle. "Her name is Amy and she's—"

"Amy Popowitz!" I intervened. "As I just said." If Brünhild thought she was going to pretend I didn't exist after what she'd just done, she had another thing coming. "And she doesn't have to explain herself here, *you* do."

But one didn't get to be Grand Matron by being easily emotionally manipulated. Ignore me she had decided to do, and ignore me she would. "Markus, please help Miss Popowitz to her feet and take her to the bathroom to wash off. Quickly. Sunrise is eleven minutes out, and you need to be on the road in six."

Friend though he may be, my cousin was still a righteous hood, and fell right back into being the perfect little soldier when the Red Matron snapped her fingers. He hoisted Amy to her feet, even as her left and right legs attempted to swap sockets. "Whatever you do, don't get any of it in your mouth. Inga was a Dracule. Very potent maker bloodline. Even a few drops could start the process."

"The process?" Amy asked, clutching his arms for support. "What process?"

"Becoming a vampire, of course." He said it like he was telling her water was wet. "Unless that's what you're after."

Amy shook her head. "I can't even eat a pink steak, I don't think I'd have much luck with sucking down human blood."

They rushed off to the bathroom, Markus closing the door behind them.

"You there." Mother pointed at Caleb. "Have you gone through rites?"

The slayer's eyes hadn't left Inga's dripping head since it had left its owner's body. "I have."

"Good." Brünhild tossed the head atop the corpse on the floor. "My sympathies for the loss of one of your own, but now is not the time to grieve. There mustn't be any evidence of her existence when the authorities get here. Is it true that your dead dissolve in water?"

"What?" Caleb seemed shocked by the sentiment. "Um, yeah. Yeah, it is."

Brünhild jerked her head toward the bathroom. "As soon as they're out, take that one's body and wash it away with haste."

Cody shifted back to his human. "Oh, come on, Brünhild. You can't possibly think you're going to be able to cover all this up in less than ten minutes, do you?"

The Grand Matron quirked an eyebrow. "How long have you known me, Cody Ryland?"

The werewolf fidgeted, which paired with the fact that he was naked, upped the awkward level. "Um, all my life, ma'am."

"And you doubt my ability to do this?"

Cody cocked a hip and shied his eyes. He may be an alpha, but he had also lived years under my mother's direct authority and worse, on numerous school field trips on which she'd chaperoned. "Um, no ma'am, sorry."

Brünhild picked up some gauze sitting on a tray at Alex's bedside and proceeded to wipe off the blood from her short sword. "I won't ask what's brought you all the way from Paradise, but we will talk on this, Alpha. Janus?"

The diminutive vampire promptly appeared at my mother's side. "Yes, Matron?"

"Markus will evacuate this lot as soon as he emerges with the huey. You and I will stay behind and handle the fall out. We need everyone to believe this was a gas explosion, a terrible accident that claimed the life of mother and child. Can you handle that?"

Yan tipped his head. "Of course, Matron. And I should advise you also that I can hear the sirens of the emergency vehicles and authorities approaching. You should probably reclaim and hide your silver."

Without arguing, my mother held up her weapon. A solid object one moment, its edges shimmered and turned in on themselves, flooding down her sleeve and under her cloak. A moment later, the flowing garment itself faded from existence, revealing an odd choice for slaying wear: a smart pantsuit. So, she was going to act the role of a huey while Yan mind-wobbled the actual humans to believe every lying word that came from her mouth, huh?

Part of me actually admired the forethought.

Markus emerged from the bathroom with Amy, her blond hair still dripping. She wore nothing but a pale pink hospital gown that clung to her curves at unnatural angles.

Her words barely managed to sneak past her chattering teeth. "I feel violated. Seriously Markus, you have no idea how to touch a woman."

"Gee, let's wonder about that, shall we?" Markus pushed Amy forward into my arms, then heeded Caleb's request to help pick up Alex's body.

Propping Amy up, I pushed the two of us forward. "Strike first, die last, is that it, Mother? Thanks to you, my one lead on where to hunt for the other asenaics in Spain is gone."

Keeping up her "Zero Geri" policy, she continued to ignore me. "Markus, are there enough cars here to transport everyone back to Triberg?"

"Yes, Matron. We have two SUVs parked outside."

"Good. Cody?"

The werewolf turned. "Yeah?"

Brünhild's eyes drifted down. "Clothe yourself." Then nodding to Markus, she said, "Take the others and go now. Only Janus and the slayer are to stay. I'll need their assistance to contain this damage."

Markus hesitated. "Matron?"

"Yes, Markus?"

Just at that second, Mina's little grunt rose through the silence, as though asking in my cousin's stead, "What about me?"

For the briefest second, my mother didn't have an immediate response. The hesitation was over in two blinks as she steeled herself. "Yes, take the baby too."

"Got it." The brawny hood clapped twice. "Let's go, crew. We got to move."

Cody, who had found a pair of green scrubs in one of the supply doors, pulled a simpering Anya to her feet. The poor dear had become the victim of her own fight-or-flight instincts in which she'd gone the unspoken third route: don't make a move, shut down completely, and hope it's all just a bad dream.

"Come, sweetheart. She's gone, and that's terrible, but we need to get out of here."

My father assumed Amy as his burden. Perhaps to help me. Perhaps out of concern for her. Perhaps just because it brought him within a few feet of his wife for even the tiniest of moments. Brünhild tracked him, but never once did her resolve crack. As the others started toward the door, following my mother's orders without question, I lingered. The anger dwelling within me had finally reached critical mass. The barrier would no longer hold.

"Wait a god damn minute!"

Stopped in their tracks, everyone swung their head in my direction. Except my mother, of course, who only let her expression fall into one of general annoyance.

But I was here, and I would be seen *and* heard. "The last time I saw you, you attacked me, banished me. You made it perfectly clear that I was nothing to you, that I was *relinquished*, disowned, an outsider to the world in which I'd been reared and raised. And now you're just going to show up out of nowhere and start commanding around my friends and commandeering my choices?"

"*This* is largely the result of your choices." *For* the first time since she entered the room, Brünhild squared her gaze on me. "Besides, isn't this what you wanted? *Not* to be a hood?"

"Yes, it was." My tone leather, my jaw steel, I chewed my words. "Only, I never *was* a hood, was I? And you knew it. But you still tried to force me into the role, tried to force me to be your little protégé, all the time knowing I was an asenaic."

She smirked in annoyance. "Your point being?"

I held my arms out wide. "How could you do that to me? How could you do it to Papa? How could you torture the people you supposedly loved when their only fault was being who they are? How could you be that much of a... a bitch?"

That one word, one I'd thought thousands of times, but never had the guts to say, finally cut a lash across her resolve. My mother towered over me, easily five inches my better, and lowered her voice in a way that somehow made it feel louder.

"How dare you? Everything I have done was to protect my family." She pointed at the corpse laying prone on the floor. "That woman, the vampire you thought was your friend? She wanted to kill you when you were four years old, but I stopped her. And have you ever asked at what price? No. She knew the Ravens would take you, use you, bleed you. You want to know why I forced you to train harder, to know more, to be tougher than even my own mother, one of the most infamous and cruel matrons ever to wear the red cloak, ever did of me? It's because making you this tough was the only way to make sure you'd survive."

I bit back tears, even though whether they were born of pain or of anger, I didn't know any more. "But what kind of mother pushes away her own child?"

"One who knew the cost if she didn't. Do you think it didn't hurt me, having to constantly hurt *you*? I ached with every cruel word and bitter pronouncement, but it had to be done. You had to be self-sufficient, self-reliant. You had to be able to run, as far and alone as necessary, to keep yourself safe. Any attachments I fostered in you would be to your detriment. If you're expecting an apology from me, you're going to be waiting a long time, because it's not coming. I'm not your friend, Gerwalta. I'm your mother. My job is to provide for your needs, not your desires, and what you need to do right now is haul ass. Now *move*."

Cody's arms around me reminded me that I still had a body. "Come on, kiddo. We're keeping the others."

Shaking out my confusion, I surveyed the room and found it was only him, my mother, and myself. And just like that, we were moving. At some point, we must have gotten into one of the SUVs. It wasn't until I was laying in the back on the impromptu cot that had been set up for Alex, the baby placed in my arms and Cody laying across the way from me, that I even became cognizant of the fact that we'd left the parking lot.

"Like old times, huh?" The werewolf reached out, rubbing my arm. "You and me, laid out in the back of a vehicle after one of your mom's screeds?"

The joke brought no joy. My soul was bleeding, and beside me lay an infant who was suddenly... mine. Mina flinched, her arms flailed, her limbs out of control.

"She's so..." *Helpless? Useful? Doomed?* "Orphaned."

His comforting smile faltered. "She is."

"Inga and Alex are dead."

In my mind's eye, the events of the last twenty minutes replayed in a loop of terror. Inga charging Alex's bed, the slayer's attempt to send a solarium at her attacker. The magic somehow robbing her of her energy, turning back on her, and her body falling limp to the cot. Caleb screaming as he dove, getting to the new mother too late. The havoc of all of us trying both to protect Anya, and not hurt Inga, who was, after all, our friend. Or so we'd thought.

The moment the vampire's body had fallen away from her head as my mother's sword cleaved her in two, because she was the only one who understood who Inga really was.

"She saved us, Cody. She flew us out of Istanbul, she… She supported Caleb, gave Tobias a job, got him fake papers to make it possible for him to stay in the US… She was our friend, and my mother just cut off her head. She's dead because I'm a… Because…"

"Because she was trying to kill you." The voice was my father's. Based on the way it projected through the car, he was at the wheel. "For the second time in your life, she threatened to destroy you. Your mother took her word once, and Brünhild does not give second chances."

Of all the faults I could assign to my mother, this might turn out to be the biggest yet. Brünhild should have let Inga kill me when I was four. I never would have lived my life, my very existence a burden to my family. Cody's father might still be alive. Tobias never would have been captured by the Ravens. And Alex… She might still be a prisoner in Vlad's harem, but she wouldn't be a corpse that my ex-boyfriend had been ordered to dissolve in a hospital shower.

This child would still have hope.

"I have no idea how to care for a baby, especially not one like her."

Cody's eyes narrowed. "Why would you need to care for her, Geri? What is she to you?"

A source of guilt? A debt I owed?

The truth brought a smidgeon of warmth to my shaken spirit. "She's pack."

The alpha's mouth quirked. "What do you mean, she's pack?"

The last few words I'd exchanged with the slayer before the doctors made the incision replayed in the back of my mind. "Alex asked me to be the baby's godmother. I said yes. And then... Cody, am I going moonmad? Is this how it starts, with delusions?"

His voice remained soft, but a lilt suggested suspicion. "Why, did you see something?"

"I'm not sure. I passed out, and maybe it was a figment of my imagination, or... It's impossible. I thought I heard Tobias's voice inside my head, like he was whispering right in my ear."

He grinned his relief. "No, Geri, you're not going moonmad. *That* was a quickening."

"A quickening?" I repeated the term like it came from a foreign lexicon, even though I'd heard the term all my life. "The weird thing that happens when an alpha accepts a new member into their pack? But Tobias is my alpha, and he's hundreds of miles away."

I tried to quell the odd thrill that ran through me when thinking of the roguish and rough Englishman in that way. Genetics and hormones made odd bedfellows.

Cody placed a finger in Mina's hand, the tiny creature gripping for dear life. "Might have been a proxy acceptance. I've heard of it, but it's uncommon. The distance doesn't matter, though. You've probably just never heard that because, well, you know, werewolves aren't exactly globetrotters in general. The quickening happens to the whole pack, not just the alpha."

"You're saying I'm acting as some kind of proxy alpha?" I asked. Cody bobbed his head. "But that can't be. One, I'm a woman. And two, I'm barely even a wolf."

"Being an alpha isn't all about the bloodline. It's about attitude. It's about who's willing to step up and do what needs to be done to keep the pack safe in a time of crisis. If that doesn't describe you, Geri, I don't know what does. Men make kings. Wars make rulers."

Even with all the crush of truth and tyranny and trouble, the thought warmed me. "Then I *did* hear Tobias, because I had a quickening. Because I'm wolf enough."

"Tell you a secret, Little Red? The day you stood up to me at the wedding, when I told you to back off of your moping, I felt a…. I don't know, some kind of snap."

"I told you, I'm not going to apologize for that."

"No, Red, that ain't what I'm driving at." He pulled his hand back from the infant's grasp and wiped it down his face. "I mean, I felt you *leave* me. Not physically, but like, metaphysically. I'd always joked you were pack, and then you up and proved it by becoming a rogue. And then damned Tobias went right after you, didn't he?"

My memories traced back through that night, to the first kiss Tobias and I had shared, a sweet recollection that I didn't understand until much later had been real and not a dream.

"I suppose he did." But any sweet delight I took in the thought of being bound to Tobias that way ceded in the larger bitter implications. "But that means I'm running out of time. I was barely able to save Tobias from lunacity once, and that was when he was with me. I have to find him, and soon. But where?"

"You said something about Spain."

"I was going to try and find the other asenaics," I said. "Igor said he'd been getting his blood from a special source there. Igor will lead the Ravens to them eventually, sooner rather than later. They've already moved as far west as Venice."

The werewolf's forehead wrinkled, but I summed up my explanation by saying only "long story."

"The hood archives wouldn't have that kind of information?" Cody asked.

I shook my head. "Our history says that Gerwalta and Andreas's baby died with them."

"But you got this inheritance from your father," Cody said. "Just trace back his bloodline, then wheel it forward."

"My dad's family immigrated to Argentina from Spain three centuries ago. I can go back and find the origins, but moving forward through the generations... The Casa de Amarillo is a few hundred hoods spread out across the western Mediterranean basin."

My finger traced down Mina's cheek. The child, strengthened perhaps by her semi-lupine body, turned her face into my touch.

"I don't have time to covertly work my way through that big of a list, and that's assuming the Yellow Matrons gave any candidates permission to talk to me. I'll need to figure something else out and quick. I can't let Tobias go moonmad, and I can't let Vlad hurt him any longer."

"Don't worry, Little Red, we're going to find him. And after that... well, I'm not sure what kind of relationship is possible for you two, but at the very least, you'll have your friend back."

I grinned at him as my eyes fell closed. "You mean *another* friend back."

# EIGHTEEN

Bitter wind bit my skin, jolting me awake. A weapon! I needed a weapon! Instinct beckoned my silver skin to yield to my command, but found it lacking. Didn't matter. I could kill with my fists. Break bone with my kick. Claw out eyes.

"Geri!" Cody yelled. "Stop! You're going to hurt Mina."

*Mina? Who's Mina?*

A tiny cough rose from a bundle of warmth beside me, opening the gates of memory that sleep had closed with mercy. Sunlight stung my eyes, pouring in from the open back hatch of the SUV, a sea of bright in which Cody's face swam. Clarity came in both mind and body as the backdrop of circumstance returned. The last time I had seen the edifice behind the werewolf had been from this same car. Then, however, a dozen hoods bearing guns pointed my direction had stood between it and the outer bailey walls. Now, there was just Cody, Amy, Anya, and my dad, all staring at me with a mix of concern and fear.

"I'm fine."

No one had asked it aloud, but they were all screaming it with their eyes. I sat up, turning to check on the child beside me. In body, Mina was fine. Except that she was hungry. And wet. How did I know? The former by some odd instinct. The latter, because the smell was undeniable.

"We're going to need diapers," I said, even as I worked to undo the bundle of soiled blankets. Would that I could wash her, but that formalities of Schloss Wolfsretter demanded ceremony, procedure. *Time.* Babies were not unprecedented or even uncommon in the keep. How could they be, when our matriarchal society put women in most the leadership roles, and demanded them to reproduce? It was also true, however, that self-reliance remained a core value. When you came to the compound, other than food and basic toiletries, you were expected to bring what you and yours needed.

"Come on." Cody tugged gently on my ankle. "Let's take her inside and then we can worry about that."

I shook my head. "She'll catch her death in cold. I have to wrap her in something dry. Doesn't someone have a coat or something?"

They wore blank expressions. We'd fled the hospital with such haste, none of us had had time to grab anything. I hoped Caleb, Yan, and my mom remembered to clean up the various things we'd left behind.

My father stepped forward, closing his eyes and drawing on his power. As he did, the threads of his ancestral garb formed about him, draping him in the yellow cloak of his bloodline. He undid the tie at his throat, spinning it around. "Here. Wrap your *niña* in this."

The offer, both of the garment and of the indication that Mina was somehow mine pinched at my heart. The act, however, made clear what needed to be done for this to be true.

"Thank you, Papa, but…" I shook my head as I turned back to the cub beside me. Since claiming my fire—though still uncertain how that had come to be—I'd not tested myself in this capacity. Now, the moment had come, and it was critical that the bloodline cede to my request. I closed my eyes, calling on the ancestors of my clan, saying internally the summoning charm I'd been taught since childhood.

*Ancestors, cloak me in your wisdom and let my bloodline be my shield.*

Its weight on my shoulders warmed, while simultaneously reminding me of the burden of my legacy. Having not even been sure I could summon my red cloak, I'd put off the attempt, afraid of what it would mean if I proved incapable. Now that I found I could, I worried what that meant for an asenaic.

My father beamed at Mina and me as we crawled from the back of the vehicle, pride of such depth one might think he was looking at his own grandchild in my arms. He shepherded us under his wing as we turned toward the open east gate of the castle.

"Are you ready? The Council will have questions, make demands."

My jaw tightened. "I have a few questions and demands of my own."

Rebecca Krantz stood at the door, a solid archive of huey pride and fortitude. Gray hair and deep wrinkles around her eyes didn't detract from the fierceness of her heart.

"Welcome home, Miss Kline." Uniformed in her custom black slacks and beaten up brown bomber jacket, I could tell she wanted to say so much more, *do* so much more. Hug me, kiss my cheek, tease me about some secret romance... She'd never had children, and so the young hoods of the Schloss had become the family she'd never bear herself.

Beside her, Chin stood, resolute and severe in every way a woman of her stature could be. The wind picked up, blowing out the trail of her bloodline's white cloak, even as her eyes settled on the bundled baby in my arms with disdain. She'd read the child as a wolf; hoods couldn't sense slayers.

"At ease, castellan."

She wouldn't even address Becky by name? What an ass. Or was she just ticked off at having to oversee a formal affair in the middle of the day when she'd much rather be upstairs in bed?

Chin continued. "Miss Kline, the Grand Matron phoned about an hour ago. She wanted us to relay to you that she, a slayer, and Janus Sousa have contained the scene, and let you know that she ordered us to relocate the other slayers from your family's private residence in town to the compound."

"Where are they?" Anya stepped forward. "Where are my people?"

Chin tilted her head in Rebecca's direction. "Miss Krantz volunteered her personal residence within the castle walls for their use. The space is not as ample as RotHaus where you've been staying, but they are making do and getting settled until we are able to figure out what comes next."

My eyes flashed to the old woman beside the matron, who stood a little straighter than before. "Thank you, Becky."

Rebecca gave a quick nod. "I'm as good in the keep dormitory, ma'am, and they needed the space. I remember what it's like to come away from prison and feel the need to have a safe place."

I motioned to those standing behind me. "Perhaps Amy and Anya could be shown to the castellan's cottage as well?"

"No, your mother's orders are that everyone in your party be kept contained until her arrival." Chin gave me one disgusted glare before pulling at the corded silver belt wrapped around her waist. With the slightest effort, it melded into a stream of silver, then quivered into its next iteration: a pair of double manacles, a set that bind both feet and hands. "I suppose we can forgo this for the pup, but for this lupine..." Chin held up her creation.

Cody coughed a laugh. "You've got to be kidding me.

What is this, the middle ages?"

Chin bristled. "*This* is the House of the Wolf-Watcher, and these are the terms. No wolf may enter here unless he be bound by silver. For you to be invited alone is exceptional. If you want to escort this relinquished ingrate..."

As Chin took a step forward, so did I, placing myself between the Matron and the alpha. "The *ingrate* objects."

Chin sneered. "May I remind you, Gerwalta, that you have no official standing here? I could order you off the property right now."

"But you let me past the gate this time," I said. "Pretty sure that wasn't your decision, which means you're not the one deciding anything right now, are you?"

She lifted the chains again. "Regardless, this is our way. Now, step aside or..."

Moments before I called on the silver rattling in her hands, Cody gently pushed me aside.

"Easy, Geri," he said. "I'm a big, bad wolf. I can take a little burn. Go ahead, Matron, then let's get little Mina here seen to, huh?"

The bravado, a display. The moment the metal arced across Cody's wrists and ankles, the smell of seared flesh tickled my nose, turning my stomach. Cody tried to conceal the pain, almost managed it. The corners of his mouth flinched, giving away his pain. I felt out the silver in my mind, willing it away from his flesh, but as we began to follow Chin from the outer bailey to the inner one, he jostled, making the task exceedingly difficult.

Amy pulled up alongside me. She'd grabbed one of the sheets from the collection in the car and fashioned herself a toga over the hospital gown. *Of course,* Amy knew how to make a toga from bed sheets. Rumor was, Amy was amazing in the sheets. My father, realizing the inappropriateness of Frat Party attire in the sacred homestead of my bloodline, threw his yellow cloak over the blond huey's shoulders.

"This is it, isn't it? The castle where they burned Red Riding Hood alive?"

My teeth ground. "Not the greatest thing to bring up right now, but yes."

"Sorry, I just like, you know…" She blew out a long breath. "You don't think they're going to do that to you, do you? Because New York doesn't go out like that. I'll kick whoever's ass you need me to."

"Thank you, Amy, but no." I looked back over my shoulder, sizing up Markus, my father, and Anya. The men, eyes straight forward, were pillars of calm and determination, but the slayer…

I decided to harbor the bundled baby in Amy's arms. "Can you hold Mina for a minute?"

"What?" She pulled back a step before rushing to recover our gate through the inner bailey. "I don't know how to… What are you… Oh, okay. I guess."

I caught the look as I turned, the one that told me this was Amy's first time holding a baby, but it wouldn't be the last. She was positively smitten, even if a little out of her element.

"Anya?"

My voice snapped her out of her reverie, and she turned to me as though surprised to discover she wasn't alone. "Sorry?"

I pulled up alongside her. "I know you're in pain. Alex's loss was sudden and unnecessary, and there will be time to mourn her. But I need your help right now."

"My help?"

I took my voice as low as I could make it, slowing our steps even more. Ahead, Cody hissed, my ability to pull the burning metal from his flesh broken by distance.

Just to be safe, I pulled the slayer into my arms, hugging her, using the proximity to whisper in her ear. "You must say that Mina is mine."

"But she's Alex's…"

I squeezed her tighter. "I know, but when Alex asked to talk to me before the c-section, it was to ask if I'd be Mina's godmother. Hoods will recognize that as old law if others corroborate it. I'll need everything in my power to keep her under *my* protection. If they learn Mina's blood can kill the Ravens, they won't see a baby, they'll see a strategy."

"Surely they wouldn't…" She shook in my arms. "But she's just a baby."

"Exactly, help me protect her." Finally, I pulled away just as my father and Markus passed us. As long as my testimony came first, neither would conflict me. I hoped. Markus, while my cousin and good friend, still walked two paths that might eventually diverge. Anya, however, had no reason to cover for my lies.

I stroked her cheek, brushing away a tear. "Please, Anya, for Mina. For Alex."

She bit her lip, resolve firming her features. "For Alex."

# NINETEEN

No one knew the exact year Schloss Wolfsretter had been erected, but the best guesses placed it in the thirteenth or fourteenth century. When it had only been the home of the House of Red and not a de facto administrative center for the whole race, the current council chamber had been the red matron's throne room. The rectangular space could easily host fifty people or more, but its current furnishings were only arranged for thirteen. The massive oaken table sat at the far end of the space, one chair for each member of the matron council, each in turn representing a bloodline. The House of Red had two seats, of course, for the role of the Grand Matron demanded her to act without regard to heritage. Or so the official line went. By consequence, the reds usually dominated.

I'd spent many an hour in this morbid place, hidden away in a corner, observing at my mother's demand. No one had ever said it aloud, because the thing was obvious and understood, it would have felt unnecessary to say. I was the heir apparent, and as such, I needed to understand the power and limitation of the office I would someday assume. Seeing how my mother could dictate her form of justice, handing down edicts and judgments that lacked humanity, had soured me on the prospect at a young age. I found no reverence, therefore, in the stone walls moored in the dark ages of Europe's past, or in the tapestries hung on them that recalled the valor of my more famous ancestors. To the right, Hlin the Conqueror's sword pierced the heart of Kroon the Konigswolf under the mighty tree that once dominated this cliff. Its stump, worn smooth and uneven after centuries of use, still sat on the far end of the room. Once, it was said, it had been carved with magnificent reliefs, antlers twisted into it to enhance its terror. The tapestry to the right held its subject in the middle, her blond hair and silver bo staff front and center. Behind her, the castle, looking then much as it did now, ruled the mountain peak, and beside it, a mighty bonfire. As a child, I'd thought it as no more than a representation of *feuernacht*, a sacred fire burned under a full moon into which a hood would plunge to assume her powers and her place in the community. Only when I'd gotten older did I notice that the fire wasn't burning from logs, but from the bones of three figures caught in its grasp, each with a spit through their bodies.

Amy's eyes took in the reds and blues of another of the tapestries, and Chin didn't let the opportunity go to waste.

"Helga the Restorer," the white matron said. "Sister of the Betrayer and avenger of her mother's death."

Amy leaned in "That's supposed to be Gerwalta Faust's sister? Boy, she needed work on her eyebrows."

Chin's own unnurtured eyebrows arched.

Amy drove on, proving that filters and she did not break bread. "How come the sister is the one who gets the credit? I thought it was the Betrayer's mother who sentenced them to die?"

"Because the wolf ate Gerwalta's mother, leaving Helga the honor of executing the sentence and bringing the offenders final justice."

Amy's nose crinkled. "So when the Brothers Grimm wrote about the grandmother being in the wolf's stomach..." Amy's voice tapered off. "Not a story."

The Matron's eyes bulged. "A broken clock is still right twice a day, even those two cuckoos."

"Kinda makes you wonder..." The huey gave the tapestry a second appraisal. "...are there other fairy tales that are true, too?"

Any chance for reflection or refuting was lost when Rebecca Krantz cleared her throat and proceeded to make an official announcement in German.

Amy leaned into me. "What did she say?"

Any need to answer was cut off by the doors to the chamber being thrown open.

My mother's command rattled the rafters. "English!"

My mother's boots quaked the floor, or perhaps it was the beating of my own heart that shook me. She marched into the council chamber, a heavy sack pulled down at her side, her red cape billowing out behind her. Behind her, Yan and Caleb, both of them looking as spent as two supernaturals could be. Caleb's anxiety eased when he caught sight of us, making his way in our direction. Anya went to him, pulling him close. They'd lost one of their own today, and perhaps that death meant more than one less slayer. A little hope must have died with Alex as well.

Yan tracked my mother, taking the sack from her and continuing his way out the other side of the room.

"From this point forward," my mother said, spinning into her chair, "everyone is to speak English! I want this matter addressed posthaste, and some of those involved do not understand German. Chin!"

The disagreeable white hood, heretofore prideful as a peacock, suddenly bowed beneath the weight of my mother's presence. "Yes, Grand Matron?"

"The slayers? Did you bring them into the castle grounds as I ordered?"

"Yes, Grand Matron. Except for this one—" Chin acknowledged Anya. "—they are in the castellan's house. We have activated all security features on your home in town as requested. If anyone further enters, it will be known within moments."

"Excellent." Sweeping her way across the room, Brünhild took the dominant seat at the head of the table.

"Security features?" I asked. "What security features?"

"The place has more bugs than a Sunday school picnic," Markus said. "Sorry, Geri, the information was embargoed."

I turned to my mother. "You were spying on us the whole time we've been there?"

No wonder she'd known to look for us at the Lahr hospital.

Brünhild ignored me, continuing her orders. "Open the council at once."

Chin's olive skin blanched. "But, Matron, it is midday, and everyone is asleep. Certainly, we should wait for..."

"Did I stutter, Mae?" I may have imagined the tiny frown I thought I saw flit across her face. "Now! There is no time to waste."

Without further ado, the White Matron swept from the room.

Brünhild's arm struck out, her finger pointed in Amy's direction. "You!"

Amy held the baby with one arm while the thumb of her left hand buried in her own chest.

"Yes, you, girl. The one with little common sense and even less intelligence."

"Okay, it's going to be like that then." Amy took three

steps forward. "Excuse me, but I don't recall asking your opinion."

"I don't have opinions," my mother said. "I have convictions. This evening, you will be driven to Munich. We will provide you the necessary papers and airfare to anywhere in the world you'd prefer to go, but it will be a one-way ticket. Henceforth, you will remove yourself from the supernatural realm. You will be kept under observation to assure this, and if there's any hint of you attempting to reconnect with anyone present or exposing our secrets, you will be dealt with swiftly. There will be no warnings."

My friend's face could light London. "Who in the hell do you think you are? You don't get to tell me who I will or will not associate with."

Part of me cheered the outburst. And part of me wanted to push Amy to the ground before the metaphorical daggers my mother was shooting became literal.

Caleb cleared his throat and took a knee. "If I may speak, Grand Matron?"

The formality won over my mother just enough to get her to agree.

"Miss Popowitz should not be forced out," the sly slayer continued. "She's a known associate of your daughter's and has already come under vampire attack once. Moreover, she's been of great assistance to my people as they've tried to adjust to the outside world. If you would defer her fate to us, and if she herself would not object, I'd like to ask that she take up residence with us. We need someone with her skills."

Even I had to quirk an eyebrow on that one. *Skills? What skills?* Luckily, I was able to keep the thought to myself.

"Very well." Brünhild's face melted around the edges. "Does the huey agree to consign herself to the community of slayers?"

All eyes fell to Amy, who had commenced flapping her jaw noiselessly and pulling the bundled child a little tighter to her chest. Finally, she managed to squeak out, "What does that mean exactly, 'consign'?"

My mother rolled her eyes. "It means that you will be honor-bound to their service until such time as both parties agree to dissolve the arrangement, if any. In short, you will be their Rebecca Krantz."

The huey followed my mother's gesture in the elderly castellan's direction, took one look at Becky's aged frame and plain clothes, and swung back, panic-stricken.

"I can still wear designer brands, though, right?"

Brünhild hissed through clenched teeth as she uttered a string of German curses.

"Okay, yes!" Amy blurted out. "I agree to consign. Or be consigned, or whatever, to the slayers. Just, please, don't send me away."

My mother raised an eyebrow. "The pact is thus made and recognized. But tell me, huey, why are you so desperate to remain among us? Surely you understand the danger this will put you in."

Amy's backbone grew three sizes. "Because they're my friends. Real friends who don't like me just because of the size of my bank account or my cup size. Well," she jerked her head in Caleb's direction, "except for that one, maybe."

Brünhild fixed Caleb in his gaze. "From what I hear, that one accepts all comers."

Before the slayer could react, Amy pushed him back with her shoulder.

Which gave me an opening to step forward. "Mother, the..."

Her hand flew up. "As has always been, in these walls, I am Matron first. Now more than ever."

I swallowed my anger, promising myself to feed from its reserves later. "Fine, *Matron*. Before the council arrives, I want you to know that this baby is now under my protection." I took Mina back from Amy's hold. "Before you and the council go off making plans for her, just remember that nothing is happening to Mina unless I agree to it."

Bitterness laced into my mother's tone. "Who died and made you its mother?"

"*Her* mother did. Before Mina's birth, before you barged in, silver blazing, and sliced off Inga Rosethorn's head, Alex asked me to be the baby's godmother. I accepted."

"Were there witnesses?"

Anya's voice was tiny. "I did, I witnessed it."

Brünhild was unimpressed. Perhaps she sensed the lie. "Let me rephrase that. Did any of the *righteous* witness this?"

I clutched at my throat. "That's never been a requirement before. A pact was made between two supes grounded in honor and witnessed by a third. Our laws should allow for that claim to stand on its own."

Brünhild's hands became fisted hammers. "When both parties acknowledge such pacts, and are recognized members of their community. This slayer's word may serve on behalf of her fallen kin, but yours must be likewise validated."

I took a step forward, my teeth gnashing. "Then rescue Tobias Somfield from the Ravens, and let him give testimony."

*Check. Mate.*

Brünhild's brow furrowed, her chest heaved as she fumed the anger in her heart. "Why would *he* know anything of this child?"

Cody's voice, evidence of his weakened resolve, cracked. "Geri had a quickening, Ms. Kline. They're bonded now, and anything you do to that baby is only going to hurt your daughter even more."

"Bonded? How would a child of a slayer bond with a werewolf?" My mother's face went ashen as she leapt to her feet. "Are you saying that child is an illustrian?"

"And by legal rights, your granddaughter!" My father, silent until now, used his words with great economy, dropping the mother of bombshells on the bombshell of all mothers.

I, however, was still caught up in what she'd said before. "What's an illustrian?"

"An illustrian is a..." Brünhild fell back into her chair, her eyes glossy. "It's impossible. How would such a thing come to be? The slayers were living in Vlad's harem, and surely this did not come about by accident. A vampire of his age and status would surely know that bringing an illustrian into the confines of his clutch would be like pouring poison into the well."

It took my mother stating what should have been the obvious question for me to see the obvious answer.

"He created it to kill Igor." The words echoed in my ear before I realized I'd been the one to say them. I looked to the others, daring any one of them to correct me.

No one said a word, until my mother spoke, clutching her stomach. "Very well. Until such time as the alpha wolf Tobias Somfield can present testimony, I recognize temporary guardianship of the babe born to Alexandra, a slayer, and an unknown wolf, to Gerwalta Kline. But, daughter," her eyes pleaded as she looked up at me. "I must point out the obvious: The child is a slayer, a race endangered and in desperate need of every one of its members. Are you sure it's in the child's best interest to be raised by a…"

"A hood?" I supplied when Brünhild proved unwilling or unable to give me even that recognition. "Was it in *my* best interest to be raised by one?"

The blow landed right where it was aimed, my mother's pride. Brünhild winced. "Are you of the opinion that I did you some disservice by refusing to let Inga Rosethorn kill you all those years ago?"

"No, of course not." I tried to swallow my fear and almost choked on it. "You did me a disservice by knowing I was different, and refusing to accept me as I was."

"I was protecting you from a knowledge that would make you a target."

"The only thing you protected me from was the lies of our ancestors." I ran a hand over Mina's soft head as the babe lay peacefully in my arms. Her eyes cracked open, searching. "I will never treat my daughter that way. She will know all that she is, because there's no shame in any of it."

"There is no shame, but there is great danger." My mother looked up. "The child could be weaponized."

Instinctively, I moved closer to Anya and held Mina tighter. "I'll kill any who try."

"I have no doubt." As Brünhild rose, circling the table, part of me wondered if this was the moment I'd have to fight my mother. Instead, only her gaze touched the babe I held, examining from a few feet away, before turning on my father. "This child is *not* my grandchild." Then, softening ever so slightly and bringing her eyes to me, she added, "But it is still an innocent. The council will not be made aware of what she is, but they will sense her wolf nature. How will we explain?"

Was she actually asking me for advice? "Tell them she's mine and Tobias's, that the request to have Petunia's help for one of the slayers was just a cover because *I* was the one who was pregnant."

I'd never gotten out of the car the day I tried to convince Chin to let me in, so she wouldn't have known from seeing me that I wasn't pregnant.

My mother fanned her fingers through the air. "Petunia attended Alexandra, though."

"She would say that was a cover, if the Grand Matron ordered her to."

"You are suggesting we lie, the very sin you just laid at my feet not three minutes ago."

My mother never spoke just for the sake of talking, and even though she could be cruel, she was seldom spiteful. I sensed that, perhaps, highlighting the conflict was an effort to ask me not to be so hasty of her judgements.

"I realize that," I admitted. "Maybe if I had more time to think, I'd have a more honorable solution. But as you like to say, honor is a currency bought over years and spent in minutes."

It was as good as I was going to get: owning up my hypocrisy while not absolving hers.

She bowed her head. "I will speak with Petunia once the council adjourns, then."

"Whoa, whoa, whoa!" Cody stepped forward, keeping his arms as still as possible to avoid the silver slipping onto unmarked flesh. "Geri, think about this for a second. The last time I checked, it would still be a capital offense for Tobias to sleep with a hood. You say Mina is the result of him and you getting together, there's no point in rescuing him from the Ravens. As soon as he's free, the council will command his execution."

We all spun as my mother let out a Disney villain-worthy laugh.

Which, for some reason, pissed me off. "Something funny, mother?"

She buried her smile  into her fist. "How could the council convict Tobias of anything? Geri's been relinquished for over a year."

Cody persisted. "Yeah, but she's a still a hood, so—"

"Not in the way that matters to them." My words cut off Cody and everything else I had been thinking. "When Tobias and I finally manage to be together, it won't be a crime." I spun on my mother. "Did you do this on purpose?"

"What? Disown my only daughter and my sole heir just to keep her from harm?" Though she tried to keep her face flat, I saw the miniscule flicker at the corner of her mouth. "That decision was made for many reasons, but none of them was to appease your heart."

"I know it wasn't." I closed the distance between us in three steps. "It was to appease your own."

And for the first time in many years, I threw myself into my mother's arms.

# TWENTY

## AMY

My mother read *Alice in Wonderland* to me when I was nine. She was drunk at the time, probably doesn't remember it, and I'm sure embellished it with her interpretation of what the mouse-in-the-teakettle and falling down the rabbit hole were meant to symbolize, but the metaphors didn't elude me the way sobriety often did Mrs. Popowitz.

Seeing Geri forgive her mother after two-plus years of non-ending under-her-breath instigations about what a sucky mother Brünhild had been ranked up on my "miracles can happen" list with painless dentistry and the legalization of pot. Yeah, none of those things had fully happened either, but they were goals people worked towards that might actually come to be totally true. I just hoped that as Geri fell down the rabbit hole, she didn't forget what had led her there to begin with.

No sooner had Geri and Brünhild had their Hallmark moment (and yes, I did hear Pietro's sniffle) and separated than the worst fashion catwalk featuring the least beguiling hooded-cloak models of all time marched in. As we collectively fell back, I heard Versace turn over in his grave all the way from Triberg. Each matron wore a different color. I'd known from discussions I'd had with Geri that the other bloodlines existed, I guess I just didn't realize how many there were: twelve in all, one of them dressed in red like Geri's mom and another dressed in yellow like her dad would have been if I wasn't using his cloak as a poncho. I tried not to think about how that meant Geri had grown up in a ketchup and mustard house, but once the thought popped into my head, I laughed out loud.

Chin slithered into her chair at the council table. "Silence, huey interloper!"

"Matron Chin!" Brünhild's voice lacked any of the softness it had had just moments before. How could she so easily flip from secretly-protective mother to badass *mutha* in a blink? I wanted to be this woman's acolyte.

The Grand Matron's acidic stare corroded the white hood seated to her right. "Surely you did not mean to insult the slayer's castellan and our guest."

"The slayer's...." Chin's throat bobbed as she swallowed down her shock. "I did not realize the slayers *had* a castellan. My apologies, Miss...?"

"Popowitz," I said. And though I had no freaking clue what a castellan was (seriously, did she tell me off?) or what my role was supposed to be as one, I wasn't about to let a shame door go unused. "Matron Chin, as the *kaz-ellen*, speaking for the slayers, and given what went down yesterday, I wonder if we can review the terms of the contract you have in place with my peeps right now."

Brünhild blinked. "Your *peeps*?"

"Yeah, you know..." I pointed vaguely behind me. "My peeps. My tribe. My *slay-yahs*."

The Grand Matron cleared her throat. "Mr. Helsing, does Miss Popowitz have the permission of the community to speak on its behalf?"

Which, of course, everyone knew was a resounding, 'no the hell I did not.' I'd just been annexed into their community not ten minutes ago – when would they have had time to do a welcome-and-please-take-a-seat-as-our-representive-on-the-student-council mixer?

Even Geri was giving me the wide-eyed treatment, but what were this bunch of silver-sycophants going to do, kill me? Come on, I had an American passport *and* an American Express Black card. Both had been left behind in Istanbul, but still... Since Geri had made me call my parents and tell them where I was at during the long wait at the hospital, I at least had contacts on the outside who knew where I was and how to raise a diplomatic crisis.

I didn't wait for Caleb to answer. "I'm new at supernatural negotiations, so I have to ask what might be obvious to other people. Is it customary to offer refugees aid only on a quid-pro-quo basis in this neck of the woods? Because where I'm from, that's called exploitation."

Chin sneered. "You'll find our customs do not often align with what the huey world..."

But Brünhild put her big ol' bitch shoes down on that squawk. "Matron Chin, is this true?"

The Asian matron guffawed. "Grand Matron, you yourself have discussed with the council many times the danger posed to the wolves by the clutch of vampires that calls itself the Ravens. Is it not our duty, therefore, to seize an opportunity to eliminate them when it presents itself? They are *slayers*, after all. That is their reason for existing, to destroy those vampires who would throw the supernatural world out of balance."

Geri stepped forward at that. "The supernatural world *is* out of balance! And don't try to act like you're suddenly so concerned with the wolves' wellbeing, either. Matron Smyth: I've heard some very *interesting* stories from one of your former lupines about the way the House of Green treats its subjects in England, which makes me think that the biggest threat to them isn't vampires, but hoods."

Chin found Markus and focused on him. "Mr. Kline, did you not report Vlad Tepeş's own claim that his intent was to dismantle the foundation of lupine society by undermining their ability to bond? How is that not a threat, then? One we must bar against by any means possible. The slayers came to us looking for help, and we've offered it, though it is not our place to do so. Did they not receive food? Shelter? Weapons? Even a physician for the delivery of that…" Chin motioned at Mina "…thing."

When Brünhild got herself a fist full of white cloak and pulled Chin's face to her own, even I could tell the shit was about the hit the fan.

"It is a *baby*, not a *thing*," she hissed. "A very special baby, as the case may be. Do you even know who the mother of this child is, Matron Chin?"

Obvs quaking in her leather boots, Chin shook her head. "No, Grand Matron."

Brünhild's eyes dashed to Geri. "My own daughter."

"Impossible." The Green Matron clicked her tongue. "The child is wolf. We all can sense it. Unless… Unless your daughter has lived up to the name." With that, Matron Smyth rose to her feet. "I call for a vote of confidence in the leadership of Grand Matron Brünhild Kline. How can she lead us with such obvious conflicts of interest?"

Geri's mom… was *piiissseed*. But, like, in a quiet way that made her more terrifying than before. It was like Hannibal Lecter had become a fairy tale character. *I'll eat your liver with some magic beans and a nice chianti.*

Yan coughed a laugh. "What conflict? Their interest is highly compatible. It is merely your ingrained biases and animal natures which sets you at such odds. Your common humanity should bring you together, not enable you to destroy each other."

Meanwhile, a woman with drop dead brown eyes and sandalwood skin, wearing a black cloak, spoke up. "*We* are not the animals, Mr. Sousa, they are. Quite literally."

"Are you not?" The vampire motioned to Cody. "Look how the blood weeps from his wrists where the silver burns. And for what? Has he committed some crime? Demonstrated some behavior which marks him as dangerous in your eyes? No, you bind him in poison merely because he dares to be in your presence."

A guttural sound ripped from Chin's throat. "It is not your place to speak on hood-wolf relations. Hold your tongue, leech."

"Leech?" The normally sedate vampire who'd even managed to make me think he was a pushover spoke in a hissy voice. Oh, fur was about to fly. Or fang. Or… whatever. Metaphors are too cerebrally challenging around supes.

"You spiteful, power-hungry wench. I am four hundred and fifty years your senior. How dare you address *me* that way?"

Brünhild drew to her feet, pulling silver out of her ass for all I could tell. All I knew was that her hand went up empty, and by the time she slammed it down on the table, she had a freaking mallet formed on the end of her fist. The ricochet of its ramming brought all tongues to a sudden standstill.

Except for Mina, who chose this moment to work a gentle whimper into a full-blown howl.

"Enough!" the Grand Matron bellowed. "This bickering achieves nothing. Let me confirm that any contract made with the slayers was done without my knowledge or consent. Miss Popowitz, tell your people that I absolve them of any expectations and that our assistance comes without strings."

I felt everyone's eyes on me. And, honestly, if I could turn my eyes clear around in my head, I'd be looking at me, too. "Um, will do?"

Brünhild bobbed her head. "Now, Matron Chin, a motion has been made for a vote of confidence. As the vice-matron, it is up to you to recognize the motion or not. What say you?"

Chin made an attempt at a backbone, straightening in her chair and turning hungry eyes on the gaggle of matrons. One by one, they turned their eyes. With each tick of her head, the ego so big she must have built up some hefty calves touting it around deflated a bit. I saw the moment she realized it was a no-go; all the features in her face melted like that horrific scene from *Raiders of the Lost Ark,* only less *liquid-y.* "I do not recognize the motion."

"Good, now that that is out of the way…" Brünhild resumed her seat. "Inga Rosethorn is dead."

Exclamations went up around the table, before a hood wearing a brown robe asked, "How?"

The Grand Matron exchanged one look with us watching in the peanut gallery and said, "Beheading."

"Good," Smyth said. "The slayers have only been back a month now, and they are already bringing balance."

"No, I am the one who killed her," Brünhild corrected.

Even the easy-going Black Matron recoiled at that. "But she has been our ally for decades!"

"No more," Brünhild said. "I have spent the last few weeks ferreting out her activities. I believe she was attempting to find a way to reconcile herself to her brothers, and rejoin their cause. She would have betrayed the slayers under our protection given the slightest chance, as she was attempting to steal the baby when I killed her."

I was so not up on the Dracule family drama, but even I knew that was bad. Looking to Geri and Caleb, I found two people who defined the expression "shell-shocked."

A matron wrapped in pink, but dressed in something

that looked more like a floor-length head dress then the other's riding cloaks, leaned forward. "Markus has briefed us on his findings in Istanbul, that the Ravens seek to undo lupine social structures in some sort of ill-conceived form of revenge," she said, sounding like that Bollywood movie that one boyfriend made me watch. "But I am confused. How is it that this involves us? Other than our protection of the slayers, and that conflict could be remedied by negotiation, why are they our concern?"

"Why are they our concern?" Geri stepped out of the shadows, her jaw hanging. "You just said it, Matron Ramathan: because they're threatening to undo lupine social structure."

The Pink Matron blinked away her surprise. "Our purpose does not include assuring that werewolves remain bonded couples and happy families. Our role is to serve as a barrier between them and humanity, and to destroy any who threaten life."

Geri threw her head to the side. "Oh, please. I am so sick of hearing that hoods are some golden, virtuous race that protects hueys from animalistic heathens. Wolves *are* human, and our oldest stories say our *purpose* was to protect *them* from humanity, not the other way around. If anything, *we're* the subhuman creatures, not them."

A hush descended over the matrons as they took the brunt of Geri's vocal bitch slap. Finally, Chin, so flustered she could barely speak, leapt to her feet, turning on Brünhild.

"Will you not punish such insolence, Grand Matron? How do you stand by and allow your own flesh and blood to desecrate our sacred calling that way?"

"By remembering that we do not have a *sacred* calling," Brünhild said, as cool as spring rain. "Nor is our history without fault. We have committed great atrocities, some even in this very building. I will not fault Gerwalta for speaking truth, no matter how bluntly."

"Atrocities?" Chin fell back in her chair. "What atrocities?"

Brünhild crossed her arms over her chest. "As if I need mention the obvious."

"You *cannot* mean the affair of Gerwalta Faust."

"But I do, Chin. I mean that very thing. It is a blemish on our race, more because of our celebration of it than the deed itself. But at least, there is a path for us to remedy some of those injustices." Brünhild paused, catching her daughter's eye. "After all, as Gerwalta so appropriately stated, our true calling is to protect lupines. We can do that by protecting those most at risk: the asenaics, the descendants of Gerwalta Faust."

That knocked them righteous bitches off their rockers. Some gasped, some gawked, and at least one of them looked like she was going to town on someone. It wasn't sexy.

Pinkie was the first to recover. "Are you saying that the offspring of the Betrayer survived?"

"Survived, thrived, and multiplied," Brünhild confirmed. "Though for numerous reasons few of that limb of the family tree endure. In truth, there are only five. And as the Grand Matron, I tell you this now: our current priority is protecting them *and ourselves* by destroying the Ravens. There is to be no confusion on this. Once this mission has been completed, then I will pass word to those five that if they wish to disclose their identities, my office will accept them openly. I am currently determining their location. I will consider who should be included on the team and notify those called for duty as soon as I reach my decision."

I wanted to look at Pietro and Geri to see what their reaction was to that, but at the same time feared doing that would be like flashing a big, huge neon sign in their direction.

Jolly Green lifted a hand. What did she think this was,

elementary school?

"Yes, Matron Smyth?"

Smyth cleared her throat. "I took a vow to serve this council and execute its agendas, and I won't pull back from that. However, the question remains unanswered. Why are Ravens so intent on finding these asenaics? Is it part of their scheme against the wolves?"

"In a way, yes, and for the moment, you need know no more."

Apparently, that statement brought the gavel down on the meeting, because when Geri's mom stood up, everyone else did too, and began filing out of the room.

"Rebecca!" Brünhild called. "Please show everyone to your cottage. I know it will be crowded, but better uncomfortable with us than at risk in the valley below."

Rebecca raised an eyebrow. "Everyone, sir?"

"Yes, everyone." Then, Brünhild paused, raising a finger. "Except for Pietro. He and I have business to discuss. Show him to my quarters. I will be there shortly."

Pietro grinned, as did his wife in return. Wow, great to see even Geri's dysfunctional parents still got their groove thing on. Maybe my parents would find a way to pull it together eventually.

Hey, vampires were real and slayers were a thing, so the totally absurd could happen, right?

"Matron?" Cody said, holding up his oozing wrists.

But it was Geri who stepped in. "Oh, my god, I'm sorry, Cody. In the heat of the moment I forgot all about that. Here, let me."

And zip-a-dee-doo-dah, she magicked his restraints right off.

Before I could look back from the scene, the Grand Matron was gone.

# TWENTY-ONE

## BRÜNHILD

I wound my way up the tower, each step a measure of my increasing anxiety as I wondered who I would find waiting above.

As an asenaic, it was not surprising that Pietro often had dueling instincts, the hood and the wolf in him in constant struggle. His ability to balance and reconcile what would drive other men insane had drawn me to him from the first time I'd met him. That did not mean, however, that he could always maintain stability. There were times, fleeting but frequent, when his lupine half placed us at odds. Luckily, that nature had also claimed me as mate, and no matter how I wronged him – and how much I may deserve his disdain – the fury that would flare up refused to endure.

I didn't deserve him.

He deserved so much more than me.

He stood by the fireplace when I entered the study, his eyes fixed on the sack Yan had left on my desk on my orders.

"Is that what I think it is?"

"Yes."

"So it is true. She is dead." His throat bobbed. "At last."

My inner grand matron pushed me to make some grandiose statement, something along the lines of *"Yes, at last the vampire who killed both your grandfather and my father, and threatened to kill our daughter, is dead. May she forever more burn in the hottest fires in hell."* But though I felt a burden ease in knowing Inga Rosethorn could no longer threaten my family, I couldn't be the grand matron right now. Not when my heart-made-flesh looked back at me with his soft, loving gaze, resolve and relief shining through. All I wanted at this moment was to be Pietro's mate, to fall into his arms and tell him that justice had finally been done. The world knew my strength, the hoods obeyed my commands. But only my husband saw my cracks, gathered together my broken pieces, and held me together.

We met half way between the door and the fireplace, my head pressing into his shoulder as his arms locked around me.

Pietro kissed my forehead. "When Markus told me you were tracking her, I was so afraid. If she had discovered you…"

"She couldn't."

"If I lost you, Brünhild…"

"You never will." I pressed my lips to his. "Like you said our first night together, we stepped off the cliff together. I'm in for the fall, no matter how far. *Siempre.*"

"*Siempre.*" My mate's hand stroked my cheek. "*Mi familia es mi plata.* My family is my silver."

As his hold loosened, I felt the air shift around us.

"*Mi Corazon,* Gerwalta is…" His words tapered away.

"Coming into her own," I said, completing his sentiment. "She has learned to harness both her lupine and hood strengths. I worried the day may never come, and now, her power is even more than I could have imagined."

A line formed between Pietro's eyes as he crossed his arms over his chest. "How, though? You stopped her from being claimed by the Casa de Amarillo. How is she able to wield her silver, having never taken her fire?"

My eyes went to the floor. "Markus says when they were in Istanbul, there was an... incident. Caleb Helsing hit her with his solarium. *Accidentally,"* I quickly amended as my husband's wolf threatened violence. "He was trying to defend her, but she was caught in the crosshairs. I don't know what to think, Pietro. Perhaps it was providence. It managed to wake up every part of her, give her the defenses she needed just in the nick of time."

Pride beamed from his eyes. "Alexandra's death was a tragedy, but it is a blessing that the illustrian baby has come here; who better to mother such a child than one whose own nature is likewise drawn from so many roots?"

There was truth in what he said, but I also knew that until we defeated the Ravens, young Mina's existence was under the very same threat Gerwalta had been for years. Vlad Tepeş saw the enhancements crossing supernatural species gave the blood of those born to multiple natures as no more than a weapon he could wield.

"She needs every ally, every strength we can give her." I paused, knowing my husband would be reluctant to believe what I was about to say. "Including having her mate at her side."

Pietro's eyebrows arched. "So you've finally accepted that Markus and Gerwalta will never wed?"

"Each other?" I asked, my voice flat. "When wolves fly."

My soul renewed with his laugh. Soon, however, Pietro continued in earnest. "We will rescue him then. Perhaps

Vlad's *serum* is a blessing in disguise. It will allow this wolf to love our daughter."

My insides curdled. "It seems at first blush, but I was able to finally track down the one who developed it, a Dracule by the name of Xin. I forced the truth from her before she died."

My husband's face screwed up, but he didn't ask. He knew my methods to procure information, even if he didn't agree with them. "And?"

"And, the results are valid. A therapy of the serum, administered regularly, will weaken the lupine bond. It does not destroy it, however, it only masks it. After the therapy is discontinued, its effects dissipate. Within a few weeks, the bonding rebounds. From Vlad's perspective, it wouldn't matter. A few weeks of unmade bonds is long enough to corrupt the foundation of lupine society."

"So even if we rescue Tobias Somfield—"

I shrugged. "He is also an asenaic, though his only hood ancestor appears to have been the Betrayer. Like the Muñezes, the residual enhancements are very weak. Still, we do not know. Perhaps having a genetic baseline, the serum's ability to hold in his system will prove stronger than with the other subject the Dracule tested."

Pietro mused a space before his head dipped in a single nod. "There is a chance then, and if a chance is all we can give to our daughter for happiness, then it shall be done. But for me, *mi Corazon*..."

He crossed back to the table, his hand disappearing inside the bag. Little blood remained in Inga Rosethorn's severed head; she must not have fed for several days before cornering my daughter in the hospital. Pietro's hands threaded her hair, pulling it high into the air. He locked me in his sight.

*"Por mi padre, por favor."*

Silver flame, fed by a bit of the metal I kept always wound around my arm, lit the air, licking across the space, and found its target with a preternatural instinct.

As the vampire's head turned to dust, a smile spread across my mate's face.

I hoped somewhere in the afterlife, his lupine grandfather found peace as well.

# TWENTY-TWO

## GERI

You'd think it was the first baby they'd ever seen. Maybe it was. Alex had mentioned there hadn't been any pregnancies for some time. Which... made me begin to wonder how I was supposed to just randomly bring up the topic that that should probably change soon.

*Hey, since you guys might be the last of your kind and you're not getting any younger, perhaps consider having sex like crazy so you don't actually die out, okay? Start now if you like, I can go in the other room.*

I mean, unless they wanted to actually cease to be a species, they'd better get to the baby making. At least they had Caleb with them. As soon as the sole surviving Helsing was able to get over our break-up, I had great faith in his ability to... well, hold the opening ceremonies.

"Isn't she the sweetest thing ever?"

Teiko was the only female slayer of Asian heritage, but like all the women, she'd been raised in the harem speaking English, Turkish, and Vlad's own dialect of Romanian. She was also one of the most beautiful women I'd ever met. Petite, but with ebony locks that would have fallen past her waist if she didn't twist the mass of it around her head like a crown. Her amber eyes twinkled, reflecting the fire burning in the hearth.

Teiko finished wrapping up Mina's diaper the way

Petunia had demonstrated when she'd stopped by earlier in the evening to also inform me she was *good with the plan*. "I can't believe Alex named her Mina. It's so cliché."

I tapped on the tablet sitting in my lap to close the map of Spain it displayed. "What's cliché about it?"

Amy sauntered in from the kitchen, handing Sergei, a ruddy-faced blond stick of a man, a cup of juice. "Come on, Geri. Even I know that one. Mina, you know? From *Dracula*?"

I shook my head. "I'm sorry, still not getting it."

The blond huey rolled her eyes. "Didn't you have to take that lit class your freshmen year? Oh, I forgot, you were a transfer. Mina is the name of the English prude old Drac tries to bone in that book by Bram Stoker."

I let out a scoffing laugh. "Everyone in the supe world knows those huey knockoffs are hogwash."

Amy fixed me with her best 'oh-really' stare as she settled on the floor at Teiko's feet. "Just like the Grimm Brothers?"

"Yes, just like the Grimm Brothers," I said without thinking. "Like the hoggiest of washes."

"I don't know about that." Amy began counting out a point on each finger. "They did sort of nail that it was a *red* riding hood, when it could have come from any of the clans. And Grandmother's house?" She motioned vaguely in the direction of the castle. "Matron's house. Eating the grandmother, the huntsman coming after the wolf and killing him? Hunts *woman* maybe, but that even sticks."

"Not to mention," Teiko added, "Bram Stoker had an affair with a slayer."

Amy's eyes went wide. "No way!"

"Totally." Teiko grinned, pleased at having an audience. I foresaw the beginning of a beautiful friendship between these two. "You mean Caleb didn't tell you?"

Amy and I exchanged a look.

Just at that moment, the indicted himself came into the room, carrying an armload of baby supplies some of the hoods residing in the castle had gathered. "Tell them what?"

Teiko rose, taking Mina along with her. "That you got an Irish writer in your family tree."

Caleb blushed. "He wasn't part of my family tree."

Even I found my curiosity piqued. "It's true, then?"

The slayer collapsed into a chair at the table next to me. "Kinda? Albert Helsing and Bram Stoker had a passionate, lustful, and *brief* relationship. They still managed to be on good terms long enough for Albert to give Bram the four-one-one on Vlad. Stoker, of course, changed the details and added a "van" to our family name, but he got lots of things right, too."

Amy's mouth dropped open. "How is that not the first thing you tell people when you meet them?"

Caleb smirked. "Tell me, Barbie, did Geri lead with 'I'm named after the famous Little Red Riding Hood and FYI she actually is considered a traitor by my people' the first time you met her?"

"No, I think she told me she'd just moved away from a place called Paradise, and I made some smart-ass comment about why would you leave Paradise for Chicago."

But the wheels in my mind were spinning. Grimm Brothers, fairy tales, the truth in our world...

"My mother in her study with the leather book..."

Everyone turned on me, Caleb saying, "Pretty sure it was Mrs. Peacock in the foyer with the pipe wrench."

I stood, putting a hand on Caleb's shoulder. "I was too young to read back then. Markus and I snuck into my mother's private office and there was an old copy of *Little Red Riding Hood*. No, that doesn't sound right. Why would *we* have a copy of a Grimm fairy tale? But it was? I think it was. I... I can't remember." I stood and started for the door. "Teiko, can you watch Mina for a while?"

"Geri?" Caleb was just a step behind me. "Where are you going? We all agreed we needed to just lay low and rest for a day or two."

"I'm not leaving the compound. I just have to go see something in my mother's study."

"Right, and where is that?"

I pointed up. "Top of the tower."

He looked incredulous. "They wouldn't even let you beyond the council chambers yesterday. You and mommy might have bridged a gap a bit, but you're still relinquished."

"I am so not relinquished, and I'll slice anyone who insists I am."

My body ricocheted off his arm as he strapped it across the door. "Exactly, you have enemies there. You can't just go gallivanting about."

I gently moved his arm to the side. "Relax, Helsing. I know how to stay hidden. I was walking these hallways before I could even crawl."

His face screwed up. "How did that work exactly?"

"Don't mark up my metaphors to full price. What I mean is, I know this castle, inside and out. I can get in from the cliffs."

Caleb blinked his surprise. "That doesn't sound very secure."

"It is, though," I insisted, even as I summoned my red cloak into being, its gentle weight falling like a hug upon my shoulders. I could get up to the tower covertly, but I still had to get across a courtyard full of young hoods in the midst of training. Looking like one of them, conveniently with my face hidden, was a golden ticket. "No one else but the Grand Matron knows about it."

"And everyone in this room who heard you say it exists."

I stifled a laugh and pulled silver I'd left in a ball on a side table over my skin, hiding it from view. "You can't open it. It requires a special key that only hoods can use."

"Hello!" Caleb clapped. "This isn't medieval times anymore. Those kind of things can be made with 3D printers. I know your kind sticks to the sticks, but you got to keep up to date with modernity."

At the door that led into the courtyard, I paused. "Excuse me? Which one of us just earned a BS in Biochemistry and which one of us thinks Penthouse Forum is high literature?"

"It was just one copy, Geri. I told you, I don't normally read those things."

But I was done arguing.

# TWENTY-THREE

A carpet of homes, shops, streets, and just... brown... spooled across the valley. The irony of Schloss Wolfsretter's secret entrance was that it was in open view. At least from the village below. Probably not so much a consideration at the time it was built, given the lack of telescopes, binoculars and zoomable cameras held by medieval laity. Night cloaked my presence, however, the maturing moon masked in clouds. The stairway that led to the true base of the tower was nothing more than a series of stones that extended out about the width of two hands from where the earth dropped away. A thin margin for error, but the twenty steps I'd need to take with nothing below me but a fall didn't concern me. That fact that the gathering storm parading across the valley sparked lightning in the distance, did.

Basic rule of metallurgy: silver is the best electrical conductor.

Hoods were mortal. We were born, we aged, if somewhat more gracefully than hueys, and we died. We were amazingly resistant to disease, counted superhuman senses and strengths as assets, and could make silver our bitch, as Amy might say. It was in that last gift, however, that we also found our greatest weakness. I'd never had to fear it before; as a nascent, the lightning would not seek me. Now, having claimed my fire, that would no longer be the case. Wolves had always known the best way to outmaneuver a hood was in a storm. We didn't dare expose ourselves to them, because when lightning struck near enough, it would reach out a finger to us and strike us dead.

Even though the storm was far away, if I took too long at my task, it would be too late to escape the same way. I'd either need to find another way out, or a place to hide inside until the danger had passed.

The silver wrapped around my arm obeyed my command, pooling into a thin stream that siphoned into a crevice beneath a stone bearing the crest of the House of Red. Liquid metal snaked its way deep into the structure, finding the lever at last when it had gone so far as to be nearly out of my command. With a shift in my mind's eye, the silver solidified, forming a chain. With a hearty tug, the lock released, and the faux brickwork concealing the chamber tilted in.

Into a tunnel of darkness even my sensitive eyes could barely distinguish. *Great*. I'd been so quick to leap at the chance, I'd forgotten basics like the need for freaking lights when ascending a foot-wide staircase entombed between two massive stone walls.

"Here, let me help."

"Holy shit!"

The brilliant light struck my eyes and nearly made me lose my footing. Caleb grabbed me just in time with his solarium-free hand and threw me into the tunnel.

"Sorry, Geri, didn't mean to scare you. Just thought you could use some help."

"Some help?" He winced as I pelted his chest, ignoring the fact that he'd plunge to his death if I did so too hard. "What in the hell are you doing here? I'm trying to be all covert and stuff. Did anyone see you? Did anyone *follow* you?"

"All the nascents were heading indoors when I passed through. I guess even if they aren't allergic to lightning, still sucks to be in the rain. I ran through fast; they probably didn't see me."

I'd forgotten that a slayer could run almost as quickly as a vamp. "Good, but you shouldn't have come. If I get caught inside, it's bad enough. Bringing an outsider into the Grand Matron's private study? It looks like my mother's matronship isn't as secure as it used to be, and that will be major capital for her enemies."

"Relax, Geri. You forget, I'm the master of sly. Besides…" He took a few steps up, calling up a solarium as he did. "…you forgot a flashlight. Pretty cool hidden door trick there, too. How did you open that before you could wield silver?"

"I didn't." The way illuminated as we began the four hundred and eight spiral steps it would take to reach the top. "Not from the outside, anyway. I've only been down here once, about a decade ago. My mother showed it to me in case I ever needed to make a quick escape."

"Does that happen a lot here? Emergency escapes?"

I shrugged, despite the fact that being in front of me, Caleb couldn't see. "I don't think so. I think she just thought that I was finally old enough that I'd keep it secret. Guess she was wrong."

"If it helps, I promise I won't tell anyone."

"Especially not Amy."

He paused, looking at me back over his shoulder. "Why would I tell Amy of all people?"

"I don't know, you two seem to have a way of getting in to one-uppings." I gave him a little push, urging him on. "Why did you do it, by the way? Offer to make her castellan of the slayers? You guys don't even have a castle."

"Maybe not, but I have a corporation. Or at least, a big part of it."

"What are you talking about?"

"You don't think I was giving Inga my blood out of the

kindness of my heart, do you?" He laughed as he turned forward. "Everything was very quid pro quo. Inga got biweekly feedings. I got a big slice of WWL ownership."

"Wait, so basically you're…"

"God-maddening rich, yes." Caleb shrugged. "Amy will be well-compensated, don't worry about that. Should finally get her away from those self-involved parents of hers, too."

"Why do you care about that? I thought you hated her."

"I don't hate Amy. I just hate being around her. And you didn't hear her side of the conversation when she called home. After the 'thank god you're alive' part, I kinda questioned if they really were. Thankful, I mean. I don't know exactly what they said, but after a few minutes, she just went all quietlike, letting them get their licks in. Can you imagine what you have to say to Amy Popowitz to make her mopey? Oh my god, how long is this staircase?"

"Just keep going. You do realize you just guaranteed being around Amy for, like, well, until you figure out how to get rid of her, right?"

"She'll be free to leave at any point. Tell you the truth, though? I don't think she's going to. Amy's a drama junkie, and being in our world has given her a steady supply. Notice she hasn't man-shopped once since we left Chicago?"

"During which time we've been hunting vampires or running from them."

"Exactly," Caleb said. "No guys. Girl just needs a new thrill every couple of weeks."

Finally, the stairs ended. The Grand Matron's study wasn't as private as the official residence on the several floors above the tower were. It wasn't uncommon for her to host meetings with other matrons or even passing hoods here, though only by invitation. While on my side of the entry, the door looked like something taken from a barn, from inside my mother's study, it was hidden behind a very large painting of the Schloss made in the eighteenth century. I pushed it gently, checking that the coast was clear.

And came face to face with my mother.

Reclining against her desk, her arms folded over her chest and wearing street clothes, I had to wonder just how long she'd lain in wait.

"Well?" she asked, a slow, impatient draw in her voice. "Coming in or not?"

Not knowing what else to do, I pulled myself erect and crawled in. "Caleb is with me, too."

"I assumed it'd be him, since I sensed no wolf. Well, hurry along, then. I do have other matters to attend."

I looked back in the portal at Caleb, jerking my head. Hesitation lingered until I gave him a death glare. "I didn't ask you to come along. Now suffer the consequences."

"You know, Geri, if you wanted to come off as the nagging wife, you really should have said yes when I proposed." The slayer stepped in, and as soon as we were in the room proper, proceeded to act like we'd just arrived for a scheduled appointment. Extinguishing his solarium, he offered his hand. "Mrs. Kline, Grand Matron, you're looking lovely this evening."

Brünhild rolled her eyes. Then, pushing herself off her desk, leaving Caleb's hand hanging, she circled toward the fireplace. "You're still officially relinquished. If my adversaries find out I've let you into the tower, they'd have my head and yours."

"I know. And I'm sorry. I know it's exceptional that I'm even being allowed to stay in the compound. But..." Why was I twisting my hands? "I think Vlad is heading to Spain, and I think he'll have Tobias with him."

"Interesting, but it doesn't explain to me why you're in my study. So, tell me, why exactly did you break in here?" She folded her arms over her chest and stared into the fire.

Caleb launched into in a seeming non-sequitur before I had a chance to come up with a convincing lie. "Grand Matron, let me explain. To start with, vampires are not, in fact, immortal. They get about five hundred years after they're reborn in the creche before becoming ash. But they can extend their lives by drinking supernatural blood. I mean, wolf doesn't do anything special for them, but a meal of slayer or hood blood every couple of weeks keeps them going."

"Which was why Vlad kept his harem," I jumped in. "They hunted down most of the race but kept a select few to breed and live off of."

"And asenaic blood not only keeps them alive, it makes them even more powerful." My mother's eyes met mine. "I know all this."

Of course, she did. She probably knew a lot more than I did about tons of supernatural lore. If only she'd ever shared with me the stuff that truly mattered.

"Papa told me he was meant to be the last of his line in the Americas. He said those words very exactly, which tells me there may be others of our kind in Spain, where Papa's family immigrated from. I know Igor was visiting them, drinking from them. I need to find out who those people are and warn them about Vlad, and I need to be there if the Ravens show up. *When* they show up, because they're already on their way."

"Really?" She arched an eyebrow. "And what makes you so sure?"

I gulped down my nerves. "Because during the quickening, I heard Vlad say as much. That was a few days ago now. They're either already there, or about to be."

If this surprised my mother, she showed no signs of it. Instead, she looked bored. "You still have not answered my question. Why are you *here*?"

I sucked in a breath and all the courage I could summon. "Because I think there's a book here that lists the history of the asenaics. I'm pretty sure it's the one I was looking at once when you caught Markus and me snooping around. I need to see it, so I know where to go."

Brünhild walked forward, bracing her hands on the back of a guest chair on the opposite side of her desk. "Last chance, Gerwalta. Why. Are. You. Here."

Confusion drew my eyebrows down as I tried to figure out what I was missing. Then, suddenly it dawned on me. She didn't mean just in this office. No, her question was so much broader than that.

"Because I love Tobias," I said. "Because I want him as my husband, and I want to be his mate."

"He already had a mate," my mother said. "Her name was Kara."

I nodded. "But Vlad's got some kind of gene therapy that's unraveling the wolf instincts. Undoing bonds. Tobias had already been exposed to it in Istanbul. I know because he... He kissed me."

Though that didn't explain it all. He'd told me he loved me before the Ravens had taken him, kissed me before he'd been lost to me, but I didn't want my mother aware of his idiosyncrasies any more than was necessary. It might give her fodder later to condemn the man I loved.

To my surprise, my mother smiled. "Finally. And if you don't remember that from here on out, you're not going to succeed at anything."

Expecting fire and getting only kindness, I found myself aghast. "You're … not … mad? All my life, you've drilled into me that hood begets hood. You even tried to convince me to marry Markus, for Christ's sake."

Caleb blew a raspberry. "As in your cousin?" he asked. "Ew."

"Such pairings are not uncommon in our society, Mr. Helsing. And given the extraordinarily small gene pool your kind will be swimming in for the immediate future, I think you'll find they'll be somewhat common in yours." Then, focusing back on me, she added. "I was trying to find you a protector, because I've always known this day was coming. Markus loves you, though sadly, not in the way I would have liked. I appreciate Cody Ryland, but I never thought of him as the kind who could be a leader. Happily, he's proven me wrong on that account. Now, Tobias Somfield… He's good for you."

I swallowed my disbelief. "What?"

"Do you not think I above all people could be sympathetic? I love your father, even knowing that I'm supposed to hate him, even want to destroy him. You need to be sure you feel that for your wolf, because even if I, the Grand Matron, accept you, that does not mean everyone will."

I was dead. Or in a coma. Whatever was happening, it couldn't be real. "Accept me?"

But in my mother's characteristic fashion, she considered the matter closed as soon as the words were out of her mouth. Pushing herself off the desk, she spun in the direction of her bookshelves. "I destroyed the book you're talking about. I cannot show it to you."

And… there was reality, crashing back down around me. All the hope I'd felt? Like pure oxygen, it caught a spark and leapt into flame. "What? Why? You… *Son of a bitch,* how dare you destroy something that—"

Caleb pulled me back, putting a hand over my mouth. "You really need to work on your communication skills. Don't you get it? She didn't destroy it to piss you off. She did it to protect you and your dad. Which, based on my limited knowledge, sounds like what she's been doing all her life."

My mother softened. "Perhaps this one is more than a shameless flirt and pretty face. Here I thought his only abilities were flattery and insolence."

"No, Matron, I can be as insolent as fuck. You could have asked Inga herself, if you hadn't killed her. Forget about the book, Geri. Remember in the council meeting when your mother said she was closing in on the Ravens' location? Your mother knows what you're after."

I turned on her, tapping a foot. "Well, do you?"

Emotions cycled across Brünhild's face. Annoyance, disappointment, finally… acceptance. "At the council, I mentioned there are five. Two, of course, you know: you and your father. Three more survive in Navarre, on the edge of the Pyrenes. Pedro, Elenara, and Indigo Muñez."

"Indigo?" Caleb's voice filled with glee. "'Ello, my name is Indigo Mon…"

His words turned into groans as I elbowed his stomach. "Not the time, Helsing."

"What is he…?" My mother looked at my ex like he was a mental patient.

"Something about vampires and slayers," I said. "They have a thing for *The Princess Bride*. Pedro, Elenara, and Indigo Muñez in Navarre. Got it. I'll leave just as soon as I have my supplies gathered."

"Just like that, you're going to flee?"

Was she kidding? "What would keep me here, our warm and sentimental relationship? You think one hug in a moment of weakness overwrites the years of disdain and cruelty? Look, I *am* thankful that you've given the slayers refuge, that you recognized my claim on Mina, for saving us from Inga. But you lost me the moment you kept me from *my* birthright. You attacked me with silver flame, mother. *Me,* your own flesh and blood. How did you know it wouldn't kill me?"

The barely visible lines on her face grew taut. "It was never my intention to hurt you. I had hoped it would… It doesn't matter anymore."

Struggling to keep my voice even, the heels of my hands bore the grunt of my frustration. "Thank you for telling me the names of the other asenaics. I'll do what I can to let them know the danger they're in."

Just as I turned, she said perhaps the only thing that could get me to stay. "There's a reason, you know, why Tobias Somfield can love you."

I tried to burn her with my glare. "Because it can't be my charming personality?"

Her jaw worked. "The book you saw? It contained more than just the details of the yellow bloodline from which your father descended. Stuck in the pages was a letter written to my grandmother in 1944 by Igor Kharmarov."

I tried to downplay that fact. "What does that have to do with Tobias?"

"Gerwalta Faust gave birth to a healthy asenaic baby. And *that* child, when she matured, had twins. The father, by the way, was also lupine."

I didn't know why that knowledge caused a pang in the pit of my stomach. I had *two* wolf ancestors erased by time? How many more secrets were hidden in my blood? "How would Igor know that?"

"Because he's the one who raised Bianca Baron."

"Gerwalta's daughter?" I scoffed. "Are you serious? Igor would have told me."

"Besides," Caleb chimed in, "a vampire would never raise another supe's baby. Especially not a Dracule. It's just not in their nature."

"I suspect he would not have done it, if he had not felt some guilt. You see, Gerwalta Faust was not, in fact, called the betrayer because of her affair with Andreas Baron. It was because she learned of a plot by the Ravens to destroy werewolves; likely the same plot they're playing out now, only enhanced by modern science and technology. She was ordered to stay out of it, but she refused to not fight for the wolves. It is Gerwalta who entombed the Ravens in jars of silver."

Someone had just shot my brain with a confusion cannon. "Wait a minute, you're saying Igor... The sweet little professor with a pet cat, raised the Betrayer's kid?"

"And her twins, until he became aware of the hyper-restorative power of their blood. He knew then that this new asaenic bloodline could restore the Ravens to power if ever they escaped. He even separated the twins, untwisting their fate. One whose nature proved more hood than wolf was adopted into the Casa de Amarillo in Navarre. The other, whose nature tended towards lupine, was sent faraway to England, where he was raised wolf."

"Wait a FREAKING minute!" I fell back into the chair behind me. "Are you telling me that Tobias and I are... That we're... I'm in love with my cousin?"

"A very distant cousin, yes," my mother said flatly, like she was only confirming it had rained that morning.

Caleb coughed a laugh. "Five minutes ago, you didn't raise a huff at the idea of marrying Markus, but someone you shared a grandma with three hundred years ago? Oh, be still my scandalized heart."

My head whipped back and forth so hard, my brain pingponged. "You're saying Tobias is also…"

But when I took two seconds to think on it, it fit. Tobias had been attracted to me even before Kara died, something that should have been impossible. He'd been able to sense me from almost as far away as I could him, more so than any other wolf I'd ever met. Most convincingly, he'd fallen in love with me before Vlad had ever done anything to him.

"An asenaic, yes." My mother put into words what I couldn't find the strength to do. "As is my husband and my daughter. You seem convinced that I am against you, Gerwalta. Maybe that's part of your wolf nature, too, or maybe we're just a typical clashing mother and daughter. But I assure you, everything I have done, every secret I have kept, has been to protect my family."

"If that's true, help me now."

For the first time since Caleb and I had emerged, Brünhild wore surprise. "To do what?"

"Include me on the team going into Spain."

"Geri, you are my daughter, and I love you. But I am also the Grand Matron, and you are not recognized as a member of this community. I couldn't possibly include you on the team. Besides, Vlad will want you above all others. I'd be handing him a gift-wrapped package by sending you."

"I know. And I know that's against our… *your* traditions. I'm asking you to do this not for my sake, but for the sake of those asenaics. I am one of them, they're more likely to trust me than the leader of the community who has shunned and ignored them for three centuries. Then I can also be there to save Tobias. Besides, no one you have here is a better fighter than me. You know that."

Her eyes went to the fireplace. "I'd need to get the council's blessing before agreeing to that."

"But I thought you were the Grand Poohbah," Caleb said.

My mother swung an acidic glare his way. "It isn't a dictatorship, Mr. Helsing. I am a queen who serves only with the support of the nobles. They have so far let go my insistence to use our resources to track Gerwalta—they are all mothers, after all, and understand my concern—but as you saw, support for my office is waning."

Daring her objections or worse, her indifference, I stepped forward, taking one of my mother's hands in mine. "Please, after I save Tobias and warn the others, I swear, I won't ask you for anything again. I will go about my life alone."

It took a moment, but at last, Brünhild's fingers hooked around mine. "I have to consider the ramifications. There are *some* matrons," her eyes shifted accusingly to the side, "who do not believe the slayers are worth protecting at all. I will not exchange your heart for a whole race's welfare. I'm sorry, but I cannot include you on this mission."

I dropped her hand and my expectations. "I see. Caleb and I can go out the way we came in." I took a few steps back towards the hidden door.

"However—"

My mother's words arrested me. I spun, my heart racing, my thoughts filling in all the ways she could finish that sentence. "Yes?"

"As I am no longer *your* matron, I cannot forbid you from being any particular place at any particular time, and if Markus, while visiting you in Rebecca's cottage, were to accidently mumble the plans in his sleep today before we depart at sunset, how could I hold it against him?"

"Are you saying—" Why was my mouth going dry when there were such salivating developments? "I can be part of the mission?"

"No, I'm saying I can't stop you from undertaking your own mission. Understand, Gerwalta, if dangers arise which force me to choose between aiding my own team or you, I am obligated to them first. However, as your mother, I cannot advise you to abandon your heart. You must do what you must do."

This tender moment died on the sword of Caleb's ill timing.

"Great, so now I have to choose between *two* different teams to be on?" He ran his hand through his perfect 'do. "Don't suppose we can flip a coin?"

"You're not going." "You're not coming."

Brünhild and I locked gazes right after our synchronized words.

Caleb took a moment to wipe away his shock before clearing his throat. "Why?"

"The slayers need you," I said. "You're too valuable to risk against the Ravens."

"Not to mention," my mother continued, "you're the only surviving male of your kind we know of who's gone through his rites. Just as with our kind, only a female matron can awaken the gifts of her clan, so too must the other male slayers rely on you to do the same when the opportunity arises. If you die, then your race ends with its current generation."

I turned to my mom. "I didn't know that."

"Why would you? You've never needed to."

"You got to be kidding me!" Caleb moaned. "Geri, look at me. I told you not long after we met that the Ravens killed my parents. If anyone has the right to go after them, it's me."

I couldn't deny his rationale, but as much as I'd be loath to admit it, my mother was right. "We can't risk it. You have to stay here and keep working with the slayers. Didn't you say you wanted to try and perform rites with some of the guys this coming new moon? You need to get them ready for that."

 "As the saying goes, I don't have to do anything but pay taxes and die, and I'm really good at tax evasion." The slayer crossed his arms over his chest. "Neither of you wants me on your team? Fine. I'll make my own team. You aren't the boss of me."

Brünhild grinned. "Mr. Helsing, I admire your drive, but if you do not comply with my order to stay settled here, I will..."

"I'll tell Amy that you have a crush on her," I inserted.

My mother spun on me, brow furrowed, lips pursed. Caleb, in the meantime, threw his hands up in surrender.

"Okay, I yield. You play dirty, Kline. So dirty."

As we grumbled our way back down the hidden staircase, Caleb in the front to light the way, he said, "Mind if I ask you about something you said back there?"

"Why not? You seem to know all my secrets now anyways."

I imagined his smile. I'd give that to Caleb, he smiled more than anyone else I'd ever met.

"When you said your mom hit you with silver flame, what did that mean?"

"I told you about that," I said, my hand tracing the wall with each step. "My dad tried to arrange for me to take my fire with his bloodline, the yellows. My mom found out, freaked out, and relinquished me to keep me from claiming my birthright."

"Yeah, you told me about that, but you didn't mention anything about silver flame. I've never heard of it."

"Of course not, it's a hood thing."

"A common hood thing?" He paused, looking back over his shoulder.

"I mean, not common. Really rare, in fact. So is flying, but she can do that, too. Hardly any hoods can anymore. It's a trait we seem to be losing through the generations."

He turned back and trudged on. "If you say so. All I'm saying is, I've never heard of silver flame until now."

And as I followed him, I had to wonder if, outside of my mother's ability, I had ever heard of it either.

# TWENTY-FOUR

I'd made many mistakes in my life, but so far, none so big as writing off Amy Popowitz as a man-gobbling, college coed more interested in getting drunk and screwing guys than being bothered with actual relationships. I'd also underestimated her grip, and if she didn't let me go soon, she might choke me to death.

"You're acting like I'll never see you again."

"What? No, I'm not. Of course, I'm going to—"

I wrestled myself out of her hold and held her at arm's length. "We don't say anything. No goodbye, no good luck. We just go do and get back."

She wrinkled her nose. "Well, you guys suck then."

I pulled back and made a final check of the weapons in my sack. Silver, of course, several bricks of it, but there was also a titanium curved blade I was itching to try out. Wooden bullets and a gun with just enough force to project them without splintering rounding out the kit. "I'm sorry you can't come along, but..."

"But I'm just a huey," she said for me. "I know. I get it. I'm getting better at the hand-to-hand stuff, but I'm not an idiot. I'm not ready to do things at your level yet. Hell, those twelve-year-olds playing Mulan in the courtyard could kick my ass. But, now that I'm a Casper..."

"Castellan."

"Whatever," she said. "I should spend my time figuring out what that means. I'm sure it involves regulating Caleb's conquests. The slayers didn't get out of a vampire's harem just to be dragged into his."

"I'm sure you'll keep everyone in line."

I turned to Anya, who held Mina in her arms. Lupines led the growth curve, but even I was shocked by what one week had done.

The baby's eyes followed me, predatory senses already developing.

"She's tracking you," Anya said. "She knows you're her m—"

"I'm not," I cut off the slayer. "Please, Anya, don't put me in that role. I'm her guardian, and that's all."

I was so not ready to be anyone's parent, let alone a mythical creature whose blood was the opposite of mine, with the power to steal the life from a vampire instead of extend it.

"Remember that Petunia will be stopping by to check in on her every day."

"Of course, we'll expect her."

"Hey, Little Red!" Cody escorted my dad up the walk, Pietro's own weapons kit hanging heavy at his side. I got a nod as my dad passed by and Cody hung back. "I really feel like I should be going along on this wild ride."

I shook my head. "Lisa's going to deliver any day. You need to be there when she does. Family first, pack second. And, frankly, neither Tobias or I are either of those things to you."

His hand cupped the back of my head. "You're always going to be family to me, Geri Kline. You're like my weird sister who I used to make out with."

"You always know how to spoil a tender moment, don't you?"

He pulled me to him then, kissing me on the forehead. "I'm going to turn on my phone the second I land in Marquette. You let me know when you're out and you got him."

"And you let me know when Lisa delivers," I said. "I want to kiss that baby when all this is over. And tell Lisa I hope she's well."

And for the first time since Cody and I had broken up, I really meant it.

From the outside, the van we were allowed to borrow to "do some sight-seeing" didn't look that different from any other vehicle. On the inside, though, it was perfect for supes. The driver and front passenger compartment had been outfitted with the same kind of glass Igor had had in his car back in Chicago, allowing Yan to sit comfortably in the middle of a sunny day without scorching. I hadn't even considered asking the vampire-in-residence to come with us, but in his improvised "sleep talking," the offer had been made via Markus. How could I turn that down? To my surprise, my mother hadn't ordered him to stay behind when asked.

"So what happens after all this?"

My father's question from the driver's seat broke me from my reverie. "What do you mean?"

"You get your wolf back, your mother kills the Ravens, and what after that?"

"I haven't really had a chance to think about it." More like I hadn't wanted to get wrapped up making plans for a future that may never come to be. "Happily ever after, I guess?"

"*Niña*, you know it's not that easy." His gentle voice wore down the edges of the harsh reality. "Even if your status means there's no official crime, the biases of lupines and hoods will make you outsiders almost anywhere you go."

"I know. But I can't plan for a world of infinite possibilities. I just want to hope for one that has a chance for Tobias and I to be together."

*As mates, a couple.* I longed to say both of these things, but feared putting so much debt into a prospect that may not pay off. Then, thinking about what that might mean, and realizing that, no matter how odd it was, my dad was one of the few people on earth who I could ask, I said, "Papa, did you *bond* with mom? Like, you know, the first time you two…"

"We made love?" He grinned and shook with silent laughter. "There is no shame in saying it. We *have* been married a very long time. Why do you ask? Are you hoping for that, or scared of it?"

No. Yes. "Tobias already had a mate, and when Kara died, he suffered like any lupine would. Maybe he'll love me because of what he is and what's happened to him, but what happens if he's the only man I can ever love and it doesn't work out?"

"That is not a question you need to ask. The only question you need to ask is, is he worth the risk? For me, that answer was yes. We've had our moments."

"Like when she exiled you from the clan?"

Dad shrugged. "For standing against her edict to aid my daughter, which I did willingly and knowing the possible ramifications. Should I have *not* done that?"

"Of course, you should have!" Despite the fact that it had also led to my relinquishing. "I just don't understand how you can forgive her."

"Ach, *niña*. Your mother did not exile me. The Grand Matron did."

"Don't start that. She tried to pull the same thing on me, too. You can't just divorce the two like that. She's only one person. What was it Abuela used to say? Don't try to be everyone to everybody, because we all only get one grave."

"Sage words spoken by another asenaic, who knew what it was like to live two lives," my father said. "You and your mother are more alike than you realize. You struggle to find common ground, because you don't realize you're standing in the same exact spot. Same view, different eyes."

In the middle row, Yan's cell phone beeped. He fished it out and read the screen. "Markus says the Muñez siblings have been moved to a secure location. The Yellow Matron in charge of the region says they've also confirmed the Raven hideout. You were right, Geri. They're there."

I'd never doubted my instincts for a second, but having them validated with so little effort wasn't completely reassuring. I tried to ignore the implications and stay focused on the matter at hand. "Where?"

"They're holed-up in an old residence of Igor Kharmarov's. It's dilapidated now, probably hasn't been lived in for years, but all vampires of a certain age who've passed this way know of it."

I nodded. "Once we're close enough, I should be able to sense Tobias's whereabouts."

Yan looked up from his phone. "How close is close?"

I shrugged. "If the location is relatively open and sparsely populated, a mile or so. With Tobias, it varies. Why? I don't know. Moon phases, moods, distraction? Maybe everything."

Did the fact that we were both asenaics have anything to do with it, like we were operating on a closer frequency?

I had to wonder. Then again, my father was also of the same bloodline, and he had never spoken about any greater ability in proximal sensitivity. Come to think of it…

"There is a chance, though, that whatever the Ravens did has changed that," I admitted out loud *and* to myself. "I won't know until I know, I guess."

My father smiled. "He is your mate. You will know, always."

# TWENTY-FIVE

We pulled off to the side of a mountain road just before sunset, into a field covered in dry grass amid a grove of tall, thin trees topped with plasticine leaves. The car used by the official hood team sat unguarded, empty of any occupants.

My dad turned to me. "Anything?"

With eyes closed, I focused on the hum of energy that presented itself whenever Tobias came into my proximity. Concentrate as I may, there was no sign.

Dad laid his hand on my shoulder. "Don't force it. We're still two kilometers from the house. It means nothing."

I got out and surveyed the view, leaving Yan in the car. He'd await the final moments of twilight to avoid losing any of his strength to the sun. In the distance, gray mountains highlighted with white patches picked up the amber shafts of light coming from the west. As soon as night rose in its fullness, this landscape would glow under the shine of a full moon. The snow wasn't deep – one would have to round up to say it was an inch – but it did serve as an archive of those who'd gone before. I squatted down, examining the contours of the footprints heading south.

"Mother, Markus... Matron Smyth, I think. These two, I don't recognize."

Pietro knelt down beside me. "I suggested to your mother that she recruit two of the local clan to accompany the mission, to avoid political questioning. More than likely, that is them."

My dad pointed to the southwest. "Igor's home is just

over that ridge. We agreed that this distance would allow us to have a sufficient staging ground."

I pressed my hand to the hood of the late model vehicle Markus had parked. "Still warm, but barely. Given the temperature out here, I'd say that means this car was turned off about fifteen or twenty minutes ago."

"According to plan," my dad added, rising to his feet. "Your mother will engage the Ravens, attempting to draw them away from the home. While they are distracted, we will locate Tobias and if we can, Igor Kharmarov, and free them."

"I'm not sure what kind of state Tobias is in." I fished out one of the silver bricks, a chunk of metal the size of a chalkboard eraser, and pooled it over my skin. "He might not be able to keep his huey form if he's too weak."

"We could always call off the mission, try again tomorrow night."

I shook my head. "You know Mom won't back down now that she's in the field. Besides, tonight is the second full moon since we've been separated. He's got to be starting to lose his grip on reality. I hate to say it, but I want his animal brain to be the one in charge of his body tonight. Instinct should get him to run when the chance comes."

*Even if that means leaving me behind.* It was something I was prepared for. Vlad wanted my blood too much. If he captured me, he might torture me, even take advantage of me as he did with Alex, but he wasn't going to kill me. To free Tobias, I'd endure that.

"Just let me get the silver and weapons I brought out of the trunk. As soon as it's dark, we can—"

The opening car door drew our attention. Dad and I turned to see Yan, his hands shoved in his coat pockets like the cold actually did anything to him, strolling across the way.

"I thought you were going to stay in the car until the sun was completely down, to keep yourself from losing even the smallest bit of strength?"

He nodded. "There are but a few minutes until then, and your father needs assistance."

Suddenly panicked, I turned to my dad still standing by the car. "Assistance with what? You look fine."

I felt the air shift around me, felt the change of direction in my soul, even before my father's head finished its fall.

With a blink, my world flipped. Yan's arms caged me. Silver threads raced through the air, a network of spider webs that laced over my arms and legs, drawing me into a hold. My mind raced even as my limbs flailed and my mind tried to comprehend the impossible. It was silver, just silver, but why wasn't it obeying me? Why did it refuse to yield to my command?

My father couldn't bring himself to look at me. "The silver is blood-claimed. It obeys only me."

I'd been named after the Betrayer, but I was the one being betrayed. Blood-claimed silver? But didn't he say the act was banned, that it caused horrific pain for the one who claimed it? Why would my biggest champion my whole life put himself through that, just to trap me? "Papa?"

The intensity of his gaze knocked the breath from my lungs. "When you were born, your mother and I vowed to do whatever it took to protect you from harm. That holds even if it means protecting you from yourself."

Every movement drew the taut threads tighter across my skin, even as my sadness turned to fire. "You have no right! He's *my* mate. He's *my* responsibility."

"And you are mine." Crossing to me, the metal about me moving at his command and allowing my legs freedom just long enough to collapse beneath me, leaving me in a sitting pose, my father's hand cupped my cheek. "I promise, *mi corazon*, I will save him. Now, no more discussion. We're losing precious time."

I closed my eyes, resigned to the fact that to struggle would only hurt more. "You're losing something far more precious than that."

My father paused, looking back over his shoulder. "Time can heal an injury, but it cannot restore the dead."

I shook my head. "Tell yourself that if you want, but the full moon is still rising."

A threat full of hope and lacking all capital. My father said no more as he and Yan made for the nearby trees. I flexed every muscle, trying to break the hold of the cords around me, but to no avail. No magic could force it either. At this point, I only had one choice.

If the silver would not yield, it would have to burn.

And I along with it.

# TWENTY-SIX

## AMY

"So this is the archive, huh?"

I examined the rows and rows of leather-bound books and piles of scrolls with all the interest of a fruit fly to Styrofoam, i.e., zero. But for some reason, the last place on Becky Krantz's itinerary for my personal tour of Schloss Wolfsretter was the one she seemed proudest of. She looked on it now like her own grown child striding across the stage at graduation to make his valedictorian speech.

"It's, um… very nice?"

It wasn't. True, it was nicely *organized*. And I'd add that it was surprising to find in the subterranean floors of a medieval castle. What was a climate-controlled high security library room straight out of a Nicolas Cage film doing in the dull patina of Schloss Wolfsretter? And what did the hoods have that was so coveted it demanded this level of Mall Cop Mecca-hood anyway?

"It is my pride *unt* joy," Becky said. "When everything arrived here in the 1940s from all over the world, it was a mess. Just boxes and boxes of records, every family using its own classification system. And preservation? The only things the hoods know how to preserve is a grudge. But now, you see. Years of labor, all for this, and it is marvelous."

What could I say? I didn't want to be a dick and not appreciate something she obviously bled and sweated for. "So I guess you know a lot about wolves and hoods then."

"Of course. I am, perhaps, the world's foremost expert in lupine and wolfsretter genealogy."

"Wolfsretter?"

"*Ja, wolfsretter.*" She nodded. "It is German for 'wolf-watcher.' Until recently, this is what the hoods were called."

"Watchers, huh? Sounds voyeuristic." Then, finding a place where maybe the old castellan and I could share some common ground, I adapted my conspiratorial tone. "Bet you came across some dirt in all these documents, huh?"

Her face curdled. "Of course, but I managed to clean all the documents without damage. I am a phenomenal archivist."

"No, I don't mean like *dirt* dirt. I mean like, dirt. Scandals. The dark underbelly of wolves and wolf-writers."

"Wolfs*retter.*"

"That's what I said." I put an arm around her, pulling her close. "Tell me, Becky, what's the juiciest thing you ever read in all these books?"

"Juicy?" She shrugged. "The hoods are not *juicy*, as a rule."

I could have guessed that, having lived with Geri for two years.

"Surely there's something." I gave her shoulders a little squeeze. "Come on, just between us castrati."

"Castellans."

"Right."

"Well... I suppose it would be the story of Hamunshet."

"Becky Shantz! You kiss your mother with that mouth?"

Becky's smile fell away. "My mother died in Auschwitz."

Awkwardness put on its gloves and punched me in the gut. Jesus, I couldn't just *not* make a joke for once. "Oh! I'm sorry... I didn't mean to..."

Luckily, the airlock around the door decompressed, and in walked tall, dark, and stuck-up, presenting me with a merciful deflection.

"Caleb!" I exclaimed like he'd just brought me to the edge of release. "Just in time. Becky was about to tell me about the story of He-Man Shits."

The castellan clicked her tongue. "There is something quite wrong with your ears, girl."

Caleb must have sensed my utter tumble into graduate-level social guffaws and allotted me a moment of mercy. "Go easy on her, Becky. You have to remember, Barbie here was raised in a place where the most exotic thing she encountered in everyday life was the halal food cart outside her hot yoga studio."

I balled my fists. "It was a kosher hot dog stand, moron."

He laughed away my retort. "Did she mean to say Hamunshet?"

"Yes, you know the story of the first hood?" Becky grinned.

Finally, someone who didn't try her patience. Caleb just charmed everyone, didn't he?

Asshole.

"If you mean the ancient Egyptian priestess who got knocked up by Aten the sun disk god and had twins? Yeah, I know that story," Caleb said. "My mom used to tell me it at bedtime when I was little."

"Well, that explains something." I cocked a hip. "No wonder you're so sex-obsessed. You were programmed to fall asleep thinking about divine boot-knocking."

The slayer squinted at me. "She put it in kid-friendly terms, of course. Only, Becky, Hamunshet gave birth to the first *slayer*, not the first hood. It's the reason we have the power of the sun, being that we're descended from the *sun disk god*."

I looked to Caleb, who looked at me, and I looked at Becky, who looked at Caleb.

"You don't honestly think that's true, do you?" I asked. "I mean, there's no such thing as Egyptian gods. Mythology is the invention of man."

"So is money, but I'm a devout worshipper."

Becky shuffled to a shelf on the far end of the room and pulled out a box about the size of a loaf of bread. "Here, I will show you."

She moved it to a table and opened it, pulling out a scroll. As she unrolled it, the fragments pasted over a clean linen cloth came into focus, looking like something out of an old monster movie. In the center, a woman wrapped in a beautiful white dress sat on a throne, the sun blazing over head and its rays shining down on her. On each knee, a baby, one who shone so brightly its features were difficult to distinguish, almost as if it *were* light. The other, robed in a blue cloak, but with silver eyes.

"There's the whole of it," Becky said. "The oldest version of the story I've been able to find. Came here from the House of Black about fifty years ago, but I've found mention of this through much of the hood literature."

I traced my fingers over the edges of the papyrus scroll. "Caleb, I'm no expert in this. I mean, a priestess impregnated by a god? Way above my pay grade. I'd laugh it off, but a year ago, if you had tried to convince me vampires and werewolves were real, I'd have said you were even drunker than me. If there's any truth to this, it means—"

"It means that slayers and hoods come from the same origin. That we're in some way… the same race."

# TWENTY-SEVEN

## GERI

A howl pierced the air, falling on us from the edge of the woods, just as the moon came up.

Local wolves, of course. If there were hoods in this region, there would also have to be lupines. During full moons, packs roamed their lands, consumed by their animal natures, more beast than man. Obligated to walk on four legs, only alphas and the occasional beta could keep their huey form under its power. I used to fear meeting one on a *feuernacht,* suspecting such a meeting could turn into a kill-or-be-killed situation.

My mother had always speculated that once I took my fire, the wolves would heed my summons. Under the light of the silver moon, I drove awareness into my soul, beckoning them, appealing to them.

*Help me. My mate is a prisoner, and I am trapped by those who've betrayed me.*

The words turned and twisted in my head, radiating out, a beacon for any help. After a few minutes, sweat beaded my forehead, even as the night descended and the temperature dipped.

The howls faded.

And then, padded paws crunched the snow.

Golden fur rimmed a brown face. Smaller than the packlings I'd been raised with, the alpha still commanded grace, his tenuous steps as lithe as they were determined. He must not have been expecting to find what he did when he'd descended from the hills, for when he suddenly shifted into his huey form, he wore a screwed-up expression.

"You're a hood," he said in a form of Spanish that sounded more lyrical than my father's.

I shook my head. "*Soy una* asenaic. Um... *Soy una muceta pero soy también una loba.*"

"Both a hood and a wolf? Is that possible?" he continued, scratching his unkempt black hair. "What did you do to me? How did you make me feel like I *had* to listen to you?"

"Please, I don't have time to explain. My name is Gerwalta Kline, and I..."

"Gerwalta?" he said, cutting me off. "The Betrayer?"

I gulped down my anxiety. "Her descendant. Her... Her heir. Please, my mate is being held prisoner a few kilometers from here. I need to get out of these silver cords and save him. Can you help me?"

His eyes swept over me, taking survey of my situation. "What is this, some trick to get me to touch the silver? Playing a joke on us, are you? There are other hoods near here tonight; we have sensed them. They must be near now, hiding. You have a bet or something, don't you? See if you can trick a wolf into getting burned."

"No tricks. I swear, I'm not lying. Please, the cord is woven too tight for me to unravel. If you'd just loosen it a bit, I could do the rest. You're an alpha at full moon, I'm sure you're strong enough to bend it. You can rip off one of my sleeves or get something out of one of those cars so you don't have to touch it."

"You are a hood, no? You should be able to will the cords away yourself."

"Normally, yeah. But these are…" I struggled for a word in Spanish I knew that would work. "Defective."

"Defective?" The alpha's face curdled. "If you are a hood who cannot wield silver *and* a wolf is not burned by it, it is *you* who are defective. I don't believe any of this." He turned. "I'm not falling for your tricks, hood. A word of advice: next time you play this game with another wolf, do not claim your name is the one all hoods loathe."

He turned tail, reclaimed his fur, and ran.

"No. No, please!"

But it was no use. I was alone, I was bound, and I was trapped. Or was I? Part of my training had been learning to get out of tight situations. Surely I could do that now? First step: to stand. Leaning forward, I folded my legs underneath me, getting ready to jump. The moment I did, however, I discovered that my father wasn't an idiot. The cords were looser at my ankles, but still restrictive, and threw off my balance. I called out as my body paralleled to the ground, the earth rising to meet me.

The moon laughed above as I rolled on to my back like an overturned armadillo. "Give it up, Geri Kline," it seemed to say. "I've seen this story before. Now just sit there like a good little red riding hood and wait for mommy and daddy to return. You're not going anywhere."

Which I might have done, if not for the fact that I knew, if the decision came down to freeing Tobias or killing Vlad, there was no way my werewolf was getting away. Through the forest and over the river in the valley, my mother and father, my cousin and his boyfriend, and even a few hoods took on the Ravens. I had to get out of here. I had to be the one there to make the right choice.

And I was going to do that... how?

I was a hood and wolf, why couldn't my strength be enough? I pulled and pushed, trying to stretch the metal. Nothing. It was too strong. I was not strong enough.

Frustration caught spark, sending anger raging through my limbs. Twisting, turning, crying out to the night until my throat was raw, I screamed. No, I refused to be sidelined. I refused to be relinquished. I *would* find a way out of this.

The cry started in my heart, clawed its way up my throat, and ripped from my body with the power of my ancestors. Soon, the fire was not only emotional, it was physical. I opened my eyes and looked down at my body, watching silver flames dance over my fingers. The melting started slow, the bands on my wrists and arms dropping to the ground. Too amazed to be curious, I pushed my palms in turn to each of the cord's stress points. My ankles, my shoulders, my arms. In a moment, I was free. The second none of the cords remained, the fire snuffed itself out.

And I ran. Across the field, through the forest, through the splashing ice cold water of the barely-a-river, until it came into view.

Moonlight clung to ancient alabaster walls of a structure more tall than wide, its sharp dimensions punctuated with arched windows and doors alluding to a Moorish past. Perhaps not authentic to the period, but the influence was there. Five or six stories high and with only one apparent way in or out, the path was clear as my feet ate up ground between the forest and the house.

When the lurch in my stomach grabbed me, stopping me dead in my tracks, my control almost abandoned me.

He was near. *He was near.*

But he wasn't moving. Not away, not toward me, not at all. The sensation remained constant, growing in strength only as I forced my feet to work. Part of my instincts told me to call out, to tell him I was coming. The wiser portion of my brain remembered that wounded animals fell first to predators stalking the night. Igor's old home lay no more than four hundred meters ahead, but the same distance to the east, my heart stood still.

I saw it then, the low rise of a masonry wall more ruin than foundation. Light footsteps carried me across the open earth. A well. Or what remained of one. Even as I leaned in to peer down, I knew what I would find, but that did not stop the pulse of anticipation and woe as I did so.

"Tobias!"

Either he hadn't heard me, or he couldn't. Even from thirty feet overhead and with the moon above at such an angle that he was left in shadow, there wasn't much of him I could see. His lupine form lay motionless, drawing my worry.

*He's not dead*, I lectured myself. *You'd know it if he were dead*.

"Tobias, answer me or I'm coming down there."

Nothing, not even a flinch of an ear or a cycle of breath. I looked around, hoping to find a rope or some kind of ladder even. Nothing but empty, cold ground. Then I remembered the silver I'd grafted under my clothes before we'd arrived. If my father could make a cord to bind me, surely I could make a rope to climb down into a hole. I reached for it with my mind, demanded it do as I willed.

Only, nothing happened. No rope, not even a tiny little string.

I pulled off my coat and looked for the metal, my eyes demanding to confirm what my senses already felt was true. It was gone. All of it. Whatever magic it was that had let me melt my father's bindings must have also claimed the silver plated against my skin.

There was nothing to do then but jump. I threw my legs over the walls of the well, took a deep breath, and let gravity pull me down. My feet planted on either side of his head.

"Tobias? Wake up!"

A rising and falling frame proved he was, in fact, still alive. My hands pulled up his maw. He was thinner than the last time I'd seen him, but his body seemed in good condition. Why was he here, and how was I going to get him out? The effort would strain my abilities, but I could probably lift him. But to do that while attempting to climb the well-worn, icy walls of a dry well? No way. I'd just have to hope I could find a way to wake him up.

I closed my eyes and tried to sense the pack that had roamed the hills, hoping if I got them to where I was, they might have greater sympathy for one of their own than their alpha had had for me. On the edge of abilities, I found their energy and gave it a slight tug, asking them to circle back to me. The alpha's direction shifted, but just as soon as the string between us pulled, it again went slack.

Suddenly, footfalls on the ground above took my attention skyward. A head blocked the moonlight from my view above. "Gerwalta?"

"Mother?" I leapt to my feet. "Mother, I found him! He's here. Tobias is here. He's okay, but unconscious and... Mom, you can fly! You can get us out of here."

The next sound I heard made my blood boil and freeze at the same time. "Oh, I don't think that will be happening, Geri."

With a shard of moonlight cast over his features, his eyes looked even more intense, his surreal beauty threatening. Vlad wore his usual cock-sided grin as he turned to my mother, who I realized had her hands tied behind her back, likely bound in electrical wire. "You see, Matron? I told you she'd fall for my trap. Never doubt the pull between mates.

The magic that binds them also makes them blind to danger."

I'd done many things in my life to invite my mother's disappointment. My days and nights seemed meted for her disapproval. Never before had she looked at me with such disappointment.

And for once, I felt I deserved it.

# TWENTY-EIGHT

Wind flew from my lungs, leaving me gasping, powerless. Electrical wires, charged by a small battery pack taped on my back, encircled my wrists, leaving my hood abilities inert and my hands bound. A moment later, the vampire threw Tobias down beside me. He was still fast asleep, knocked out by whatever drug Vlad had given him. I struggled to survey the area around me, searching desperately for the others, but all I found was Vlad and my mother seated at a table, both with cups of tea.

"Miss Kline." The vampire raised his cup my direction, saluting me. "I wonder if you now regret refusing a place in my harem?"

I rolled onto my back and managed from there to sit up, despite the ache in my ribs. "My only regret is not slicing off your head when I had all those swords around me."

"Ah, yes, that would have led us down a different path for sure." He took a sip, smacked his lips, put the cup down. "Your mother and I were just talking terms, but ones concerning you were just wishful thinking until you arrived. Thank you for your haste."

"Terms?" The question was directed at my mother, who had the gall to be stoic. "What terms?"

But it was Vlad who answered. "The offer on the table is this: you will stay with me, provide me and my clutch with your blood, and I will allow you and your wolf to live a rather comfortable and accommodating life under my protection and let all the other fools we've captured tonight go free. Refuse me, and everyone else dies...while you? You will only be able to wish that you were."

I mused silently for a moment. "Sounds awful, like the one the sultan gave you. Life in a gilded cage, comfort but no control. You think I don't see the insult?"

"What do I care if you do?" Vlad snipped. "It will not render your choices altered."

"Why am I so important to you?" I spit back. "You have my mom at the table. Offer to trade me and Tobias for your whole harem back. You can set up your little breeding compound where you like and feed indefinitely."

My head swung back to my mother, but her expression revealed nothing. Defiant and uncompromising, she'd admit to no fault, whether or not there was one to be had. Was she a prisoner too, or had she gone in with the intention of meeting Vlad as her equal? Where were the others? Markus, my dad, Yan? The two yellow hoods? I searched her expression for some tenderness or clue, but found none.

Vlad's eyebrow perched curiously. "Your mother tells me Inga is dead, that she turned on you. Tell me, Geri, how well did you know my dear, departed daughter-turned-sister?"

"Well enough to know she hated you." I spit out the blood pooling in the side of my mouth. "Makes two of us."

"Ah, and you're witty. I shall enjoy your humor in the years to come." Vlad stood, bringing his teacup along with him as he paced in my direction. "Truth is, Inga never should have been turned. She didn't have the constitution for an immortal life. I blame myself, really. You see, when she was no more than my *human child,* I neglected her. Abused her, even. She grew up with what I believe your generation calls daddy issues. She's spent her eternal life running between two father figures. Me and Igor, Igor and me. The last turnover was about twenty years ago. I didn't realize that when she was giving regular checkups to my young slayers, she was also slipping a little something extra into their vitamin shots. Left all the male slayers infertile. Oh, Inga was kind-hearted. As much as a vampire can be, anyway. She didn't want to *kill* the slayers to keep me from feeding. She just wanted to make sure I wouldn't get my hands on any more. Then, the cycle flipped, and she was off with Igor again. She was on her way back to me soon enough. Inga always came home again."

A swirling of emotions made it impossible to react. What Inga had done was horrendous, but was it the best possible solution to an untenable situation? How many more slayers would have been bred in captivity if she'd not sterilized the males? How we'd remedy that in the future was a problem for another day.

"So you see, Geri," Vlad continued, "while I adored my slayers, would have been happy to keep them forever, I've known for some time that source of sustaining blood had an expiration date. I was so delighted when Caleb wandered onto the scene. One vibrant, fertile stud for all my lassies. Inga thought it would make up for her previous transgressions. I was starting to worry, thinking I might finally die… in sixty or seventy years, when my slayers died out. But then, my sister surprised me with one final offering."

In a blink, he dropped the tea cup, crouching down beside me and pulling me up by the hair. "Hamunshet's gift. Oh, dear one… I *would* take your father. I would keep the Muñezes. I would even barter back my slayers for the right offer. But all of them put together aren't worth a single blade of your hair. All I need is you. Oh, and the children you and this asenaic—" His head jerked in Tobias's direction. "—will produce. And your children's children. And *their* children's children… Perhaps with the occasional outsider thrown in to keep the gene pool healthy."

Confusion swirled in my soul. "What makes *me* so special, Vlad? What makes *you* so deserving?"

My mother cleared her throat, pivoting in her seat. "I think that what my daughter means is, while it's true her veins carry wolf blood, we're three centuries down the line. Whatever elixir asenaic blood seems to be for you, surely the effect would be increased by a fresher coupling."

Vlad, amused, pulled back. "Are you offering me an alternative, Grand Matron? Unless the offer is the illustrian I was breeding—"

"I told you," my mother interjected, "I killed it. Her and her mother."

What was she talking about? Mina was alive, and Brünhild hadn't killed Alex. Alex's death had been a tragic consequence of forcing so much power into an attack when she was already so compromised.

"And Inga all in the same swoop," Vlad acknowledged. "Yes, I recall. You have a remarkable sense of bloodlust. And all this leads me back to Geri."

"The pick of any under the command of my office, every twenty years!" The mirror cracked, and my mother's inner demons took control. The words flew from her lips with a passion I'd rarely witnessed in her. The air of desperation clung to each syllable. "And the forced acquiesce of an acceptable wolf mate, in perpetua. I can make that happen."

Venom laced my tongue. "Mom, you can't!"

Her eyes drilled into me. "Silence! You are not a righteous hood. You have no say in my decisions."

Vlad stood, taking two steps to my mother. One of his long fingers traced a line down her cheek. "The time for feigning ignorance is over, Brünhild. You know as well as I do why I want Geri. I've tasted her blood; I know what she is." He leaned in, his tongue darting out. A slick line of saliva marked the path Vlad licked up my mother's jawline. "And I know what *you* are."

I saw everything and understood nothing. For the first time in my life, Brünhild Kline was... scared.

Her words trembled over lips gone white. "She doesn't know. No one does."

"Know what?" I inched closer to the table as well as I could in my position. "What is he talking about?"

"Funny thing, supernatural blood," Vlad mused, backing away. "It's a genetic chemistry lab, all the ingredients stable on their own, but mixed together in different proportions, and BOOM!" His clap made both of us shake. "Explosive results. Huey blood keeps a vampire alive until for some reason, after half a millennium, the magic just dries up. I can drink slayer blood and that's, well... yummy, really. Hood and werewolf blood, a little more gamey, and not quite as powerful. But cross a werewolf with a hood or a slayer, you get liquid life and death. And I thought *that* was the ultimate cocktail. But then... Then I tasted the blood of one who had all three creatures running in her veins."

My mother's eyes fell closed.

"All three?" For some reason, I took the question to Vlad, who seemed to be the only one willing to give answers. "That's impossible."

"Hood begets hood." Brünhild's loathsome words melted through a sighing resolve. Her eyes shone as she lifted them to meet mine. "Words I tried to drill into you. Words my own mother drilled into me. She never wanted me to repeat her mistake."

My world turned red. "No. No, that's impossible, Grandpa Germain was a hood."

"Yes, Jacques Germain *was* a hood," my mother said. "But he was not my father."

The words echoed in my head, but repetition didn't bring clarity. Three bloods ran in my veins... The hoods of my mothers, the wolves of my fathers, and the slayers... My grandfather was a slayer? My *mother* was *half-slayer*?

Suddenly, Caleb's words while descending from the tower came back to me.

*All I'm saying is, I've never heard of silver flame until now.*

When I pressed my brain, I realized that I hadn't heard of another hood with the talent either.

Except for… me.

Vlad held his hands to the sky. "And truth, like a blanket, grows heavy and smothers out our misconceptions." The vampire refocused on my mother. "Geri and the wolf are mine, payment in kind for my slayers."

The monster returned to my side and reached down, his cold, bony fingers threading through my hair, pulling me to my feet by the scalp. I refused to offer him the pleasure of my cry, and filtered the pain through clenched fists and ground teeth.

"What say you, Miss Kline? You, your wolf, and eternal comfort, or just you and all the others be damned?"

My acidic glare met his. "How about neither and you go take a long walk on a sunny day?"

"Do you need further incentive?" His chin lowered into his chest. "Very well."

At the far side of the room, where there may have once been shutters or a pane of glass, only a window frame remained. Vlad pulled me to it, forcing me to look down below, to a clearing where a man stood tied to a tree. For a moment, I assumed it must be one of the local hoods. The cloak distinguished the captured as a member of Casa de los Amarillos, but I couldn't find familiarity in the swollen, broken skin or the blackened, bloodshot eyes. Only when I noticed the patch of solitary gray hair just above his right temple did I realize the truth.

"Dad! Let my father go, you fuc— *Ah!*"

Vlad yanked me back, his cold cheek pressed against mine, sending a pain shooting down my neck. "Do you know what happens to a vampire when he does not feed, Geri?" he asked, his voice distorted by fangs. "I think it's much like what wolves experience: a form of madness. The onset is quicker, though. It's been seven weeks since Istanbul, when you were kind enough to leave my father behind, who I've made certain hasn't had a drop of blood in all that time."

I shook my head. "Igor's strong. He can endure it."

"In his prime, perhaps, but at his age?" Vlad laughed. "If not for his kinship with your distant cousins here in Navarre and their blood, he would have disintegrated long ago."

Below, guided by two other vampires I assumed to be members of Vlad's clutch, Igor emerged from out of my line of sight. Ragged, pale, skin on bones, he was a fading echo of the vampire I'd come to know and trust over the last two years. His brown eyes found me, and a momentary sadness made the depth of his suffering reverberate.

As he turned his head, Igor saw my dad. Like an unrepentant criminal being led to the gallows, he bucked, struggling against the hold of his captors, crying out words in a language I didn't understand.

"What are you doing?"

Vlad grinned. "Have you ever been to a zoo, Miss Kline? I haven't, but I understand animal feeding times are quite a draw."

"Feeding time?"

It didn't make any sense. Vampires didn't need so much blood as to kill their prey. Such deaths were usually the result of intent, or the consequence of inexperience.

"Is this a threat? This will only make Igor strong again."

"Oh, make no mistake, as hungry as *my* father is, *your* father will not last long. Even when he is restored, Nicolae and Petru, my Ravens, will easily overpower him."

Fear kicked in at last, my heart pounding like a wild thing in my chest. The decision was in my hands, but its implications burned. Say yes to Vlad, and my father lived. Say no, and watch as he methodically killed every person he'd captured tonight and force me through who knew what kind of tortures until, at last, battered and used up, he disposed of me, too.

*"Niña!"* My father's eyes caught mine from below, blazing courage. *"Te amo. Siempre te amo.* Tell your mother, I forgive her."

"Pietro!" My mother's voice broke in its fierceness. "Vlad, no. I'll do whatever you want. I'll—"

Vlad waved his hand, and the two vampires below let loose their charge.

I closed my eyes, for even what my ears heard overwhelmed. My dad's cries gargled through blood, and my mother's through terror. But despite refusing to see it, I suddenly *felt* it: his anguish, his despair, his life ebbing away... The wolf within my father reared its head, let out one last sorrowful howl, and fell into darkness.

My knees gave out on the spot just as the vampire released his hold, letting me collapse. "I forfeit."

He curled a hand around his ear. "What was that, Miss Kline? Do speak up."

"I said, I forfeit!" I threw my head back to fix him with a stinging glare. "Tobias and I will stay with you. We'll... We'll *breed*. But let the others go, and swear you'll leave them be forever."

"Not so fast." Vlad crossed to where my mother sat,

her face covered in tears but her expression molded by hate. "Your word as well, Brünhild. Your daughter and her mate remain my guests for life, and you will forget she even exists, understand? If I ever catch a whisper that you or any hood under your command is so much as looking for me, I'll destroy you all."

My mother's words came through restrained tears. "None under my command shall pursue you. I swear this as the Grand Matron of the Wolfsretter."

A drunken grin spread across Vlad's face. "Ah, the old names. I do like them. Ladies, we have an accord. Hurry up now, Matron. Time for you to grab your little commandos and be on your way. Oh, but before you go…"

The vampire crossed the room to where a shopping bag had been left on the floor. I'd thought it garbage, some bit of refuse left behind in the rundown abode by a squatter. I should have known better. Vlad crossed to my mother as his hand went inside the bag. What he pulled out seemed impossible. A blade. A *silver* blade, one only a few inches long with tiny jewels encrusted in its hilt. As a weapon, it was useful, though not big enough to do any serious damage to a vampire. As silver, it was useless. For the first time in my life, I understood why such an object had been bequeathed to me instead of merely being recycled into another form: it was my grandmother's dagger, and the silver must have been blood-claimed by her.

Vlad used the dagger to slice away the electrical cord binding my mother before turning the hilt and shoving it into her weapon hand. "A token of good faith. Your daughter left this behind in Istanbul. Take it with my good wishes."

The self-proclaimed sultan snapped, and with that, a fourth and fifth vampire walked into the room. Reality hit, punching me the stomach. All five Ravens were here. If I just had a way to attack, we could take them all down now.

*And leave Tobias unconscious and open to attack,*

*trusting in the honor system that they wouldn't go after him? Smart move, Kline.*

The only way we'd take them out like this was if we set off a bomb. As a rule, supes didn't deal in explosives. We were of the old world, and fought with its rules. Only, as I thought about all I'd learned tonight, I realized, we *did* have a bomb. Two in fact, and now that Vlad had unwittingly given my mother a fuse to light them, the plan forming in my head just might work.

"Mircea," Vlad said to the vampire on the right, who couldn't have been any older than me when he was turned. "Escort our guests to town. Do not release their bonds until daybreak. Mihnea?"

The other vamp, a man who could have been Inga's brother based on his looks, dipped his head. "The sedative we gave Mr. Somfield should be wearing off soon. Once he's awake, please see him and Miss Kline to a containment chamber before daybreak. They will have much to speak on once they are able to talk."

Mihnea bowed. "Yes, Sultan."

I struggled to my feet and then, with all the mock obeisance I could muster, bowed my head. "Your Grace?"

Vlad, on the edge of leaving the room, turned, his face aglow. "Ah, see. She is learning. Well done, Miss Kline."

"Thank you, Sultan," I continued, my eyes kept low. "You won, I'm yours. But please, let me say goodbye to my mother. It's the last time I'm ever going to see her."

He weighed the request, his eyes tipping from side to side, before ceding. "Very well, but quickly."

Playing up an inability to move, the restraints on my arms and hands stretched with my efforts. "Can I hug her?"

"My, my, aren't we suddenly sentimental?" With a jerk of Vlad's chin, Mihnea followed unspoken orders.

Brünhild Kline felt light in my arms. A spirit, a shell, a hollowed heart that beat despite its owner wishing to die, all hidden behind a brick wall. I wouldn't question it; I was barely holding on myself. But grief was a luxury I could not afford.

I wrapped my arms around her, pulling her drifting form into my hold. "Please, mom. Please."

No response, not even a sigh. My chin on her shoulder, I looked to the silver in her hands. The dagger my grandmother had left to me, *my* dagger. Would it be enough?

"Mom," I sighed. "I'm going to be okay. *We're* going to be okay. You have to relinquish your love for me, just like you did before. Do you understand?" I squeezed her even tighter. "Relinquish it *the same exact way*."

God willing, Vlad thought nothing of the tiny gasp my mother made, nor understood its significance. No wonder there were no other hoods who could command silver flame. It wasn't a *hood power*. It was a unique skill commanded by a rare individual. My mother's silver flame must be some kind of solarium, and *that* was the craft of slayers.

"I know it seems impossible with what's happened, but is it something you think you can bring yourself to do?" I pulled back to find her red eyes as wide as saucers.

She nodded, looking as astounded and shell-shocked as any widow should. Was it subterfuge, or sincere? Could it be both? "I know you'll persevere," she said. "You are strong. Stronger than I ever dreamed. But your... mate?"

I nodded, my confidence drawn merely from earnest hopes and solemn prayers. "He's strong..." I leaned in the tiniest amount. "...like me, remember? And tonight I realized, in the ways that really matter, *I'm just like you*."

Her eyes went to the comatose wolf on the floor, then back to me. She opened her arms, inviting me, even as Vlad huffed in the background.

"My daughter, my child."

A raw energy crawled over my skin, leaving gooseflesh in its wake. Then, suddenly, heat. Warm, hot, burning, *blistering*… My mother's power electrified the air, making the hair on my arms stand on end. The last time she'd hit me, the shot had robbed me of my abilities for months. Then, I'd only been a nascent. Now, I was so much more. Hood, wolf, mate. Mother.

If I lived.

She kissed my cheek and—

"I relinquish you."

—silver flame lit the room.

# TWENTY-NINE

Flames licked my limbs, then bore deeper. Down, down, down into the very marrow.

"Gerwalta!"

My mother's voice was so close, and yet, distant, mottled.

"Gerwalta, run!"

A hard smack brought my attention to the pain, reared my instincts to defend. Focus summoned me back to the present, to a place where I was under attack. Run? From what? Oh, yes. From Vlad.

From Vlad.

With a gasp, I plunged back into reality, falling to the floor where Tobias lay, awake but confused. As was I; he was no longer in his wolf.

"Geri?" Sluggish, he pulled himself onto his elbow. "Geri, what are you doing here?"

I pulled him to his feet. "No time. Run."

All around us were howls of pain, cries of anguish. One particular wail stole my attention, and when I looked, I couldn't explain what I saw. It was a vampire, one of the Ravens. Only, where there had been flesh and bone, all that remained was sinew and blood. The image of charts hung in my Human Biology lab back in college resurfaced in my body, and I knew what I was seeing: the human form, ripped from all flesh.

The vampire surveyed himself in disbelief, trying to come to terms with what had happened. He was a walking anatomy model, a cross-sected corpse that nonetheless was still living. Another monstrous body stumbled into view, its front side scorched as well as peeled, and they took to confirming their worst beliefs.

My mother tugged on my clothes. Clothes? How did I still have clothes when we'd just managed to peel the flesh off of four of the world's most powerful vampires in a single blast?

Explanations would come later, when we weren't dead or prisoners.

I scanned the room as my mother helped me get the werewolf to his feet. "There's only four."

"Vlad smoked away a moment before the blast." She shook her head, pulling Tobias's arm over her shoulders. "I don't know if it hit him or he got away. Hurry!"

"Silver flame, mother… It's—"

"Later!" she yelled as we raced down the stone stairs, emerging at a terrible scene.

Igor and my father, both tied to a tree. The vampire, staked through both shoulders and at the hip, blood still smocked across his chin. My father, his head lulling to the side, half of his throat missing.

"You!"

Tobias stumbled as my mother dashed away, crossing to the vampire with terrible, ferocious speed. She drew the stake from Igor's stomach. The vampire cursed, calling out for a long dead saint.

"Please, do it!" he wept. "Kill me. I deserve death. I deserve *much worse.*"

"Mother! Mother, we don't have time." Even as I said it, I was shuffling as best I could with Tobias in tow. "We have to run."

Shrieks erupted in the house behind us, hideous bemoaning wails that soon took on depth and breadth.

"The vampires," my mom said, snapping her gaze. When she looked back at Igor, and at the stake in her hand, poised over his heart, it was as though she were discovering both fresh. "Redeem yourself!"

Igor swallowed his cries as best he could. "How?"

"You're going to die tonight, Igor Kharmarov. Either by me stabbing you now, or by you attacking your brood. Which will it be?"

He whimpered his response. "I can… only kill… one. Then… I die."

Without asking him to say more, Brünhild dropped the stake in her hand, took the other two stuck through Igor's shoulders by the heel of her hand, and yanked them out of him. Igor fell to the ground.

"One life then for the one you took from me. Survive, Igor, and I will hunt you to the ends of the earth and destroy you slowly."

No words from the broken man I'd once respected as a mentor, just a silent nod of acknowledgment. Her eyes fell then on my father. Brünhild lifted his head with the palm of her hand, pushing a kiss against his white lips. *Siempre, mi amor. Siempre.*

"Mr. Somfield!" And like that, she was all business again, all emotion gone from her face. "You'd best take your fur."

"Do you think I'd be in skin if I could bloody take my fur?" he snapped. "Something happened. I can't pull myself through."

Another bellow in a tongue my ear did not know, this one closer to the front door. They were coming. The walking corpses were on their way.

"Mother, the Ravens!"

Brünhild pointed to the trees in the distance. "Take him and go. Do not wait for me."

"What?" Was she serious? "But the Ravens will…"

"There is another pit around the back of the house where they threw Markus and the yellows assigned to help us out. Yan went there to rescue them. I will rendezvous and we will make for the cars together."

"What? How do you know that?"

She held up her hand pulling down her sleeve to show me some kind of electronic device strapped on her wrist. "The Ravens didn't even think to look. He was listening the whole time. Until we used the silver flame anyway. We had codes for different contingencies worked out in advance."

More rambunctious curses from voices dipped in pain, and their forms appeared in the doorway. "The bitch matron dies last and slowest. Kill the rest. Kill them all!"

My mother's eyes went wide as she pushed us in the right direction. "Go!"

They started for her before she even turned, their advance slowed by their condition. They didn't notice Igor's presence until he was on them, the snarling, yipping fight happening at a speed my eyes couldn't comprehend.

Tobias assumed his own feet and wrapped his hand in mine. Moments later, we were running as fast as we could. Weighed down with sorrow and the effects of silver flame, we drove forward, pushing beyond our limits, until Tobias doubled over, his hands on his knees.

"What's happening to me?" he said through gapping pants. "Why can't I take my fur?"

"Silver flame."

His wide eyes looked up. "The stuff your mum hit you with when she relinquished you?"

I nodded.

"I don't understand what that means."

"I don't either."

In the distance, wolves howled out. Under the light of the full moon, a pack was only as tame as the alpha demanded. An alpha could be reasoned with, as I'd experienced earlier, but if any other wolf encountered us, they'd be just as likely to attack us as not.

Taking to Tobias's side, I tried to pull him along faster. "We have to keep moving."

He jerked up when a second howl came. "We should ask them for help."

His feet trudged. One step. Two steps. Three...

"They won't help. I tried."

The moon above became playful, skipping its way across the night sky in and out of patchy clouds, making the forest a patchwork of blues and grays, blues and black, over and over again. Perhaps that is why I didn't see the cloud of smoke rushing toward us.

"Tobias!"

It came upon us like a swarm of wasps, encircling us, blinding us to direction. We swatted the air, trying to push away the assault, but every movement only made the blanket around us tighter.

"Geri!" Tobias shouted out. "Take my hand."

I reached but found only air. A moment later, the man I love called out for me, his voice trailing on the breeze, growing distant.

"Tobias!"

No answer came, even as I grew dizzy, turning in all directions, arms out, desperate. The taste of ash on my tongue, I coughed, until finally, everything rushed to a stop. I opened my eyes. My hands were empty, but on the ground a few feet away, hideous charred lips drew back in a sinister grin.

"Now, you are ours."

The monstrosity of bone and sinew bared his fangs. Nicolai? Mihnea? The others? I didn't know which Raven it was that seized me, and it didn't matter. They were all equally deadly.

"You did this to us!" he hissed. "Give me your blood, and undo it!"

"No, wait, I—"

Cries broke the air as fangs sunk deep into my neck. *My* cries, I realized, though the beating of my pulse in my ears dampened the sound. My hands planted on the monster's chest, trying to push him away, but I could feel my strength draining away, pouring into him, healing his temporary wounds. The thrum of my heart drowned out all other sounds, and soon, echoed in the vampire's chest.

He was killing me. Or at least, he'd bring me as close to

death as he could. I knew the vampire wouldn't really let me die, he'd only make me wish I could.

Only when he'd had his fill did he pull back, grinning. Even as my eyesight blurred, I could see it: the transformation. Fresh flesh spun in webs over him, stitching together a plane of perfection silver flame had singed. His hair, mussed and scorched, became fine and flaxen. Those smiling lips rejuvenated, taking on a rosen glow even a vampire couldn't hope to achieve.

Almost like he wasn't a vampire at all.

If not for his hold on me, I may have fallen to the ground. The very next moment, I did. Not because the monster had let me go, but because he pushed me down.

One fang curled over his bottom lip as he paced my direction, even as I made a feeble attempt to back away, my elbow pushing me up.

His hand went to the button of his slacks. "You need to be taught your place, girl. You are ours now, and we will have you in any way and every way we desire."

"No." *Jesus, no.*

Any normative calm was gone. The vampire growled his words. "*Anything* and *everything,* you insolent, mortal cur."

No fucking way. I refused. I REFUSED. But what could I do? Even as my mind raced, routing a dozen solutions, finding ways to escape, nothing would work without a weapon or at the very least, my strength.

In a moment, he was on me, pulling at my clothing, robbing me of my security. The world began to fade. Trees, sky, ground... all narrowed into a pinprick of light. This was it. I'd failed. Not just Tobias, but everyone. Mina, Amy, Caleb and the slayers... even my mother.

Cold wind and icy snow pushed into my naked flesh as his renewing body covered mine, pushing my shoulders into the ground and pinning me at the hip with his weight. I closed my eyes, helpless, telling myself that I'd do no one any good as a martyr. This was not death. I would survive this, and in time, the vampire would pay. They all would.

I bit my lip and tried to think of anything else but this place and this moment. If I had stayed present, I may have heard it: the rustle of leaves, the approaching of a foe. My eyes shot open when the vampire's weight flew off me, and the sound of conflict filled the air.

A few feet away, my attacker, mounted by Igor Kharmarov, stared up at the wooden stake poised for his heart. Igor closed his eyes, his weapon arcing through the air, and plunged it into the vampire's chest.

The Raven didn't last another breath, his limbs going numb within a moment. Igor, chest pumping, looked down at the body in amazement before turning to me.

"Did he… Did he…"

I shook my head. No, he hadn't. I'd escaped. Barely. I was, however, injured. Broken ribs, dislocated shoulder, a neck still dripping blood. But it could have been worse. Far worse.

Igor staggered to his feet, and it was then that I saw it: his true age coming over him. He'd held the youthful face of a man in his late 30s for hundreds of years. Whatever magic that bound him to the survival of his progeny, however, began to take back what fate had given him. Igor himself realized it too, holding up his hand, watching the wrinkles appear before his eyes.

"I'm dying," he said. "As I should. My debt has gone unpaid for too long, and I killed your father."

He had, and I should have hated him for that. I should've

killed him myself. I couldn't, though. I wouldn't.

"You couldn't help it," I gasped. "They starved you."

"I gave in to the monster." His black hair lost its shine, then its color. Sixty had come and gone, and his body drove onward, the vitality of his face fading, bags forming beneath his eyes. "Geri, you must kill them, all of them, or they will hunt you to the ends of the earth. They will hunt Tobias. They will... They w..."

A curdling noise cut off his words as the brown of his eyes turned black. Igor's feet gave out from under him. His ripped and tattered clothing coughed the dust he became as he hit the ground.

I didn't know how long I lay there, bleeding, naked, scared, alone. When movement caught in the corner of my eyes, all I knew was that it was him.

My wolf.

I knew he spoke, because I could see his lips move, but only a dull palate of sound pressed against my ear. Tobias's arms pushed under my frame, lifting me into his hold, carrying me through the forest.

"Igor..."

He stopped, looked down at me, mouthed "what?"

"Igor saved me. He's dead."

A swish of red, and suddenly I began to warm. A cloak. A hood's cloak. I turned my head, only vaguely aware of the pain in my neck, and saw Markus. I could feel Tobias's voice vibrate his chest. No, not his voice. He was growling. Growling because Markus was trying to pull me away.

"No!" I shook my head. "I stay with him. I'll *always* stay with him."

Markus mumbled something I couldn't make out. A cloth pressed into my neck. From where? I didn't know. It staunched the flow of blood, but even I could feel my lightheadedness. Perhaps the loss was already too much. Could I be dying? Could my world be fading from my sight? It didn't matter. I'd saved Tobias, and that's what I'd come to do.

"Geri?"

His hands pinched my chin, turning my face to his as my eyes fluttered closed.

"My hearing must be coming back." I smiled. "I heard you say my name. Say it again."

"Geri…"

Geri…

*Geri…*

# THIRTY

## AMY

Three quick taps on the door before Caleb's head peeked in.

"What's the point of knocking if you're not going to wait for me to say if you can come in or not? We might want to add etiquette lessons to the slayer training program."

Tall, dark, and presumptive smirked. "If I were here to see you, I'd have waited, but I'm here to see her." He pointed to the bundled baby in my arms.

As if Mina understood she had a gentleman caller, her tiny little blue eyes opened, scanning the room, finding the arrival. I swear, that child was already smitten with her Uncle Caleb. He was going to spoil her rotten.

"You seem to have taken to being an auntie pretty well." He settled down on the bed beside me, reaching up to stroke the billowy puff of red hair on the baby's head. "I thought you said you wanted nothing to do with babies."

"I don't. But Mina isn't a baby. She's... like a little kitten."

"She's half-werewolf."

"Fine, puppy then. My point is, she doesn't scream and shout and act like the world is ending because of a wet nappy or anything. She's special. And I like her just fine."

Who was I kidding? I loved the little thing. We all did.

Hell, even the hoods who saw her in the courtyard when we'd taken a walk earlier went gaga over her, and according to Markus, most of them were so high-and-mightiest, they questioned the reverence of saints.

"At least tell me you're here because you have news. Did they finally say Geri and Tobias could have guests?"

The sparkle in his eyes dulled as his hand and eyes dropped away. "No, they're both still isolated from the others at the top of the tower. No one's allowed up there except Brünhild and Petunia. Even Markus says he's embargoed."

Damn it. It had been two days since they'd come back from Spain, since the horrific word that the mission to kill the Ravens failed. Well, wasn't totally successful, anyway. Three had been whacked, I'd heard from Yan. The Grand Matron managed to take out two during the escape, and Igor Kharmarov had given his life to destroy another. That left three, one of them being the Big Bad Daddy Vamp, Vlad Tepeş. As sad as that was, worse news came later: Geri's dad had been killed during the mission. Officially, Pietro had been exiled at the time of his death, so he wouldn't be allotted any memorial. Which, IMHO, was sucky on the hoods' part. I mean, damn. But unofficially, his death painted a gray cloth over everything and everyone, most of all Brünhild, who'd left the compound soon after getting back to Triberg, and hadn't been seen by anyone since.

Mina grunted, her little lips puckering and drawing me from my reverie. "Looks like someone is hungry again. I swear, at the rate this child eats, she should be the size of a sewer rat by next week. I better make up some more formula."

But before I could get three steps to the door, Caleb swooped her out of my arms. "I got her. You get some rest. It's late."

"It's only 1 AM."

"And you're still a huey," he said. "All good little girl and boy humans should be tucked up in their beds by now."

"I'm not good. Or little. And if there's any word from Geri, I want to know."

"I promise, if anything comes before morning, I'll let you know. Get some shut-eye. The others and I will be on Mina duty through the night." He shifted the baby from the cradle of his arms to his shoulder, giving her a little bounce. "We'll count on you to handle the day shift again."

"In that case, I think I'll grab a few hours then. You guys might sleep during the day, but this little one doesn't seem to give a damn that she's supposed to be nocturnal." I extended my arms over my head, inverting my steepled fingers and feeling a beautiful stretch down the sides of my midframe. "Thanks, Buffy. Sometimes you don't totally suck."

"That might be the sweetest thing you've ever said to me, Barbie."

Little Mina's eyes caught mine as the slayer turned away. I'd blame being tired for why the shut off key in my brain didn't turn in time.

"You'd be such a good daddy."

Caleb froze. Turned his head halfway back toward me. Turned it back toward the door.

And left.

# THIRTY-ONE

## GERI

His scent filled my senses. My hand reached for his, which was stroking my cheek. "Tobias…"

Slowly, the world came back into focus.

I opened my eyes to see beauty. My love, my wolf, my mate, smiling down at me. He'd grown a full beard, which, combined with his usual mess of shoulder-length hair, made him look like a lumberjack who'd escaped a Pacific rainforest, but I didn't care.  I'd take him bald or wild, just as long as I had *him.*

I reached up, tracing my finger over the significant beardage. "Hi there."

His eyes closed as he huffed out his relief, his forehead falling to mine. "Bloody hell. I thought I lost you. I thought you'd never wake up."

"I rescued you," I said, like that was the perfect counterargument to being comatose. "I came for you."

He grinned as he pulled back. "Yes, you did. You total badass, you did."

But with consciousness came memory, and the realization of the cost for his delivery.

"My father…"

His smile dissolved. "I'm sorry, Geri."

Panic struck my heart. "Markus? My mother?"

"They're okay. Mourning, but alive."

"And the Ravens?"

He shied away his eyes. "Your mother killed two. Igor a third. Three, they presume, fled."

I pushed myself up by the elbows, ready to jump to my feet, but stopped when I realized I was in a bed.

With Tobias.

I sat up, observing the space. No doubts about where we were. The carved wooden bed frame, the dark velvet bed curtains, the large oval window that opened out to the view of the valley below.

"This is the Grand Matron's suite. This is my mother's bedroom." I turned to Tobias. "And you're here."

The lupine blushed, pushing himself off the bed. He adjusted the bathrobe tied around him as he took to his feet. "I swear, nothing happened. I've been in my wolf most of the time, just as soon as I was able to do it again. I only took on my skin when I noticed you were waking up."

"No, it's fine. I—"

I threw off the blanket and discovered I was dressed in a white nightgown that ran down to my feet and its sleeves to my wrists. A bandage covered a patch of skin where I suspected an IV line had dripped a steady bead into my veins.

"How long was I out?"

"Three days under. But that was only because Petunia induced it. She wanted to make sure the worst of your injuries healed before you could argue with her. I guess everyone thought you'd fight your way back to Spain if they'd woken you any sooner. Good thing hoods heal with superhuman speed. It's still red and swollen, but the skin has closed over."

"Three days? I've been out for three days. And you've just sat there the whole time? How did you get up here? Wolves aren't allowed in Schloss Wolfsretter without being bound in silver. To have a wolf in the tower, though? I'm surprised the council didn't riot."

He smirked. "I'm sure they weren't happy, but no one's going to attack the decisions of a grieving widow."

His words trickled off just as my sadness rose anew. My dad. If he hadn't bound me in blood-claimed silver, I would have been with him when he'd been captured. Maybe I could have fought off the Ravens with him. Maybe things would have been different. Maybe... so many things. Nothing could be done when a page was turned. The story stopped for no one. His was just another name of the fallen now, joining Igor, Inga, Kara, and Alex.

Alex!

I leaped up. "Oh my god, Mina!"

Tobias's mighty arms caught me as I tried to fly by. "Hold up now, explain yourself."

"Mina, the baby," I said, pulling back. "She's... It's complicated. But she's mine. *Ours.* I mean, she's pack. Our pack. She's our..."

"Daughter?" The wolf grinned, pulling me into his embrace. "Is that the word you're looking for, Geri? Our *daughter*?"

I swallowed, even though his scent was making me dizzy. "I'm her godmother, and, well, her mother died, so I just assumed... We can talk about our kids... I mean, if you ever wanted to have kids, but with Mina, given the situation…"

Tobias brought his hand between us, pushing a finger against my lips. "*Shhhh.*" A moment later, his mouth replaced the hold as the werewolf brushed a kiss across my lips. "I felt the quickening, too. I knew she was ours. And if that is as a daughter, then we have a daughter."

The girly parts of me wanted to swoon, but the hood parts of me were doggedly practical and wanton of formality. "We're not even mates yet. Not in any real way. Seems like things are out of order: first kids, then becoming a couple? Assuming, that is, that you meant what you said in Istanbul. And that whatever happened to you these last weeks hasn't changed…."

"You and I will have a proper munch later and discuss what happened. But let's get this set right from the get-go." Another brush of his lips, this one softer, and yet, more intense, chased by another. "I love you, and I have every intention of mating you just as soon as we can make the arrangements."

"I love you, too…" Another visit of his mouth on mine, and I was positively melting in his arms. "…but is that even possible?" I threaded my fingers through his mangy hair, pulling him closer, deepening the connection. "Can we be together, that way?"

He bit my lip before pulling back to examine me. "There's only one way to find out."

His hands gathered the nightgown as he inched higher, building a delicious anxiety with every bit of territory he claimed.

I licked my lips. "There's no rush, Tobias. After what you've been through… If you need time to…"

"I don't need a moment more to know how I feel about you." He paused midway, kissed the rise of my hip bone, dotted the planes of my stomach with his lips, the white folds of cloth filling his hands. "And if there's one thing I've learned, it's not to waste time doing what's proper, when you could spend your time doing what's *possible.* I love you. I am *in love* with you, and I don't want to lose you again. I want you as my mate, my friend, my lover, my companion. I want you as the mother of my pups."

Logical and rational Geri tried one more hostile takeover of my brain. "They'll never understand. Not the hoods, not the wolves, no one. Our lives will be..."

He paused, looking up from where his two fingers had hooked around the top of... when had someone put underwear on me?

"Hard as hades?" he said, pulling down the cotton band with aching deliberateness. "Yeah, I know. But at least at the end of the night, I'll be with you."

No panic, no pain, no sudden anxiety. Nothing but peace. His eyes stayed locked on mine as he pulled himself over me, and as his mouth closed in on mine, so did his heart.

He was my wolf.

And I was his.

# EPILOGUE

I bit my lip, sensing in every fiber of my being what even the patch of sky I could see through the windows above had yet to acknowledge. Dawn was coming.

*She* was not.

Tobias pulled me under his wing, squeezing my shoulder. "It's not about you or Mina. She's grieving the loss of her mate. She needs time and space to do it however she needs to."

The old familiar streak of guilt ran the length of me. *Kara.* Tobias's words weren't derived from assumption, but from experience. But he was a wolf; my mother was not. My mother was the Grand Matron, head of the House of Red, and one of the toughest women ever to walk the earth.

"I just wish she'd let us know she's okay," I said. "I mean, I know she's not *okay,* but that she's safe. We don't even know where she is. And if something happens to her..."

"*Shhhh...*" The lupine pressed a kiss against my forehead. The shift of my body made Mina flinch in her sleep. Tobias kept his voice low, trying not to wake her. "Nothing will happen to Brünhild Kline. And now that I'm back, nothing's going to happen to her daughter either." He ghosted a finger down Mina's cheek. "Or *our* daughter."

A rush of warmth filled me. *Our daughter.* Tobias and I had had one of the quickest progressions to establishing a family in history. Here we were, parents, despite the fact that we'd only slept together for the first time two nights ago.

And the second time the same night.

The fifth through eighth times, in the past twenty-four hours.

His lips claimed mine for a kiss that was all too brief. Barely had we touched when the doors leading to the courtyard of the inner bailey opened and Rebecca shuffled in.

The grin on her face brought a blush to my cheeks. "Are you ready, or do you want me to watch the baby and tell everyone to wait so you can sneak a quickie in the armory?"

Tobias cleared his throat and pulled back his focus to the ground. How curious that a wolf was so prudish when it came to a little raucous humor.

Then again, he *was* English.

"No, Becky," I said. "The sunrise waits for no one. Thank you, we're coming now."

The castellan winked and left us alone, leaving the door open in her wake.

Formal affairs required formal attire. My cloak materialized into existence with my beckoning, falling over my shoulders and covering me down to my calves. I shifted Mina so I could cradle her with one arm and offered my free one to Tobias. "Bailey or call Becky back and head to the armory?"

"Stuck in a room surrounded by silver weapons?" Dousing the residue of his blush, he hooked his arm with mine. "Even with you, I'd pass. I'm still chuffed they let me stay without chains. But... maybe you could wear *that*—" His free hand motioned vaguely at my cloak. "to bed? Like, *just* that?"

"Tobias Somfield, are you telling me you have a hood fantasy?"

"No, Geri Kline, I'm telling you I have a little red riding

hood fantasy. And I promise, I *will* try to eat you."

Shivers went down my spine. If not for the pink beginning to tickle the horizon, I'd hand Mina off that very second.

Though we wouldn't get as far as the armory.

Markus planted balled-up fists on his hips, personifying the concerns of the slayers, hoods, two asenaics and two hueys paying witnesses. "Anytime *please,* or we're going to miss the sunrise."

"Okay, okay!"

Despite the nip of the early winter air, all the research Yan and Markus had done in the few remaining slayer texts suggested the ceremony required the child to be naked. Amy took up the blankets as Caleb unwrapped our illustrian burrito, holding them at the ready to swaddle Mina the second the ceremony concluded.

"We gather today to welcome a new beam of light."

An uncertain Caleb Helsing was an amusing sight. The slayer clutched the index card in his hand as though it was his lifeline as he managed a newly-awoken-and-more-than-a-little-confused-about-being-naked baby in the crook of his other arm. Caleb's shiver didn't go unnoticed, and it wasn't because of the cold. Even Amy had noted the very thing I was coming to suspect: as the only awoken male slayer and the only one with substantial defensive training and world experience, he had defaulted to being the leader of his kind, and that prospect scared him to hell.

"As the sun falls upon her now," he continued, the formality sounding like a foreign tongue on his lips, "may it fill her with life, lighting a path of righteousness and honor, and into a world where she is known as…"

*Cue: my line.*

"Mina Alexandria Petra Kline," I said. "May the sun blaze her name into the hearts of her people, and light the path of righteousness—"

"Yeah, righteousness and honor," Caleb mumbled over my words, cutting me off. "I already said that part."

He pivoted, just as the sun peeked over the eastern ridge of the sky. Its amber light seemed to be drawn to her, the beam setting my daughter aglow, the baby golden in Caleb's arms.

"Mina Alexandria Petra Kline, you have been accepted by the sun. All here bear witness, a slayer is born."

"A slayer is born!" said every single slayer in the compound, standing in witness.

As the clapping and cheering arose, Amy's patience snapped. She swooped in, coating Mina in folds of wool.

Tobias waited until the clamor had died away before clearing his throat, calling the crowd's attention. "And as alpha of the..." He turned to me. "What pack are we?"

A good question. Packs were generally identified by the region or town in which they lived. But where did Tobias and I live? We didn't have a home anymore, and who knew when we would again.

But we did have *something* in common that bonded us together, something which very few others could claim.

"I believe that's the asenaic pack, dear."

He grinned. "Bloody right we are." A swooping kiss sealed the deal. He turned back to the crowd. "As alpha of the asenaic pack, I claim Mina Alexandria Petra Kline as one of my pups, under my protection and the protection of all my packlings."

"So just you and Geri then?" Caleb couldn't help a little sarcasm.

I turned my face up to Tobias. "For now."

I mean, we were having lots and lots of sex, so things could happen…

The subtext of my comment didn't fly over Amy's head. "Finally! Okay, now that you've gotten over that hurdle, I need to educate you on advanced practices."

A growl rumbled through the chest of the alpha beside me.

The blonde huey threw her hands up in surrender. "Fine. But if a copy of the *Kama Sutra* should show up in Geri's library someday, you'd thank me for it."

Before I could frame up a witty response, my words died in the air. The rays of the sun took on shape, an object that seemed distant in one blink solidified the next into meaning. My mother landed in the midst of the bailey without pretext.

"Mom, I—"

Tobias pulled me back, shaking his head. Had he sensed something I hadn't, or did he just want me to give her space?

Brünhild took in the scene through a confused expression. "What is this?"

"A slayer naming ceremony," I said. "We're doing it as best we can figure out from research. Mina has just been recognized as a member of the slayer community."

"And as a member of my pack," Tobias said. "She's slayer and wolf, and we'll all protect her."

"An illustrian will need such protection," my mother concurred. She looked at the baby in Amy's arms. "And who will protect the protectors?"

Tobias and I exchanged a look. "We'll watch out for each other. Wherever the slayers go, Tobias and I will follow. We'll... We'll make our pack where they settle their pride."

"A *pride* of slayers?" Caleb asked. "Is that what we're calling it now?"

Teiko called out, "You're sure as hell not calling us a harem anymore!"

"I like pride," the normally silent Sergei nodded. "Like lions. We are fierce."

My mother, I could tell, did not agree, but with the slayers at least she understood where her opinions should cease. "Very well. But your *pride* and your pack will not be alone. This child is the daughter of my daughter, by cause if not blood. By this, she is also hood."

"But, mother," I pulled away from Tobias. "I'm relinquished. How could Mina be—"

"I decree it so," she said, cutting me off. "You are restored. From this day forward, all asenaics are recognized members of their houses." Her eyes went to Tobias. "Do you understand my words? *All* of them."

I turned back to my alpha. "Tobias, I think she means you."

The werewolf blanched. "Me? I ain't no bloody hood, and don't you dare go..."

"*All* asenaics, Mr. Somfield," Brünhild cut in. "Remember, our laws still dictate that a wolf and a hood may not join in union. I can acknowledge those with documented bloodlines, even if they're not wholly hood, but my power to change the laws are more limited, especially in current circumstances." My mother grinned as she walked past him, patting his shoulder. "Welcome to the House of Red, *son*."

"Reclaim my father!"

My sudden outburst arrested Brünhild in her tracks. She turned her head back over her shoulder part way. "That I could, Gerwalta, but Pietro's crime was not his heritage. As I said, my ability to change laws is..."

"But does anyone know why you exiled him?" I cut in. As matron, she didn't have to explain her actions unless she chose to, and knowing how much my mom loved my dad, she never would have spoken a word against him like that.

The corners of her mouth lifted. "Disobedience is the only notation I made on the decree."

"Then say it was a lie," I said. "Say you did it because you discovered he was an asenaic. Grandfather him into your decree. Don't let him die in shame."

"It will not bring him back in any way. It does not change what happened."

"If it is written down, then it does." I crossed to my mother, laying a hand on her arm. "Gerwalta Faust *wasn't* Gerwalta Faust when she died. She was Gerwalta Baron. She was a wife, a mother, an alpha's mate: things I never understood until I saw her grave marker. The writing made her truth real. Don't doom my father to dying a criminal when the only thing he did wrong was try to help his daughter."

I didn't know if I asked too much. My mother's leadership had been so strained already, but if I didn't try to move her on this, the cost would be so much more than her matronship. She stood to lose the honor she felt in being my father's wife.

Slowly, the Grand Matron nodded. "Very well, I hereby

pardon Pietro Kline of his crimes and restore him as one of the righteous."

"Thank you, mother." Later, I'd talk to Rebecca about arranging a formal remembrance, but one step at a time. "You know he's worthy of it."

"I know he is," she agreed, "but am I worthy of being a martyr's wife? I... I do not think so."

As she turned, crestfallen, and made her way into the castle, I prayed that was a question neither Tobias or I would ever have to ask ourselves.

Kendrai Meeks was deported from the American Midwest after graduating college, and held against her will since in California. She really hates sarcasm. She first published in 2011, and has since put out books in romance and science fiction. In 2017, she decided to return to her first love, urban fantasy. She is the founder of the Bay Area Allied Indie Authors group. She has also been a featured speaker on a number of conference and industry panels on topics ranging from Fanfiction, to Audiobooks, to Serialized Fiction. She is a world music devotee and loves to travel (just hates to fly – a conflict, for certain). She enjoys twisting the extant into the exceptional, often basing her work on historical themes or legendary folk tales and mythology.

# Acknowledgments

A special thank you to Chantell Reed and Erin Fraser, who help by finding uncrossed t's and undotted i's before releases. Chantell apologizes needlessly for her generosity in doing so. (Chantell, babe, you don't understand how much that means to me and what a big help it is. STOP SAYING YOU'RE SORRY.) To the pre-readers: who devote time with kindness, and suffer through enough typos to fill a book, literally and literarily. To my friends who keep me going in difficult times, and to my daughters.

RIGHTEOUS
RED CHRONICLES BOOK 5

"But you *must* see that the best way forward is together. If we don't ally as one nation against the Dracule, then…"

Mother's words cut off as hysterical curses poured over the phone line. She passed a look around the Council Table in the Schloss's former throne room. Instead of other matrons, however, only Markus and I were seated there to lend silent sympathy.

With a huff, Brünhild continued, "I would remind you, Yanyu, that regardless of half of the Council's retreat from Germany, I am *still* Grand Matron. Think of that twice before threatening me again."

Once upon a time, I would have believed in fairies before the idea that someone would try to out-bitch Brünhild Kline. Now, our allies in the Hood Houses had fallen away like flies. The first to bolt: no surprise. My mother had barely finished decreeing that all asenaics were now recognized members of the community when the House of White's matron showed Schloss Wolfsretter her backside. The Greens followed in her wake fast enough to share a cab to the airport, taking away the Atlantic seaboard on both sides of the ocean as safe zones. God willing, Vlad didn't decide to head to NYC because the Big Apple was now a Brünhild-Kline-can-suck-it designated zone.

Pressing her forehead against a balled-up fist, Mother waited for the other voice to a give her an opening, and then…

"Of course, I understand that what I've done has gone against centuries of tradition by treating werewolves as our equals, but we both knew the day was coming. When the most powerful and vicious vampire in the history of creation declares war, you find your allies where allies are to be had. What better time to move us forward? And if you'd just listen to reason, then…"

The other side went dead.

Markus's words wrapped around the lollipop he sucked. "Guess the House of Orange is a no?"

Brünhild closed her eyes. "Indeed." She cycled a breath, then turned to me. "Where does that leave us?"

I examined my notes. "So… pretty much all of Asia and the UK have told us to go to hell. Casa de Amarillo is still with us, though that's probably more because they're the ones who helped hide the asenaic line all these years. And… the blues are confirmed, so if the vampires invade either the Fjords or Minnesota, we're golden."

My attempt at comedy was a drop of water on a hot stove. Pushing off my sarcasm, I set aside my notebook. "It's a fifty-fifty split, but *Mädchen*, that's more than enough. There are only three ravens left, and Vlad's just one vampire against, what, a few hundred of us?"

"He's not just *one* vampire, Gerwalta. He is *the* vampire. And with Igor Karmarov dead, he's now the paterfamilias of his bloodline. It's a position many still revere." Brünhild let out a long exhale as she planted her hands on an old, ornately carved chair and leaned into a stretch. "And I fear he may be targeting the other asenaics now."

Behind us, sitting on the side of the room, Tobias coughed a laugh.

The Matron spun. "Something amusing you, Mr. Kline?"

"Mr. Kline? My name is…" Tobias's face screwed up. "No. No dice. You are not going to stick me with my mate's family name just because you decided it's convenient if I'm one of you now."

I crossed my arms. "And what's wrong with taking the wife's name? Or did you assume that because you're a man, I'd take yours automatically?"

"Why wouldn't you want to be a Somfield? It's a great

name. Geri Somfield. Gerwalta Somfield. *Mrs. Somfield.* Rolls off the tongue like sugar now, don't it?" He stood, walking... no, *stalking* toward me. Tobias raised his hand to trace a finger down the bridge of my nose and over my lips. "Don't you want to be my missus, *Mrs.* Somfield?"

Behind me, my mother chocked on her annoyance. "You two must learn quickly there is more to marriage than constant sex."

"Oh, I know that, Matron." The corner of Tobias's mouth pulled up. Given only a few days, he'd learned all the best ways to piss my mother off. "I hear it also comes with tax benefits in your country. Maybe even a green card."

The chair legs groaned as Brünhild pushed them into the table. "I hope that at least you're using protection. This is hardly the time to knock up my daughter."

And she, it turned out, had learned how to push all of Tobias's buttons.

"You're very crass for an old autocrat, you know that? What I was laughing at," he said, like that part of the conversation had been on pause and all he had to do was hit play again, "what made me so giddy, is that I guess it should come as no surprise that there are other asenaics you know about and we don't. You were covering up quite a few things, it seems."

"Yes, I was." Brünhild crossed her arms. "If I didn't, old school traditionalists like Zhu and Smyth of the House of Green would have hunted them down and killed them long ago. So, you're welcome, Tobias, for my efforts which kept you and your family alive all these years."

I sucked in a breath through my teeth as I turned to watch the crater of that verbal shell form.

Tobias's hands balled into fists. "Last I looked, I'm the only one left standing. Dracule killed my brother and my da.

And, oh, my mate, too, so… tell me again why I should thank you?"

My mother's eyes tracked to the floor, a gesture anyone who didn't know Brünhild Kline the way I did would take for shame. Only, my mother didn't do shame. There was only ever one reason for the matron to not look you in the eye.

"Mother, you're hiding something."

She didn't deny it. Why would she? It was her privilege as the unquestioned—well, until recently unquestioned—leader of our people to keep whatever secrets she wanted.

I stepped forward. "Fess up."

"What do you think she can tell you, Geri?" Tobias said. "That my father and brother *aren't* dead? I buried them myself. That Kara isn't dead? You were there for that funeral with me."

An image of Tobias's first mate's grave in the Paradise cemetery flashed in my mind.

"No, Tobias, I would not tell you they're alive, nor deny that I was aware of the possible target they represented for the Dracule as soon as the Ravens were set free and began to regain influence and power. But there is at least one other member of your bloodline who carries the asenaic traits, and more than the fear that Vlad may come for her, I fear that she may welcome it."

My mate was the picture of a man who stood on the edge of a precipice with the balance about to be knocked from his feet. "I don't have sisters, aunts… Both my grand-mothers are dead. Who possibly could there still be?"

Brünhild lifted heavy eyes. "Your mother."